DESTINY GIFT

THE EVERLAST SERIES BOOK 1

JULIANA HAYGERT

COPYRIGHT

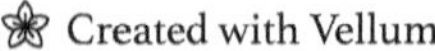 Created with Vellum

AUTHOR'S NOTE

I HOPE YOU ENJOY READING *DESTINY GIFT*!

DON'T FORGET TO SIGN UP FOR MY NEWSLETTER TO FIND OUT about new releases, cover reveals, giveaways, and more!

If you want to see exclusive teasers, help me decide on covers, read excerpts, talk about books, etc, join my reader group on Facebook: Juliana's Club!

1

───────

WHEN I WAS LITTLE, MY GRANDMA TOLD ME, "NADINE, BEFORE THE sun left us, you could look up and estimate what time it was just by the position of the sun in the sky."

Holding my breath, I walked out of the subway station into the street and looked up. All I saw were tall buildings, most of them in need of some love and care, reaching up to thick, dark gray clouds, the same ones that had been a permanent fixture in the sky for my entire nineteen years.

I wasn't sure why I kept trying.

Exhaling, I focused on my task, on why I was uptown and not safely behind the gates of the university. To be honest, I wasn't letting myself think about it too much. Otherwise, I would freeze. I would turn back around and flee. I would go home and pretend everything was all right.

One measured step in front of the other, I walked from the subway station to the next block. All the while my eyes stared straight ahead, and I breathed through my mouth. Even then I caught a sniff of the rotting smells of the city; my eyes drifted to the broken sidewalks, to the fallen street lamps, to the dying trees and dry dirt, to the homeless people hiding at the edge of alleys.

I swallowed the fear building inside me. As far as I knew, this had been a nice neighborhood until a couple of months ago. As nice as a neighborhood could be in this world. Larger companies and businesses moved out as soon as it started getting bad —poverty and robbers and bats—but not everyone could afford to pack up and move.

Like the psychiatrist I had scheduled an appointment with.

At first, I pushed my problems aside. I ignored them. But now I couldn't anymore, and this was the only psychiatrist from the over twenty I called who had an appointment available. The others wanted to put me on a wait list at least three months long.

No, thank you.

I stopped at a corner and waited for a green light to change. I glanced up at the tall building with a mirror-like exterior across the street, reflecting more buildings and the dark clouds. There. Right there was the psychiatrist who would be able to help me with my problem.

The faint sound of wings flapping echoed through the street, and everyone looked up. Including me. Among the reflection of buildings and dark clouds, I saw the blurred line of a bat cutting through the sky. Thankfully, it disappeared with my next erratic heartbeat.

These damn bats ...

The people in the street seemed to relax all at once.

A sigh escaped my lips.

But the bats weren't the reason I was here, coming to this shady neighborhood after a psychiatrist. I needed help because I had dreams.

Dreams was the word I used to calm my mind. Visions was a more appropriate term.

The first one happened right after my arrival in New York nine months ago. At first the visions came once a month or so, but now they assaulted me once a week. I blacked out every time I had one. I could be cooking, studying, walking down the street, and I would simply zone out. I saw whatever the vision brought me, then I would wake up as if nothing had happened, as if I had not spent the last thirty seconds or fifteen minutes daydreaming.

I was reluctant to call my visions hallucinations. Yet now, heading toward a psychiatrist's office, I guess I should. Hallucinations could be stopped with medication, right? That was why I was here—to ask the doctor to put an end to them. The visions were hindering my life. Last semester, I failed a class because I had visions during too many lectures and exams. Three days ago, I dropped a tray on a customer at the café where I waited tables. My boss almost fired me, accusing me of being distracted all the time. I was losing control of my life, and that made me scared.

On the other hand, if I stopped hallucinating, I would stop seeing *him*.

Every time I forced myself to think about this, about the dilemma of my life, I felt my soul ripping into two big chunks. But, in the end, *his* chunk was always bigger.

I could feel the smile taking over my lips. It was impossible not to smile when thinking about my Prince Charming.

A shove cut through my thoughts, and I scrambled to keep my balance.

"Move," a deep voice said. A big man walked by with long steps, rushing through the crosswalk.

"Crap," I muttered, gathering my wits and hurrying before the light became green again.

There weren't many cars on the streets anymore, but people had gotten crazier. More violent and aggressive. Drivers didn't respect pedestrians like they used to. Or at least that was what I was told.

A shrill cry brought a chill to my spine, and I froze in place, halfway through the crosswalk. Oh my God, it could only be the bats.

"Rain!" someone shouted. "Acid rain!"

Screams rang all around me. Everyone started running.

Another shove sent me stumbling back and into someone else. "I'm sorry," I said, turning around to whoever I had bumped into, but the person had already dashed away.

My heart sped up and my hands shook.

Then it happened.

A little drop of rain fell on my cheek, burning as if I had extinguished the end of a cigarette into my skin.

The pain radiated over my face, jerking me awake and into action.

With erratic movements, I pulled my jacket over my head, trying to keep my hands under the leather, and raced back to the sidewalk. There weren't many places to hide as most shops weren't open to the public anymore, so I ducked under the awning of a small newsstand, pressing myself into a sea of bodies, just as the rain intensified.

The sizzling sound of the rain hitting metal and the people who still ran for cover was agonizing. I shut my eyes, wishing I could silence my hearing for a minute too.

Small and thin, I was easily pushed back and pressed against the cold wall of the stand. I laid my hand flat against it, realizing it was made of metal. I sure hoped there was something else underneath the metal, or that this specific kind of rain didn't melt this kind of material as it sometimes did. It was impossible to know until after it started and caused damage. Meteorology was a profession from the past; no one could predict anything about the crazy weather or the world anymore.

Something bright above my head caught my eye and I looked up. A set of wooden numbers was nailed high on the metal wall. From the three numbers, only the eight shone as bright as a lantern.

"Help!" A broken scream reached my ears, and I forced my attention away from the freaky shining number eight. "Please, help me."

I tried looking out through the crowd in front of me, but I was too short. Instead, I crouched down and saw it. A young woman, probably my age, on her knees right at the beginning of the crosswalk, howling in pain as she held up a backpack, trying to shield herself from the rain.

A gasp ripped from my throat, and my hand flew to my chest. Fighting against the rain washing over her and the water accumulating on the road, the young woman tried pushing herself up, only to stumble and fall on her knees again. Her foot seemed twisted.

"Help!" She croaked again. Her skin was marred with tiny red spots, her clothes were sizzling away, and her backpack was practically melting in her bruised hands.

I looked at the big men in front of me. "Do something," I said over the heavy sound of the pouring rain. Nobody paid attention to me. "We have to do something."

A tall man, who looked to be in his late thirties, looked over his shoulders, his eyes never meeting mine. "She's lost. If you want to help her, it'll be your doom too."

I clenched and unclenched my hands as rage built inside my chest. I couldn't believe these people would just stand there and watch.

I didn't think; I just acted.

Adrenaline shot through my veins and propelled me as I pulled my leather jacket back over my head, pushed the big men aside, and ran into the rain. I rushed to the girl, who whimpered and trembled and cried desperately. Little droplets of rain singed the skin of my hands as I reached for her and, holding to her drenched clothes, pulled her up.

"Come on," I said, biting back a scream of my own. "Help me so I can help you."

I grabbed her arm and pulled it over my shoulders, not caring if it was over my skin or my clothes. Thankfully, the girl had more strength in her than I thought, and she carried most of her weight as I half-dragged, half-guided her back to the newsstand.

However, using their jackets and bags and even their shoes, the big men pushed us away.

"Hey, let us come under the damn awning," I cried. But they just pushed us back again.

The rain continued falling, and my jacket was only scraps of fabric by now. My chest tightened as I realized we couldn't stand here and keep fighting. The girl and I had to move. So, without wasting another breath, I tugged on her waist and guided her to the building behind the newsstand. There was no awning in sight, no porch or cover, and the ones I saw at a first glance seemed full of people. I didn't want to waste time asking them to let us squeeze with them.

Instead, I went directly into the narrow alley beside the building. There had to be a place to hide in there.

I was right. The moment we stepped into the dark alley, the rain was gone. I looked up and saw balconies jutting out from both buildings, providing cover.

Relieved about our good luck, I helped the girl down to the dirty but dry ground, and she slumped against the wall. My breath caught as I knelt in front of her and looked over her. There were nasty red blisters everywhere, mostly second and third-degree burns. Her clothes were in tatters—her pants were gone from her knees down, and her shins were bleeding in several spots. Her shoes weren't in much better condition, and I bet her feet were in even worse shape inside them. Even some of her hair seemed to have been burned away with the acid rain; blood soaked in her scalp. Her face … I gagged, realizing her face would never be the same.

"T-thanks," she croaked, her eyes half open.

This girl needed medical attention right now. "Hang in there." I fished my phone from inside my purse and—

Her hand shot up, grabbing my wrist and pulling it down. Her touch, still slick with the water from the rain, burned me and I bit back the scream that rose in my throat.

"T-talk to me," she whispered.

"I would rather call for help." I jerked my hand free from hers so I could call 911.

"It's too late."

"Don't say that."

"What's your name?" I blinked. This girl was crazier than I was. Why the hell did she want to know my name when she was too hurt to even talk? "Tell me," she insisted.

"Nadine. My name is Nadine Sterling. Now, just rest and hang in there. Save your breath. I'm gonna call for help."

"I'm Rose," she said, her voice a thin murmur. "T-thank you, Nadine, for coming for me. You're a good person." Then she closed her eyes. Heavy, her head rolled to the side and her body followed.

Mouth open wide, I just stared at her limp body. A sob rose in my throat, but I swallowed it. I hadn't known this girl; I shouldn't care. Except that I did. I always cared. I hated seeing innocents get hurt, and this girl had done nothing to deserve this horrible, horrible death.

I didn't know how long I stayed there, staring at her, wishing I could have helped her sooner, wishing I had seen her before I had first reached the newsstand. Then maybe, just maybe, I would have been able to help her.

Eventually, the rain stopped and the people and traffic started moving again. As if nothing had happened. As if they weren't hurt at all by the few droplets of acid rain that had hit them, as if there weren't debris of melted awnings or signs in the middle of the streets, as if there wasn't a dead girl in this alley.

Hands shaking, I stood and took a large step back.

I inhaled deeply as something sharp prickled my skin.

"No sudden movements," a deep, coarse voice said from behind me. I didn't move, but I could feel him. A tall man with a knife in his hand, pressed against my back. I whimpered. "Hand me your purse."

"Okay," I muttered, trying to clamp down my fear. Slowly, I reached for the strap across my shoulders. I sucked in a sharp breath and prayed the man was paying attention to the hand over my shoulder, and not the one I snuck inside my purse. My fingers wrapped around my pepper spray, and I slowly drew it out before pulling the purse over my head. "Here."

The sharp sting of the knife loosened and I acted. In a rush, I stepped away from the man and turned around, swinging my purse in his direction. He raised his arms to block the attack.

"What the fuck?" he yelled, reaching for me. I had the pepper spray ready and sprayed it all over his face. "Bitch!" he screamed, clawing at his eyes.

I ran.

I ran for several blocks, zigzagging through sidewalks and streets, just in case the man wanted revenge, and finally hopped into the subway to go home. I sat down on an almost empty cart, my heart heavy, my mind jumbled, and my stomach in knots. What the hell had happened? A sob lodged in my throat as images of the girl dying in the rain filled my mind.

Five minutes into my subway ride, I gasped. I had left uptown without having set foot in the psychiatrist office.

My shoulders deflated. Damn it. All the trouble I had finding an appointment that didn't conflict with my classes, lying to my roommate, and getting some time off work.

But maybe ... maybe it was a sign. With the acid rain and the robbery to distract me, to stop me, I was almost convinced I wasn't supposed to go to a psychiatrist and put an end to my visions.

Maybe I was supposed to be crazy.

Or maybe I was reading too much into the situation and should get off this subway and run back to the psychiatrist's office before I lost my appointment and had to go through all this trouble again to get another one.

And just like that I was back in my dilemma: being crazy and having my Prince Charming, versus being normal and losing him.

I blew out a long breath, already sure of my choice.

I didn't care that every Saturday night my roommate gave me a lecture about being young and pretty and smart, about going out, having fun, and making out. I had happily exchanged those parties she'd wanted to drag me to just to see my Prince Charming. And I would do it again.

Saying goodbye to him scared me, but it wasn't the only thing that made my stomach shrivel. What if I was really insane? What if I was sent to a clinic under heavy sedation? What if I was given those shock treatments horror movies pictured so often? I couldn't be incarcerated in a freak's clinic—not willingly at least.

And I couldn't lose my Prince Charming either.

2

——————

"Espresso at table six," my coworker Adam said. He shoved the tray over to me, peering myopically through too-thick lenses, then wiped his hands on his button up shirt. "A chocolate cupcake too."

I took the tray, an espresso, and one of the cupcakes.

Frowning, I went to serve table six. My frown dissolved once I saw Cheryl waiting for me in her usual spot. I'd met her my first day in New York, about nine months ago. At the time, she'd also been a newcomer, and we'd hit it off instantly despite our age difference.

Cheryl was gorgeous, with brilliant blond hair neatly combed into a bob and silver eyes. She was wearing one of her impeccable suits, a to-die-for designer purse, and matching shoes. She was now thirty-two years old, and I had asked her at least twenty times why she hadn't become a model instead of a psychologist working for NYU.

Before going to the psychiatrist's office—and running away from it—I considered talking to Cheryl about my visions. I'd given up when I realized she was one of the few friends I had and couldn't afford for her to think I was crazy. She might never come to see me again. That thought scared me.

"Hello there." Cheryl smiled and patted the chair beside hers. I glanced around. Adam was busy, and my manager was nowhere I could see. "Is spring semester over?" she asked as I sat, hiding my hands under the table.

I hadn't told anyone about what happened last week—about me trying to go to a psychiatrist office and ending up caught in the acid rain. And witnessing a young woman dying from her wounds and almost being robbed. I still had nightmares about it almost every night.

Besides my ruined jacket and boots, my hands had been bruised and burned, but nothing some first-degree burn cream couldn't take care of. I made sure to wear fingerless gloves on the first two days so my roommate wouldn't notice it—thank goodness it had been chilly and she didn't question it.

"Not yet," I finally answered. "One more exam tomorrow, then it's over."

Being accepted into NYU with financial aid made it possible for someone like me, who came from a poor background, to get a good diploma. Since it was rare to get financial aid to such an esteemed school, I figured my education should be the priority in my life.

"Deserved vacation, huh?" Cheryl munched the cupcake with inexplicable grace. Somehow she never got crumbs down her blouse the way everyone else did.

"Vacation?" I chuckled with a forced dreadful tone. "I'll be working full time during the next two weeks, till summer classes start."

"I get that you have to work." She folded her napkin neatly, and I wondered if she had been a princess or a queen in a previous life. "So why not get a job doing what you like?"

"Like singing? In a bar or some other place?" I was in the pre-health program, but my true dream was to sing for a living. My voice was good, but I'd chosen a career path that would give me stability and guaranteed money. I felt like I owed it to my parents, like I should do this to please them and give them a better life when they got older. They'd sacrificed so much for me, and now it was my turn.

"I bet it pays better than waiting tables at the university café."

I glanced through the large windows and sighed. It was mid-afternoon and the streets were already too dark, too full of creepy figures lingering outside the campus walls. I couldn't risk singing in a bar, working until late at night, having a vision in the middle of a street, and waking up robbed, or raped, or being attacked by a bat.

So I offered my second excuse. "Most of my classes are early in the morning. I would never be able to keep up with them singing late at night."

"That makes sense." A slight crease appeared between her salon-perfect brows. "But you could work with something that added to your resume."

"Like work in a medical facility?"

"I saw an opening for a Patient Care Technician at Langone in the newspaper and remembered you have that certificate."

"I do."

"I bet they have regular shifts." Her gaze fixed on mine, as if she were trying to spy on my soul. "So, what's holding you here?" Without a good answer for her, I shrugged. "Promise me you'll at least look into the position."

I knew she wouldn't rest until I agreed. "I promise."

Her eyes gleamed in victory before she abruptly changed subjects. "Now, why didn't you go out last week?"

I gaped. "Raisa put you up to this, didn't she?" My naughty

roommate loved a good party, and she never understood my reasons for skipping them.

"She's looking out for you. You're young and beautiful. You should go out more."

"No." I raised my hand in protest. And quickly hid it away. The worse of the burns were gone, but if someone looked too closely, they would know. "Not you too, please."

"Someday you'll meet a guy who will rock your world. He'll ask you out and you'll barely be able to mutter a yes."

"We'll see," I said, my mind yearning to meet with the guy from my visions. I missed him so much. I imagined him by my side, drinking coffee before my classes, his arm around my waist, pulling me close to him.

I glanced at Cheryl. While I imagined him with me in real life, I had never seen Cheryl with anyone. During the time I'd known her, she'd never mentioned a boyfriend, or talked about her family and friends. I'd never tried pushing her to tell me though. Who was I to demand the facts of her private life when I didn't share all of mine with her?

She reached for her tablet over the table. I hadn't noticed it there before, but now that she swiped her finger over the screen and the main page of CNN showed up, displaying many horrific headlines, I couldn't stop staring.

"This is so sad," Cheryl said, leaning in closer and allowing me a better view.

In Australia, a terrorist entered a train station and blew himself up, along with hundreds of innocent people. In Brazil, the gangs of favelas in big cities had declared war and innocents were caught in the crossfire every day. In Canada, rabid doves invaded a church, killed the priest, and injured several devotees. A new virus was discovered in Africa that seemed worse than Ebola. Everywhere, assaults, robberies, killings, and other horrific events plagued the world.

Perhaps I should have been used to the disasters, but I wasn't. I was born into this world, this cruel, dangerous, dark world—the world of chaos, as my mother called it—and yet, I was always shocked by the tragic events.

Cheryl looked out the window. "I wonder if we'll even see blue skies before we die." She turned to me with a small smile. "My mother used to tell me that the rivers were clean, there were trees and flowers everywhere, and summers were warm and sunny. People could actually walk down any street and not be afraid of being robbed. Now we have to be careful of muggers and giant bats." I flinched. Cheryl knew I had been robbed once and attacked by bats a couple of times. "My mother also used to say that God gave up on us. Thirty years ago. He left us and the world changed."

Her words echoed in my mind, bringing forth an old memory. My grandma and little me strolled through the field where my dad worked. The lake had dried out, and the plantation was dying from lack of water and sun.

"The water is dirty but serves its purpose nonetheless," she explained as our feet crushed the dead stems. "The owner doesn't make enough money to keep paying for the sun lamps to warm the herbs and make them grow."

The image was forever etched in my mind: the darkness of the sky, the grayish of from the ground. Even the rotten smell of dead vegetation made its way into my memories.

I had looked around, confused. This was my father's job. How would he support our family if his work was dying?

"You know, dear, I believe God abandoned us," my grandma continued. She halted and looked at the dark clouds. "I pray and hope He'll forgive us and come back someday."

"Don't you think?" Cheryl's voice brought me back to the present.

I shook my head once, clearing my thoughts. "I'm sorry, what?"

Cheryl rolled her eyes at me. "You and whatever is inside your head. You seem to always prefer it in there." She poked her finger on my forehead. I shrugged, not wanting to lie to her. "All right." She shoved her tablet inside her purse and stood. "I gotta work too, you know. See you later." She threw me a kiss and left, strolling through the coffee shop like a famous actress crossing the red carpet.

And I went back to work.

I recognized a lot of the faces that came for a coffee, a snack, or simply to hook up their laptops and work all day long, even if I didn't officially know them all. But there was another girl I knew here today.

I approached her table and smiled at her. "Hi Sarah, what can I get for you?"

She looked up at me from her laptop. "Hi Nadine. Just a black coffee. Got keep my energy going while working on this paper."

As a fellow pre-med student, Sarah Cunnings was in most of my classes. Though we had never exchanged more than small talk, she seemed like a very nice girl. If I hadn't had so many walls around myself, I thought maybe, just maybe, we could have been good friends.

I dipped my chin in a nod. "I hear you. I'll be right back."

After grabbing Sarah's coffee, attending to some other tables, scribbling down orders, and passing along the requests, I returned to the back of the café, inhaling deeply. I loved the strong and rich coffee scent of the place. I was crazy about coffee and blamed my addiction on my mother, who made the best black coffee I had ever tasted. She always had a mug ready whenever I wanted one. Because of it, my parents' kitchen had a permanent coffee aroma. Delicious.

I peeked out the door. In the front, Adam talked to the girl working the cash register. The manager was out again. I could hide out for a few minutes.

With my chemistry book under my apron, I sneaked into the dark and humid storage room and closed the door. I shouldn't be studying during work, but I still had one more exam before I was done with spring semester. I had to study if I wanted to pass organic chemistry this time.

I opened the book to chapter eight, ready to read about Aliphatic Hydrocarbon. The number eight shone, almost floating off the page. I disregarded it. Another hallucination probably. I read, trying to concentrate.

A light stab inside my chest spiderwebbed through me, carrying warmth and a rush of adrenaline down my arms and legs, tingling all over my skin. The world spun around me, enveloping me in darkness. I blinked and let the pull of the vision carry me.

Butterflies danced in my stomach. What type of vision would this one be? Maybe it would be a ghost-like vision where I only observed other people's actions, or maybe one where they interacted with me. I preferred the latter, of course, but I was always happy with the ghost visions too, since I was able to watch over the man who had stolen my heart.

All my visions were about the same perfect and gorgeous guy. My dream Prince Charming was named Victor Gianni. He was twenty-three, tall and athletic, with light brown hair streaked by some natural honey-colored highlights, brilliant sea-green eyes, and a smile that always made my heart somersault.

Yes, Victor lived only in my visions, but I was in love with him.

I had been seeing him for nine months. Because of him I had blown off too many dates, said no to too many guys. I had become unsociable, buried in my own fantasy world. But I didn't regret it.

One simple flicker of my eyes and I found myself transported to the world my visions created. The scene adjusted and I smiled. I was in a candlelit ballroom. Harmonious music came from violins and harps. A beautiful, deep red gown replaced my usual jeans and tee.

Curious, I touched my hair. Two side braids met at the back of my head. The rest of my long, light brown hair fell loose in soft curls.

I was here, in the world where Victor existed. I'd made the right choice leaving that psychiatrist's office. I needed to be with him. Always.

"Is anything wrong with your hair?" His melodic voice came from behind me.

My heart flipped furiously. I turned to face him and took in the perfection of his body clad in his black tuxedo and his honey hair, gelled back to show his face. I swallowed, my mouth suddenly dry.

"Hello, my favorite girl." He flashed one of his award-winning smiles. "How are you?" He came closer and took me in his arms, sweeping me into a dance without asking. He knew he didn't need to ask.

It was so easy for him to render me breathless. "I'm better now," I whispered, falling into step with him, letting him guide me through the ballroom.

"I've missed you." Serious now, his eyes bored into mine.

"I've missed you too." I stared up at him, struggling against my own mind so as not to lose myself in his face. He let go of my waist, guiding me through a graceful spin under his arm, then caught me again, pulling me back to him.

"Is your grandmother any better?" I asked.

Despite the fact that the world in my visions was not real, he had a life and a history in here. The setting where we found each other—a ballroom, atop a mountain, a classroom, a cruise ship, a bistro—changed often, but his daily life remained the same, in a world of his own, inside my mind.

After nine months having these visions, I didn't question their authenticity anymore, or why they felt so real and normal. They were a part of my life, like going to class or work.

However, his world wasn't quite perfect. His grandma had stomach cancer, and the diagnosis wasn't good. She was the only family he had left.

His face fell a little, but he kept spinning me across the floor. "She woke up better this morning, but the doctors want to transfer her to a larger hospital. One with a specialized cancer center."

"What are you going to do?"

"What can I do? If they think the move will be better for her, we'll go."

"The scholarship you were offered to join that school's research team ... It was for cancer research, wasn't it?" He was finishing his second year of medical school. Three months ago, he'd grown excited about the scholarship, but had not accepted the offer. He didn't want to leave his grandmother alone. At his nod, I added, "You could talk to them."

"I already did. I explained the situation, and they agreed to take my grandma. We'll be moving in about ten days."

"Good." I smiled and my breath caught. How could I have thought of leaving? I could never, ever stop having visions with him.

He spun me around once more. "Still, I've been worrying."

"About your grandma?"

His brows knitted. "About my purpose," he said simply, knowing I would understand his words. Since my first vision, Victor had stated his presence had a purpose. He wasn't here just for my enjoyment. Though I knew, we barely talked about it. We'd much rather spend quality time together.

"You don't know what your purpose is yet."

"That's what worries me," he said, slowing the pace. "The fact that we don't know. I've been feeling like I should know it already, like I should be acting on it. And that feeling only grows." He paused, caressing my face with his smooth fingertips, making me shiver. "I feel like something is going to happen. Soon."

"Something?" I forced myself to forget his warm, soul-flipping touch and focus on what disquieted him. "You don't know anything? Not even a clue?"

"Nope." He stopped dancing, but his grip around my waist tightened. "I have this feeling." He paused and put his hand over his chest. "This increasing sensation we should be ready." He chuckled, startling me. "Though don't ask me for what. I don't know." Lowering his head, my Prince Charming kissed my forehead. "You will be by my side, won't you?"

"You know I will. Always," I whispered, closing my eyes and relishing the touch of his warm lips.

"Sing for me?" he asked in a low, husky tone, his warm and fresh breath brushing against my skin. I shivered. "I love it when you sing."

"I will." I wanted to do this for him. Give him this gift of music he loved. I wanted him to feel my love for him through my voice, my singing. I inhaled deeply and prepared my throat to voice his favorite song.

"Nadine!" My eyes shot open, and I let out a yelp. A furious Adam stood before me.

Oh no, please, I wanted my vision back. I wanted Victor back. I put my hands over my temples and willed my mind to drift away, to go back to my Prince Charming. I tried to force the vision to take over, but I couldn't control it.

"What is up with you?" Adam asked.

This wasn't the first time he'd found me during an episode. He could tell our manager I had spaced out during work hours. If I wasn't fired today, it would certainly be another day if I continued like this.

"Nothing." I hid my chemistry book behind me. Yeah, like Adam would care about my studies after seeing me completely out of it. "Did you call me?"

"Yes! These freak shows are getting longer, Nadine. I've been calling you for the last ten minutes."

"Sorry," I mumbled. He didn't know why I zoned out, but based on past experiences, he knew it wasn't something he needed to worry about and call for help since he had seen me like this a hundred times.

I stood and took a deep breath. Love and hate were truly only separated by a thin line. I loved having my visions and spending time with Victor, and I hated I couldn't control when they happened and the inconvenience they caused me.

"Get back to work before I tell the manager you were hiding."

Why he didn't rat me out and laugh while I got fired, I'd never know. Perhaps because he knew, like him, I needed the money.

I left the storage room under his she-is-such-a-freak gaze and went back to waiting tables, planning to study tonight, even if I had to stay awake until morning.

That is, if a vision didn't rescue me.

3

My eyes didn't betray me. The most perfect, peaceful sky blanketed the hill that lay under it, and a bluish green ocean rolled in fierce waves. A soft breeze blew, bringing the scents of salt water and sweet flowers, and carrying with it the sound of the water breaking on the rocky shore. It was a perfect, magical, Kodak moment, as the older people used to say, and I didn't have my camera with me.

Wait. I patted my jeans.

I had nothing with me. A vision? It felt different. Too clear, too bright, too eerie. And where was Victor?

My last vision had been almost two weeks ago, and I already missed him. I couldn't wait to meet him, to talk to him, to feel his touch and warmth, and to tell him I passed organic chemistry. The spring semester was finally over and now was the time to celebrate. With Victor.

Looking for my Prince Charming, I pivoted, only to see a palace—but not one of stone like those seen in history books. Instead a palace made of crystal loomed before me. Shimmering. Shiny. Radiant. A step away from my feet, a crystal path wound up the mountain, leading to the palace's entrance.

Perhaps Victor was inside? But why would he be inside a palace? Hmm, perhaps he had already organized a celebration for me for passing the semester.

As I followed the path, I gawked at the palace. Its peculiarity was due in part to the many different structures that composed it: Greek columns, Roman domes, Nordic round towers, Egyptian pylons, English strong walls, Chinese colors, and Islamic ogee arches—all made of shiny crystal.

I reached the front steps and tilted my head, looking to the upmost point. Suddenly I felt small, like an ant on a human's threshold.

Then I heard voices.

"Hello? Victor?" Was this a ghost-type vision, or one I could interact with? I hoped not a ghost vision. I missed Victor.

Twirling a strand of hair around my finger, I followed the voices through a high, long corridor to another grand archway. There I froze.

Five men and five women stood around a circular reflecting pool, right in front of imposing crystal thrones. The sound of their soft steps was overridden by their firm voices. They appeared to be in their forties, clad in modern suits or gowns, each holding intricate, sparkling crystal staves.

The air around them smelled of flowers. Gardenias. They were planted in several tall, round crystal pots next to the thrones.

The elegant men and women argued and didn't seem to be aware of my presence. I let out a slow breath and tension eased from my joints.

A ghost-type vision. And one without Victor apparently. How odd. But what did this mean? I tiptoed closer, confident they couldn't see me. While I was here, I could at least figure out what was going on in the crystal palace.

"The humans are losing their faith," one of the males said,

his voice melodious and stout. His face was rough but incredibly beautiful. His dark eyes looked like deep black flames. The orb topping his stave shone with a daunting black light. "They don't believe in us anymore."

"Mitrus is right," an elegant female spoke. She had black hair that flowed to her knees and skin so pale it was nearly translucent. The color inside the sphere on her stave was purple. "The humans think those Greek or Roman gods are the real ones, when the truth is very different."

"Not only Greek and Roman gods, Imha," a man with a goatee and scruffy brown hair added. His white suit was crumpled and his jacket opened. He paraded with a rolling gait, like he rode a horse. A bright red orb topped his stave. "The humans even invented that one almighty god they speak of. The one with a capital G. Soon we'll be forgotten."

Who were these people? And where the hell was Victor?

Another man came into view. He was tall with tanned skin, broad shoulders, long golden hair, and light green eyes, like two precious demantoid garnets. He had a fine stubble beard that emphasized his chiseled jaw and squared chin. As the others he looked about forty, but a hot forty, like a famous movie star.

One of his hands was buried inside his pant pocket while the other gripped his white-orb scepter. His gaze focused on the reflecting pool. "I know, Omi," he said. His voice was strong, sure, and smooth. "I wish we could do more, but we cannot interfere with their lives."

"Nevertheless, we can prove our existence," Mitrus said. "Think about it, Levi. We need to do something."

"We won't cease to exist, Mitrus." A graceful woman stood beside Levi, her wavy hair white blond and her eyes clear blue. She held a stave crowned by an orb that emanated baby pink light. "We just need to craft a plan, without exposing ourselves."

"I agree with Ceris," Levi said, taking the woman's hand. "We should start talking about plans to increase our popularity among humans. We need to get them to believe in us again until they realize the gods they have believed in do not exist, those gods were myths based on our true existence."

Ceris smiled at Levi. "Well said."

"Are you blind? We have to punish those puny humans!" Mitrus raised his voice. "They deserve to feel the pain they inflict on us for forgetting us! We're weakening without their belief. We'll become powerless immortals."

"A little chaos." Imha let out a hollow chuckle that sounded heinous, while playing with her hair. "I like that."

"Yes, chaos," Omi said. "And death and destruction until the entire world comes to us, on their knees, begging for our mercy."

Wait, what? They were talking about destroying *my* world? Could my world get any worse? I hoped whatever they were and whatever they were saying was a figment of my imagination, or just another hallucination.

"Listen to yourselves!" Levi let go of Ceris's hand and faced Imha and Mitrus and Omi square on, no fear on his features. "If we scare them, they won't trust us. We have to help them, bring them joy, show them that every hard time will be compensated."

"I don't want their trust," Mitrus exclaimed, fisting his hands. My stomach clenched. Was it just me, or had the crystal walls shook? "I want their reverence, their obedience."

"You won't get those without their trust and respect," Levi said, his voice low, but embedded with steel.

"Only you care about their respect," Mitrus shouted.

"Of course I care about their respect." The muscles on Levi's neck corded and bunched. "You should too. Every good thing in life comes with respect. Civilization can be organized and just only if people respect each other."

"I don't know how you can be in charge," Mitrus spat

between gritted teeth. "You're weak and pitiful, like the humans."

"I think it's time for a change in our leadership," Imha suggested with a wicked smile. The cruelty of it, added to the ardent shine in her eyes, sent goose bumps over my arms. I embraced myself as if I could protect myself from her.

"You know it's not that simple," Levi said, letting his shoulders droop. "Being the leader is not my preferred pastime, but it is one I take seriously. I'm the balance between us. If we change that balance, the whole world will change."

"Not a bad idea," Mitrus murmured. With a sudden but subtle movement, he cast a shadowy bolt of energy at Levi. The bolt hit the god in the chest, and Levi fell on the crystal steps.

I gasped. Ceris cried out, and Imha laughed.

Before I could blink, Levi was on his feet again, holding a white bolt in his palms. "We are immortals, Mitrus. We cannot die. Why waste time with foolish fights? It'll only slow the important decisions."

"Perhaps we *can* die," Mitrus said in a controlled tone. Imha and Omi came to stand beside him. "Perhaps we only need the right weapon."

Together, one after another, the three of them hurled heavy black bolts toward Levi. I shouted for them to stop, disregarding the fact they couldn't see or hear me.

My pulse quickened. Damn it, I was in the middle of a fight, and there was nothing I could do about it. There was no way I could interrupt it. Why the hell had I entered this palace in the first place?

Ceris tried to protect Levi, but was flung back several feet. Levi had been disarmed. Each new assault hindered his attempts to stand.

She ran to him, waving her stave, casting what seemed to be

a magic wall around Levi, giving him enough time to sit up and take a deep, shuddering breath.

"Come on, love. Respond." Ceris rested her hand on his shoulder.

He stood. "Stop it, Mitrus. We're just wasting our stamina. You know these bolts don't hurt."

"But they annoy and weaken." Mitrus took out a black spike from his pocket. The spike had sharp ends, like a stake, and was no more than ten inches long with carvings that shone white.

Levi gaped at Mitrus. "You didn't."

"I did." Mitrus held the spike between his hands and squeezed. As if he summoned power, his palms turned bright red. The ruby glow transferred to the spike, its carvings now shining. Mitrus threw it at Levi.

Levi whipped around and cast a shield before him. He grabbed the spike with his hands before it could hit his body. He turned the spike toward Mitrus, putting it in the center of a huge white bolt, and hurled it at his foe. Mitrus did the same with another stake he had hidden.

At the same time, Levi and Mitrus were pierced by the spikes. Both stood, wavering, staring at each other with fury in their eyes, then their bodies shivered, shimmered, and disappeared.

All the noise and the movement in the room ceased.

For a couple of moments, nobody breathed. The gods seemed petrified.

Levi and Mitrus were gone. Not just dead, but gone. Bodies and staves, just gone.

"I can't feel them," Imha whispered, as if she hadn't trusted they would be able to kill Levi. Though, I was sure, killing Mitrus hadn't been a part of their plans.

A scream, desperate and piercing, ripped from Ceris's throat.

I flinched and closed my eyes, unable to bear the pain and the wrath carried by her cry.

"Nadine," someone called me. "Nadine, wake up!"

My eyes fluttered open. Cheryl. My rushing heartbeat waned.

"Hi," I muttered as I scanned my surroundings. We were in the university bookstore, and I stood before a shelf, a book opened in my hands. It took me a moment to clear my mind. I remembered I had finished my shift at work, and Cheryl had invited me to the bookstore. Then I had spaced out and the insane vision overtook me. Could any of that have been real? I had never seen anyone but Victor in my visions until now.

"Are you okay?" she asked, her silver eyes anxious. "I have been calling you for over fifteen minutes, and you didn't even blink. You freaked me out. I was about to call 911. What happened?"

"I-I'm not sure," I said. My head spun.

It had been the longest vision ever. Who were those people? And the crystal palace? It felt so real, so powerful.

"Come on." Cheryl grabbed my arm and led me toward the coffee shop inside the bookstore. "You should sit down."

"I'm fine." I pushed her hands away but didn't offer any more protest. I needed some time to think about what I saw.

Oh God, was I losing it? Besides visions of Victor, now was I going to see gods and goddess I had never heard of? I sighed and considered telling Cheryl, who sat across from me looking as if she expected me to blurt out some horrible news.

I opened my mouth. Nothing came out.

"You know you can tell me anything, right?" she said, her expression pleading.

I so wanted to talk to her about the visions. I really did. The thought of losing her friendship won over though, and once more I let the opportunity slip away. There was no way she could understand. She'd think I was mental.

I averted my gaze. "I know."

She patted my hand. "I'm gonna get us some coffee." She stood and went to the ordering line.

My mind spun through the images of the crystal palace and the impeccably dressed gods. Not that I knew why I had visions about Victor, but why the hell had I seen those gods?

4

I WALKED OUT OF THE UNIVERSITY CAFÉ INTO THE STREET AND took a deep breath. My nose wrinkled from the foul smells flooding over the walls. I tried to ignore the stench. I was too wound up for anything to bring me down. I figured I'd better head home and give myself a break. Maybe I was working too hard. Maybe the visions were from exhaustion, not some psychiatric disorder. Maybe I just needed to sleep the whole weekend.

After ten days of working ten-hour shifts, I was relieved it was Friday and I had the weekend off. To keep my spirits high, I had to block from my mind the knowledge that on Monday the summer semester would start, which meant more studying, more work, and more crazy-hour shifts. But maybe soon I'd be working with something more satisfying than coffee grounds and bagels. Following Cheryl's advice, I had applied for the Patient Care Technician position. I was told I'd hear from them in a few days. For now, I planned to chill.

I greeted the security guard at the university's gate with a quick nod and stepped outside the protected area. I always felt safe inside the walls. Besides providing students with an outstanding education, the institution emphasized security, earning the vote of trust of many parents throughout the country and around the globe—including mine.

After the darkness took over, NYU changed too. Before, its campus had been spread through Lower Manhattan. Now, the university was confined to the area around Washington Square Park, the entire site contained within a five-block radius, protected by thick sixteen-foot walls. Cameras and security guards kept watch. Only Langone Medical Center was outside, but it was also heavily protected and watched. At least my apartment wasn't far.

When NYU moved to one location and closed itself in, many apartment buildings were built around it, and their owners hoped they would be used by the students who were not able to get a university dorm.

During my first semester at NYU, I was in a dorm inside the walls and that was where I met Raisa, my roommate. Raisa and I decided to move to one of the apartments close to NYU so we could have more privacy and larger rooms. We chose a building with a good security system, only one block from NYU's south gate.

Even so, I hurried and glanced over my shoulder many times to make sure nobody or no bat followed me.

I stopped at the newsstand on my block, pulled in by the large picture of an exploding volcano. The headline read: *Volcano in Mexico deemed dormant erupts and sweeps surrounding cities.*

The tragic news didn't stop there. In Australia, a containment wall ruptured and the massive waves washed away several cities and ended hundreds of lives. Without the full strength of the sun, the agriculture crisis was rapidly scaling up, causing many farmers to become criminals—yesterday the most feared gang robbed five banks in Chicago—and the tri-state area population of giant bats had grown by thirty percent in the last four months.

I shuddered, thinking about the bats. No one knew if they were a new species of bat, or if regular bats evolved and become larger somehow.

"I wonder when we'll find a good headline." The owner of the newsstand grabbed a newspaper from the pile.

"Me too," I whispered. I turned and ran the thirty feet to my building's door and quickly put my index finger on the biometric lock. A second later, I was inside the foyer, inhaling the fresh lemony scent from recently applied floor wax.

"Good evening, Miss Sterling," the concierge welcomed from behind his tall desk.

"Hi, John," I greeted him and entered one of the elevators, noticing his attention had already returned to the screens under his desk, where he monitored our building.

As the doors of the elevator opened again, I glanced at the floor number printed on the wall before me. I always tried to avoid it, but the more I fought against it, the more the pull to stare at it grew stronger.

Number eight. Shining brightly, even though it was painted a dull gray on the white wall.

I sighed and stepped into the corridor, wondering if it was time to face a psychiatrist once and for all, but then I heard my neighbor Olivia's voice—lilting and warm as she sang one of my favorite songs. I smiled. Singing with Olivia would be a perfect way to relax. I rushed toward the end of the corridor and knocked on her apartment door.

Her beautiful singing died. "Who is it?"

I could already see the small frown forming over her round brown eyes. She was always suspicious of everything and everyone. Who wouldn't be living in this world?

"Your partner," I answered.

The door flew open and Olivia stood before me, her face split by a huge grin. "Come in!" She pulled me inside her loft and disappeared into the kitchen. I followed, then stopped.

In the kitchen she drained a soda, then put the can down on a pile of dirty dishes and draped a towel over the mess. I winced, though part of me wished I could drape a towel over all the messes in my life. But dutiful daughters always did the dishes.

"When was the last time you cleaned your apartment?" I asked, pushing a pile of shoes to the side, trying to make room so I could sit on the couch. I forced myself not to look at the rest of the apartment. If I did, I would start cleaning for her.

I moved a guitar to the side and pitied the many instruments she had. If they were mine, I would take good care of them, not dump them in a pile.

"Hmm," Olivia said, putting a finger on her chin. "When I moved in, I think."

I rolled my eyes and sat down on the little space I was able to create. "Almost two years ago."

Olivia shrugged and flipped her wild chestnut curls. "It's not bothering me." She sat on the floor, crossing her legs.

"I heard you singing." My voice carried a dreamy tone. It became like that whenever I spoke of music. "Were you rehearsing?"

"Not really. Just killing time."

"You're so lucky. I wish I was in the music program with you."

"You aren't in the music program because you don't want to be. With your voice, your audition would last twenty seconds, tops."

"I can't. You know that."

"What I know is that you like to play the Good Samaritan." Olivia grabbed one of her Spanish guitars. "If you were a little selfish, you would follow your dreams."

If I could follow my dreams, I would wake up and see Victor by my side every day.

"How is the new piece going?" I changed subjects, drawing her attention away from my lack of backbone and to her upcoming composition class.

"It's good, but I need a break." She handed me the guitar, an impish smile radiating across her face. "Let's sing."

Smiling, I took the guitar and positioned myself at the edge of the sofa so I had better control over the instrument. Olivia got up and went to the keyboard crammed against the wall.

I ran my fingers over the chords. "What do you want to sing?"

"I'm open to suggestions. What inspires you today?"

An image of Victor smiling at me flashed in my mind. I named a popular love song featuring deep, haunting melodies and a seductive tone.

"Hmm, romantic." She winked and I blushed.

We sang and played as the world outside melted away. While singing, there was no chaos, no violence, no darkness. I closed my eyes, and the world was almost perfect. Only missing Victor.

Olivia and I were a good duo, not only while singing and playing, but in our friendship too. I met her when Raisa and I moved in next door. I couldn't believe my luck when she had told me she was a music major and had invited me to sing with her. Every now and then we would get together just to sing. But on weekends, Olivia usually went out with Raisa. The two of them insisted upon my presence, but I always declined. I preferred to remain home and wait for a vision.

We were on our fourth song when a knock on the door made us stop.

"Who is it?" Olivia asked, getting up.

"The only one who can bear you two singing," Raisa said.

Olivia went to open the door and paused. "Apologize, or you

can't come in," she threatened, portraying a faux-serious face. I laughed.

"Ah, get out of my way." Raisa barreled in. She stuck her tongue out and walked past Olivia, winking at me. She was a tall brunette with hazel eyes and short brown hair—she had almost killed the poor hairdresser who took off too much, then demanded her money back. Olivia wished I had Raisa's strength and would go for what I really wanted—to major in music. But Olivia didn't have a family in need. Medicine would provide me with enough money to help my family.

"Bah, I'm gonna call your parents. Where are your manners?" Olivia asked, pretending to be outraged.

"I left my manners at their house when I moved here." Raisa pushed a pile of books from the love seat, not caring when they scattered across the floor, and sat down. For a moment, I wondered if Olivia would complain, but observing the state of the rest of the loft, I doubted it.

Raisa took off her shoes. "Do you have anything to eat?"

"Raisa," I said, amused. "There is plenty of food at our house."

"I know, but it's always the same stuff," she complained. "Olivia has some different snacks and candies."

Laughing, Olivia beckoned toward the kitchen as she sat back on the stool. "Help yourself. If you want to wash the dishes too, I won't protest."

"In your dreams," Raisa yelled from the kitchen, already opening the few cabinets, digging for whatever she could find. "So, there's a party tomorrow. You coming with us, Nad?" She came back into the living room carrying a bowl of chocolate-covered cookies.

I chuckled. "You know I'm not coming, but I admire your persistence."

"I'm going to give up on you one of these days." Raisa threw a cookie at me. She'd been saying that for almost a year now. "Come on, just this once. I know you'll love the party."

And that was when I saw her. The world flew away and her flawless face appeared, almost hovering in front of me. "Go," Ceris said, her voice firm, chin set, eyes flashing. Determined.

Then gone.

"Hello, Nadine?" Raisa snapped her fingers in front of my eyes. "Everything all right?"

"Yes," I mumbled, looking around to make sure Ceris had been just a vision.

"I hate it when you do that," Olivia said, kneeling before me. She must have approached when I was out. "Are you sure you're all right?"

I detested having visions while in the girls' company, but it was inevitable. I couldn't pick when and where they took over.

Though, at that moment, hating that I had no control over the visions was the last thing on my mind. I had seen the goddess, Ceris, and she'd specifically told me to go to the party. That had never happened before—a vision telling me what to do. What did that mean? That I was truly becoming insane?

But curiosity about what could happen at the party won out, even over the nervousness. I had to know what the goddess wanted.

Now, for the first time in months, I couldn't wait to go to a party. "I'm going," I said, not quite believing my own words.

"What?" Raisa squealed, surprised but pleased. "Are you serious?"

"Yes. I'm going with you two."

Giggling, she threw herself over me, hugging me tight. "Yeah! I can't believe it!"

Olivia smiled. "Me neither."

"This is going to be great." Raisa sat beside me again, but she jumped up and down on the cushion almost bursting with excitement. "I can't wait!"

Olivia and I started playing a song and singing, and Raisa settled down, joining in—her voice sounding like a flapping chicken—while my mind swirled around Ceris's image and the possibilities of what could happen at the party. Sleeping the weekend away was a dim memory.

***

"NAD, ARE YOU READY?" RAISA KNOCKED ON MY BEDROOM DOOR again.

I had been ready for almost fifteen minutes. I was hiding in the dim light of my table lamps, afraid to look in the mirror. It had been a long time since I'd gone to a party. And tonight, a Saturday night, I was going out.

My hands shook, but I wasn't about to give up. I had a purpose behind the simple I'm-going-out excuse. I had to find out why a goddess, vision or not, wanted me to go to this particular party. What did she want me to see?

The truth was I wanted to make sure I wasn't going crazy. If I went and there was something there for me, then I would know.

I'd tried on multiple outfits, the result of which lined the floor of my room. My hand itched to pick up, to organize, but I forced myself to step over the mess and join Olivia and Raisa in the living room.

"I am," I said.

"Ooh, la la," Olivia exclaimed, approaching me and pushing at my shoulders, causing me to spin around in place. "Nad, you should dress up more often."

"She should, shouldn't she?" Raisa sounded proud. Of course it had been her hard work that put me together for the occasion.

"Is it too much?" I asked, looking down at my outfit. Skintight, low-rise black jeans with a few rhinestones running down the sides, an olive backless top, and black peep-toe pumps—the last two items provided by Raisa, the fashion diva—completed my outfit. She also supplied the makeup.

"No, not at all." Olivia smiled at me.

"You should wear green more often, Nad," Raisa said, coming over to us. "It emphasizes your eyes."

"It does," Olivia agreed.

I glanced at the mirror near the entrance. Yes, I could see the green in my eyes from across the room.

The intercom rang and Raisa went into the kitchen to answer it. Seconds later, she was back.

"Our cab is here!" She clapped her hands, excited. "Let's go." As we dashed to the door, she added, "You guys are bringing your student cards, right? Without them, we won't be able to get in."

"Yes." I was thankful for the heavy security anywhere we went, but sometimes it was a true pain in the ass.

"Can we go now?" Olivia pushed so we exited the apartment more quickly.

The phone rang, and I returned to pick it up.

"Don't answer that," Raisa snapped from the corridor. "Whoever it is can figure out we aren't home and call our cells." She reached in and dragged me out of the apartment.

I looked at the phone on the side table. "What if it is important?" I'd been waiting for that call from Langone and didn't want to miss it, though I wasn't too sure they would call on a Saturday night.

"The important thing right now is us getting to that party," she objected, trying to close the door.

True, but work was also important. I had a responsibility to myself, to my family. I drew away from Raisa and marched to the phone. The number on the caller ID was my mom's, not from Langone, but an important call anyway. I picked it up.

"Mom, just a second," I said, then covered the speaker with my hand and spoke to the girls. "It's my mother. You guys go. I'll catch up in a few."

"And how are you getting to the club?" Olivia asked.

"I'll call another cab."

"No way," Raisa said. "This is another excuse. I won't let you escape this easily."

"I'm not escaping," I assured her. "I haven't talked with my mother for over a week. It'll take only a few minutes."

"Then we'll wait." She stomped her foot on the carpeted floor.

"No, no." I shook my head. "You'll miss the cab. You guys should go and get us a nice table."

"Nad, please."

"Come on, Raisa." Olivia pulled my roommate by her wrist. "You know we won't be able to change her mind."

Raisa sighed. "I know." She glanced at me. "Find us when you get there."

"I will." I winked and blew a kiss, then gave my attention to my mother.

I was the oldest of four children—two girls and two boys—but we were supposed to be five. And that was why my mother called tonight.

"Ten years today," she said.

"I know," I whispered. How could I forget the main reason why I was letting go of my singing dream?

I had been the *oops* baby. My parents had just started going out when my mother got pregnant, but they'd decided to give marriage and parenting a try. My mother left her teaching job and moved to the farm where my father was an employee. Life on the farm wasn't easy, especially since the agricultural crisis was getting worse. Our shack was small, simple, cold, and huddled together with the other employees' houses—like old tenement houses we used to see pictures of in history books.

Being an only child, my mother dreamed of a huge family—though, in my opinion, poor families shouldn't have more than one child. How were parents supposed to care and provide everything for their children?

I was eight when my mother got pregnant again. Once I went to the doctor with her. A rare visit, as we had so little money. The doctor told my mom she wasn't eating well, and the baby would be born underweight. What did he want us to do? The farm wasn't doing well, and my father struggled to keep our plates full.

Troy was born weighing only three pounds. Soon after his birth, he began losing too much weight. Since she was malnourished, my mother's milk wasn't nutritious enough, the doctor said. We couldn't afford baby formula. He died before he was six months old.

"I went to his grave this morning," my mother said, yanking my thoughts from the past.

I wiped the tears away, thanking Raisa for her waterproof makeup.

"Yeah, Mom, that's good." I cleared my throat. The pain ate at me the way it did when he'd first died. She quickly changed the subject and filled me in on what my three siblings were up to. I listened, halfhearted, still remembering Ceris's message from my vision, wondering if my vision world could be linked to the real world. At a pause in the conversation, I finally said, "Do you need anything? Want me to send more money?"

"Oh no, we're getting by just fine. I still have a little from what you sent last time." I heard a sharp breath intake. "I'm sorry you have to worry about us so much."

"It's okay." I shifted on my seat. I didn't like talking to her about this. Not so openly. "Listen. Raisa is waiting for me. Call you tomorrow, okay?"

"Okay." She sounded disappointed. God, I hated making her sad.

We said goodbye and hung up. Fifteen minutes after the start of our conversation, I was calling the cab company.

"One hour to get a taxi?" I asked the dispatcher, outraged.

"Or more, lady," she said.

Huffing, I disconnected the call and twisted my hair with my finger, wondering what to do. I could stand at the sidewalk and try to holler down a taxi, hoping it was a proper one—there were several reports of people being kidnapped and abused by false taxi drivers. I could wait one hour—or more—for the company to send a cab. Or, I could run the six blocks to the club with my pepper spray in hand. A crazy idea that could get me in trouble.

But I had to know. I had to find out what Ceris wanted with me. She had been in one of my visions, and suddenly she popped into my real life, telling me to go to a real event. It sounded so crazy, so insane, that I had to know; I had to find out if I had finally lost it.

Or learn what she had to show me.

5

I GOT MY JACKET AND MY PURSE FROM THE CLOSET, LEFT MY apartment, and marched toward the elevator, not believing what I was about to do. I felt the pull to look at the number eight painted on the wall but resisted. I had a party to get to—a party a goddess told me to attend. No shiny numbers or lack of taxis would stop me from finding out what she wanted me to see.

Downstairs, Paul was on duty. The concierge stood up when I walked past him on my way to the door. "Miss Sterling, are you waiting for a cab?"

"No, my friend is coming to pick me up," I lied, flashing him a false smile I hoped was convincing enough. I had my hand inside my purse, clutching my can of pepper spray. "She called and is already coming around the corner."

"Would you mind waiting inside?" He looked anxious with his brow creased.

"That's okay. I can see her from here." I left before he could say anything else.

I looked both ways. Nobody outside, good or bad. I darted away.

I hadn't run a full block when I decided I couldn't take the high-heeled pumps slaughtering my feet. I cursed and tried to ignore my shoes, but the pain was too much. I halted, stashed the pepper spray inside my purse, and took off the shoes to find a newly formed blister and a bloody scratch on my left Achilles tendon. Damned heels!

The flapping of wings froze me in place. My heart rate accelerated. Shit. I stopped without thinking about the consequences, and now bats hovered nearby. Why did they always come for me? As far as I knew, they didn't attack every single person they saw when flying around, but they did attack me whenever there was an opportunity.

I scanned the area, trying to find some people, even foul-looking ones, with whom I could mingle and mislead the bats. Nobody. The streets were deserted. When were New York's streets *ever* deserted?

I didn't know whether to remain frozen and hope the bats confused me with a statue, retreat to a doorway and hide, or run back to my building. Even if I hid, they would find me. I decided for the third option and bolted.

The flapping noise increased. Oh no, now there was more than one. Another bad decision. I glanced over my shoulder to see how many there were and gasped. My legs wobbled and collapsed. I fell onto my back to the paved ground, fear choking my throat. There were no less than *seven* bats coming for me!

They were hideous and nasty, as large as a person. Their bony bodies were covered by a viscous gray skin, countless teeth bared and sharp, and wings large and bristly.

I cringed, unable to scream. Four of the bats landed before me and hobbled closer. Their talons scratched against the concrete surface of the sidewalk, making a dreadful screeching sound. Their fetid stench of slobber and decay and rotting flesh reached me, and I fought the urge to puke.

I crawled a few feet away and watched in horror as three

other bats landed behind me, blocking my only escape route. I was surrounded.

I recalled my pepper spray inside my purse. I carried it for muggers and robbers, but my *weapon* had saved me from these creatures before. Of course pepper spray hadn't hurt the bats, just bought me some distraction so I could run away. And I had never been attacked by more than two bats at once, but it was worth a try.

With trembling hands, I reached inside my purse. But as my fingers stroked the can, a bat lunged at my back. Yelling, I covered my head with my arms. The animal clawed, tearing into my jacket.

I tried to roll over and crawl somewhere, anywhere, but was pushed down by a potent blow. I hit the concrete, hard, and gasped as the air flew out of me.

Tears brimmed in my eyes. I struggled to hash out a new plan. Nothing. My mind was a ball of pure terror and I couldn't think through it.

I raised my head and looked over. Two more bats glided up to me. I could see in their crimson eyes they were done playing. This time they would strike for real. There was nothing I could do. I held my breath and braced myself, feeling a slow tear trickle down my face.

Their talons scratched my already torn jacket. I waited, wondering if I'd die or be injured for life.

Then ... Nothing.

My eyes shot open. Was I having one of my hallucinations? Were the bats really retreating? I sat up and rubbed my eyes. The bats withdrew, their wings folded behind them, but they seemed to be recoiling from something—or someone. I turned around and saw the back of a tall man. He stood about ten feet from me, his head held high as if a defiant attitude would send the bats away. The odd part was—it did. The bats avoided looking at him as they slowly retreated. Seconds later, the creatures unfurled their gargantuan wings and flew away.

I gaped at the back of the mysterious man.

When the bats were gone, the guy pivoted and stared at me. I couldn't see his face in the dark, but he looked menacing and I wasn't sure I was better with him or the bats.

Without taking his gaze from mine, he stepped forward.

I clambered back.

He stopped.

"It's okay," he said. His voice was strong and sure and entrancing. He had an accent, something between Arabic and French I couldn't identify. "You're hurt, aren't you?"

I didn't answer. Instead I scrambled to my feet and almost fell over, nauseated. I didn't though, because the mysterious guy caught me. His strong hands gripped my elbows.

Until then, I had not felt any pain, but his palm was wrapped around one of the wounds. "Ouch!" I pulled away and bent my elbow to get a better look.

"Let me see," he said, gently taking my arm and slipping off my jacket sleeve. "It's not too bad. Did they hurt you somewhere else?"

His deep, dark eyes bored into mine, and my breath caught. Unkempt jet-black hair framed the rough edges of his fair face, and broad shoulders were bracketed by his leather biker jacket. Despite looking frightening, he was gorgeous.

I wasn't sure what was happening. Why I was letting this guy help me and even strip off my coat? I could barely reason, but I ended up nodding. "My back."

As if he were an old friend, the guy turned me around and removed the rest of my jacket. I shivered, both from the cold and from knowing his intense gaze scrutinized my bare skin.

"Hmm. These gashes are a little worse, but nothing some rest and care won't fix."

Self-conscious, I put my ragged jacket back on, tightening it around myself, and turned to face him. "How did you get the bats to back off?"

His eyes narrowed. I guess he hadn't expected my question. "I'm not sure."

"How can you don't know?" I almost shouted, irritated with his calm stance. Who the hell was this stranger? And how the hell was it he didn't know how he'd saved me? "You just came over and those bats fled. They were scared of you!"

"I don't know why they keep their distance from me, but that's been happening lately." He extended his hand. "I'm Micah. And you are?"

I was surprised by his statement. Was he lying, though? I couldn't be sure. I frowned at his hand, not sure I should take it. But then again, he *had* just saved my life.

"Nadine." I took his—*Micah's*—hand, and cold clutched my skin where it contacted his. I quickly pulled my hand back.

His eyes were wide. "You felt that too?" At my nod, he whispered, "That's odd." He stared at his hand as if it had been contaminated by my touch.

Hmm, perhaps my hand was contaminated too. But by what? What had been that cold jolt? My adrenaline finally settling down? I looked up at the sky again. No bats. That was something. But it was still dangerous outside, and this guy was a stranger. Who knew what he was up to?

I twined a strand of hair around my finger. "I should get going." I retreated a few steps, fighting to stay upright against the pain. "Uh, thanks."

"Wait." Micah came up to me again. "You shouldn't be outside alone. Those bats seemed to like you." The corner of his lips twitched, as if the situation were funny. I glared at him and he grew serious again. "I can give you a ride."

"That's not necessary." I resumed walking, but a jolt of pain ricocheted through my back and arms. I winced and tripped, almost collapsing.

"Come on." He grabbed my wrist. "If you don't want to fall or get attacked again, it's important I give you a ride."

"All right," I mumbled, hating myself for accepting his offer.

"Over here." Still holding onto me, he walked to the other side of the street, where a black and red Harley Davidson was parked.

"That's your ride?" I gaped. Wow. The motorcycle was stunning. I had never seen a Harley before, other than in pictures. There weren't many bikes around since it was easy to get robbed or attacked when riding one. And Harleys were especially rare.

He offered me a grin. "Nice, huh? It's my baby." Without releasing my wrist, he put his other hand on the small of my back and gently pushed me forward. "Come on, let's get you home."

If he hadn't assisted me, I wouldn't have been able to cross the street. Each step sent painful jolts through my back. I winced, then squeezed his arm, which I only realized I held after I dug my nails into his jacket. He let out a chuckle.

"Sorry," I mumbled, conscious of the heat growing in my cheeks. I loosened my grip, but didn't let go.

"No problem."

He hopped on his bike and helped me sit behind him. I avoided looking at his looming body and crossed my arms as if it were forbidden to touch him.

From over his shoulder, Micah glanced at me and laughed. It was one perfect sound.

"What?" I snapped, tightening my arms over my chest.

"I won't bite," he joked.

I had no intention of moving until he reached behind his back, grabbed my arms, and put them around his waist, pointedly resting my hands over his rigid abdomen. I had a hard time controlling my breathing, his sweet scent was intoxicating, the impulse to run my fingers over his lean muscles, and the urge to scoot closer to him.

He turned the Harley on, and it revved to life. "Where do you live?"

"At the next block." I pointed behind us. "A white and blue building near the corner."

"You were attacked one block from your home?" He sounded amused. I remained quiet. At least he wasn't accelerating, and I didn't have to hang on tighter. "Boy, those bats must love you."

"Shut up," I snapped, then felt my cheeks burn with anger and embarrassment.

"Sorry." He suppressed a chuckle. It only irritated me more. He drove the bike over to my building and brought it to a stop in front of the main door. "Is it here?"

"Yes." I released him and got off the bike, but I had to lean against him when nausea and pain assaulted me.

He tugged me to him. "If you weren't in such a rush to get rid of me, I could help you."

I grunted and let him guide me to the door. I used the biometric lock, but Paul had already seen me and rushed up.

"Miss Sterling, what happened?" He glanced from me to Micah to my torn jacket.

"Bats," Micah answered for me.

"Again?" Paul asked. I struggled to free myself from Micah and let the concierge help me.

Micah glanced down at me. "Again?"

"I guess bats like her," Paul said. He chuckled and Micah grinned. I glared at them. "Sorry." He straightened and took me from Micah, hooking my arm over his shoulders to steady me. "I'd better get you to your apartment."

I turned to Micah. "Thanks again."

"Yes. Good night." He bowed and smiled, making my pulse faster. Then, he turned and strode out the door.

After the concierge helped me to my apartment and left me alone, I took a warm shower and sat down to clean my wounds. I had scratches on my back and arms and a purple bruise on my belly.

Because of the previous bat attacks I had experienced, I kept rabies vaccine in my medicine cabinet—it wasn't something pharmacies sold over the counter, but being in the pre-health program facilitated a few perks. I gave myself a shot and took three ibuprofen pills for pain.

I was leaving the bathroom when I caught my reflection in the foggy mirror. In front of the glass, I brushed my long, light-brown hair—it was the feature I liked most about me. I smiled, remembering how Victor liked my hair too.

That was when I recalled the reason I had gone out on the streets in the first place.

The brush hit the floor, producing a loud thud. Holy hell! Because of the bat attack, I'd ended up not going to the club and finding out what Ceris wanted to show me.

Worse, I drooled over Micah and forgot about Victor.

My heart sank, and I was unable to shake the feeling I'd cheated on the man from my vision.

6
———

Raisa wanted to beat me after she got home from the club at three in the morning, but when I showed her my wounds, she grew worried and yelled, saying I was the most stupid person alive—I had to agree with her—and she would never leave me behind again.

On Sunday, I slept almost all day. Raisa and Olivia checked on me several times. Then on Monday, I got up early to go to work before my first day of summer classes. I had to take two ibuprofen pills to be able to stand. I just wanted to get through the day without remembering the bat attack and feeling sick to my stomach. I purposefully avoided Raisa and slipped out of the apartment without her or Olivia noticing. I'd had enough of my roommate's lectures.

Cheryl strolled into the coffee shop. I smiled at her, admiring her beauty and elegance. Every time I looked at her, a good feeling—like a sense of familiarity and completion—filled my chest. It was a shame her frequent trips out of town for work limited our conversations and time together. I felt lost and alone whenever she was gone.

All the tables were taken, mostly by students, so she sat on a tall stool at the counter.

Without having to ask, I handed her what I knew she wanted: a tall espresso and a chocolate cupcake.

"Yummy." Her silver eyes shone as she bit into the cupcake. "Did you apply for the position at the hospital?"

"I did."

"Good. Now it's just a matter of time."

"You say that as if you're certain they will call me."

"I know they will." She winked, taking another bite of the cupcake.

I wished I could stay and talk, but instead I pushed myself off the counter and worked my rounds, rushing around the café, serving tables, scribbling down orders, and occasionally helping the manager with the mess in the storage room.

Near the end of my shift, Raisa arrived and sat beside Cheryl. She told Cheryl about the university party on Saturday. The one I'd missed. Flickers of fear touched my stomach at the memory.

"Nadine was supposed to go too," I overheard Raisa say as I walked past them. Anger crept over me. I wanted to avoid being lectured, but here at work I was trapped.

"Supposed to? Why didn't you go?" Cheryl asked, sounding disappointed I had missed the only party I had agreed to go to in almost a year.

I grunted, hating to remember the reason.

"Oh, the brave Nadine decided to go alone. And on foot," Raisa exclaimed, outraged. "She was attacked by bats."

Cheryl's eyes widened, and she nearly choked on the cupcake. "Again? You have to be more careful. Promise me you won't wander alone like that anymore." Her silver eyes conveyed worry and concern.

Shame warmed my cheeks. First Raisa's lecture, now

Cheryl's. I hated to disappoint them and hated appearing childish and immature and incapable of making smart decisions. "I promise," I mumbled, trying to hide behind my apron and tray, still ashamed of my poor choices. And more ashamed at the memory of my visceral response to hot, hot Micah.

For some reason, I hadn't told my friends about him. The truth was I was trying to pretend he didn't exist. That I had not met him. My heart still contracted every time I thought about Victor, as if I betrayed him by noticing how handsome Micah was.

When my shift was over, Raisa and I walked to the science building for the first class of summer session. I sometimes struggled in biology, but I needed to ace this class to keep my grades up. No medical school would accept a student who flunked biology. Besides, I needed the distraction to stop thinking about Ceris, the bat attack, and Micah.

Being on campus always felt uplifting. The sidewalks were clean. The fake flowerbeds were colorful and released a sweet scent—part of the perfume stored inside the plastic plants. The streetlights were brighter and the safety was incomparable. If only the skies weren't so dark and the June air wasn't so chilly.

My eyes were still skyward when I heard cawing. I stiffened but remained alongside Raisa. Could it be a bat? On campus? But bats didn't caw. Then I saw it. A raven, soaring right above us. The bird was almost imperceptible against the dark gray sky.

Heedless of the raven's presence, Raisa chatted about the latest collection of the newest fashion prodigy, whoever he or she was. I didn't bother showing the bird to her, even though birds weren't easily spotted anymore, and forgot all about it when we entered the classroom a few minutes later.

Raisa and I took seats along the back wall, where some of her friends sat. As expected, she engaged in a detailed conversation with them about guys, clothes, and makeup.

To pass the time, I whirled my hair around my fingers while humming one of my favorite songs.

"Oh yeah." Raisa turned, including me in the conversation. "I forgot to tell you. We saw the hottest guy ever at the party."

"Really?" I asked, pretending to be interested but wanting to get a head start on the upcoming lecture.

"Oh yeah, he was gorgeous."

I suppressed the urge to roll my eyes. "Cool. Did you guys meet him?"

Raisa's smile faded. "No. He may have escaped this time, but he won't for too long. The buzz is he's a new graduate student."

I frowned. They were talking about a new student. Micah was new, and he seemed a few years older than me, like a graduate student. Plus he was majorly attractive. "What does he look like?"

"Tall and hot, with dark blond hair and light blue or green eyes," Raisa said. "He wasn't too close to us, so I couldn't get a good look at his eyes."

No, this guy wasn't Micah. Internally, I condemned myself for feeling relieved.

The instructor entered and started the typical first day of summer school speech, which saved me from having to hear more descriptions of a supposedly hot, unknown guy.

Suddenly something else saved me from my boring biology class.

I felt the familiar pang in my chest, the spreading of warmth through my veins, and the tingling over my skin. Then, I entered the vision.

I found myself in the middle of Washington Square at the center of NYU's campus. The scent of flowers and trees surrounded me. Like all my visions, the sky above me was blue and the day was warm. A surge of joy rushed through me. I'd see Victor. I'd missed him so much; the weird encounter with Micah only reinforced how much I cared about Victor. I couldn't wait to spend time with him and reconnect the way we always did.

Despite the sameness of the sky, in each vision the setting was different. My clothes normally changed to match. This time, I frowned when I saw myself dressed in my usual attire: jeans, snug tee, a thin jacket, and ballet flats. Yeah, it screamed "relaxing day in the park," but I was hoping for more. I didn't want Victor to see me dressed so casually.

"What's with the pout?" I heard his voice and brightened. There he was, coming toward me, in jeans, a fitted button-down shirt, and casual shoes. But he didn't look simple. He looked like an expensive apparel model during a photo shoot.

"Hi," I was able to utter. My heart pounded so fast my chest hurt.

He halted a foot from me. His tall, elegant frame loomed over my petite form, and his delicious scent wrapped around me, making me dizzy. He smiled down at me. "Hi." He pushed a lock of my hair out of my face, his fingers caressing my skin. I shivered. "So. Why the disappointed face? From knowing you'll see me?"

I giggled. "Yeah, right." God, I had to get a better hold of myself when around him. Sometimes I thought I was under a love spell or something. "I was disappointed with my clothes." I motioned to them. "I would rather be wearing a ball gown or a cocktail dress."

His sea-green gaze swept me from head to toe, and I blushed.

"I don't see anything wrong with how you're dressed." He stepped toward me and wrapped his arms around my waist. The air ran out of my lungs. "In fact, I think you look beautiful," he whispered in my ear.

I shivered again. His warm breath washed over my neck, making butterflies dance in my stomach. His lips touched my skin, setting it on fire. I could faint.

I went to lay my head against his shoulder but he pulled back, although keeping his hold on me.

"Unfortunately," he said, "I have to go."

"What?" I yelped. Victor leaving me had never happened before. He always stayed with me until someone yanked me out of my vision. "Where are you going?" I heard the frustration in my voice.

He smiled. "Don't worry, Nadine. We'll see each other again."

"But where do you have to go? Can't I come with you?"

"I don't know." He retreated a step and extended his hand. "Want to come?"

I took his hand. "Of course." I walked to his side, ready to go, but he remained in place, still staring at me, a pleased smile over his full lips. "What?" I asked. I liked when he stared at me like that, but I never could stop from blushing.

His fingers traced the skin over my nose. "I like these," he said, probably referring to my faint freckles. "They are one of your many charms." The heat on my cheeks increased. "I like when you blush too." He chuckled and drew me closer. "I like everything about you."

Oh, I was taken.

He ran his hand through my hair, and then leaned toward me. *Oh God.* We had flirted and acted like boyfriend and girlfriend for over nine months, but he had never kissed me. Now he kept coming closer. I found myself standing on my toes, waiting for his lips to meet mine.

A blaring caw diverted my attention upward. The raven. In my vision?

"I don't understand," I said as I stared at the winged creature. The thrill of almost kissing him faded away.

"Yours?"

"No. But I saw a raven this morning, when I was going to class."

"Is it the same one?"

"I don't know."

"Come." He took my hand again. "Forget about the bird. Let's go."

It was almost impossible to pretend the raven wasn't soaring near us, but I tried. I took his hand and let Victor lead the way.

"Do you know where you're going?"

His brow creased for a moment. "Not exactly. I know the direction I have to go. I can feel it in here." He touched his chest.

"Do you think this feeling has something to do with your purpose?"

"I hope it does." He offered me an encouraging smile.

Side by side, we walked toward NYU's north gate. In my visions, even the world outside the protective campus walls was clean, warm, and perfect. There were trees and flowerbeds, all alive and well. The people who strolled through the streets seemed happy and friendly. Pleased, I squeezed his hand.

"Where to?" I asked after we crossed the north gate.

"I feel as if I should go that way." He pointed northeast.

We were crossing the street when Raisa's voice cut through my vision. "Nadine."

I looked around and found myself back in the now empty classroom, empty except for me and Raisa.

"Nadine, wake up!"

Damn it! Victor was showing me where he wanted to go, whatever that meant.

Wait. I took a deep breath. Why was the feeling Victor experienced—the one telling him where to go—now inside *me*?

Raisa shook me, making me focus on her. "Hi," I said lamely.

"You were out." She paced frantically from side to side. "Again!"

"Sorry." It was the only thing I could say. I didn't want to talk to her about this. I needed to be alone to follow this irresistible pull, to follow it in order to find what Victor was after. But first I had to reassure Raisa all was well. "I guess class is over."

She plopped her hands on her waist and shook her head. "For over five minutes now. You know, I promised you I wouldn't worry about these episodes, but I'm not sure anymore."

"Did the others notice?" I asked, worried I would soon hear rumors I was insane.

Then again, wasn't I?

"I don't know. Some might have." She threw her backpack over her shoulder.

I stood. "I'm sorry."

"Whatever," she mumbled as she accompanied me to the exit door. "I'm going to sociology now. See you at lunch?"

"Yeah." I watched her walk down the corridor until she left the building, headed to her next class.

Instead of going to my chemistry class, I marched toward the exit that would lead me to the north gate. The feeling inside my chest, the odd sensation, threatened to explode if I didn't follow its directions.

Outside, I stopped and looked skyward. Where was that damn raven? I waited a few moments for the bird to show up. Nothing. Had I imagined it before? Had it been an innocent bird just passing by? Had the raven appearing in my vision been left over from seeing one before?

I shrugged and started walking again. The chilly air of the dark exterior made me shiver. Thirty years ago, New York would have been sweltering this time of the year. Now I had to tighten my jacket and cross my arms over my tote bag to stop the persistent shivering.

It hadn't been my intention, but I halted at the north gate.

The streets of the city never ceased to make my insides turn: few streetlamps, some broken, caused the streets to be dark on a scary level; litter all around left a tainted scent; homeless people peered out of every corner; shady figures with suspicious and malicious eyes ambled by. Shattered sidewalks, barricaded windows, and steel gates on every door completed the urban decay look.

I swallowed hard and summoned what was left of my courage. I needed to follow this pull I felt inside, this sensation that would lead me to where Victor wanted to go. I needed to know if there was something for me there too, if I was going to find the pot of gold at the end of the rainbow. But what would be my pot of gold? The answers to why I had the visions? Or maybe the answer to how to stay in them with Victor forever?

I took a step forward and bumped into something, like a hollow wall that somehow neutralized my feelings. Someone blocked my way. I looked up.

"Hi again," Micah said, wearing a sly grin. I had forgotten about him—about how dangerously handsome he was. At my silence, he asked, "Won't you greet me?"

"Hi," I blurted, somewhat irritated. I didn't like the way I reacted around him, the way my heart lurched, or my palms dampened.

"How is your back?" He buried his hands inside the pockets of his leather jacket.

I shrugged. "Better. I've been on painkillers."

"So ..." He glanced at my tote full of heavy books, then over my shoulder to the campus. "Skipping class?"

"Maybe. And?" I didn't like the way my subconscious responded to him, making me annoyed and on the defensive.

"Nothing." His smile widened. "Actually, I'm glad you did, otherwise I would have had to wait until you were done with chemistry and math. And, I would have had to time it right to catch you before the start of your shift at the university coffee shop."

My eyes bugged, then narrowed. "How do you know my schedule?"

He advanced one step, towering over me. "I go after things that interest me."

I shivered. "Wh-what do you want?"

He frowned. "To be honest, I don't know." His voice resonated, deep and somber. His gaze found mine, but I could see he was hiding something.

Oh heck, he'd piqued my curiosity. "What do you do, Micah?"

"You mean, for a living?" He was back to his shrewd and charming self. I nodded and he leaned against the campus wall. "Well, nothing."

I laughed, figuring he was joking. He didn't laugh with me. "You're serious. How do you—oh, I don't know—pay your bills? Or do you still live with your parents?"

His eyes darkened. "My parents died when I was eighteen," he said, his strong, foreign accent clearer.

I put my hands over my mouth. "I'm so sorry."

"That's okay. That was five years ago. I use my inheritance to pay my bills. And, at the moment, I'm living in a hotel room."

One of the things I most hated about myself was my intense curiosity. Right now, it itched under my skin. "Where are you from?"

"Israel."

That explained his heavy accent. "And what brought you to New York?"

He chuckled. "Aren't we a bit curious?"

I whirled my hair with my finger. "Sorry. It gets the best of me sometimes."

He didn't answer but instead kept staring at me. Self-conscious, I leaned on the wall beside him and pretended to watch the dreadfulness of the city. We stood like that for a few moments, quietly observing the movement before us.

"It's like this everywhere, you know," he said, sounding sorrowful. "I've traveled quite a bit since ..." He swallowed, affected by his parents' deaths, I guessed. I felt the urge to touch him, to comfort him. "You know, there are some places that are better, others much worse, but they all have a sameness. Dark, cold, dangerous."

"My grandma's theory is that God gave up on us. He was so sad with our acts and with our direction, He decided to leave us."

"Not a bad theory." Micah glanced at his feet. "I don't know what to think, though."

I could almost hear the wheels inside his mind whirring, but I held my tongue. Showing how curious I could be would do no good. But why was I worried about what Micah thought of me?

The clock on my cell phone beeped. Chemistry was gone, and my math class would start in ten minutes.

"I gotta go," I announced, pushing off the wall and turning toward the campus gate.

"Wait," he called out. My pulse quickened, and I turned to him. "Can I have your hand?" he asked.

"Excuse me?"

He laughed—a delicious sound. "No, not like that." He ambled up to me, his sly grin adorning his flawless face. "I want to hold your hand." He extended his hand, and I scowled at it. "Just for one second. Please."

His cryptic black eyes pleaded in a way I couldn't resist. I gave my hand to him and, as our skin met, the same cold shock from the other night stung me. My gaze flew to Micah's face. He stood still with his eyes closed and both hands over mine, then he took a deep, soothing breath. I battled the urge to yelp and pull back when I saw his intensity.

Five seconds later, he released my hand, and maybe it was only me, but his stance seemed more relaxed.

"Care to explain?" I asked, afraid he was planning to suck my soul out through my hands.

He shrugged. "I don't think there is an explanation." He smiled, then bowed and walked away.

I remained there for a few more minutes, gaping at his receding figure.

"Lady?" I glanced over my shoulder and saw the gate guard looking at me. "Three minutes until the next period. If you have a class, better hurry."

"Shit," I cursed under my breath. "Thanks," I yelled as I ran past him, headed toward my math class.

Ten feet from the classroom door, I skidded to a stop. Wait. Hadn't I gone outside and skipped class to follow the path Victor told me about? But then Micah showed up and swept me off my feet, causing me to forget about my intention—again!

I pivoted. I'd follow my original idea—skip class and follow the pull that invaded me when I'd woken from the vision. I had to find out where Victor wanted to go, but I found the interior pull was gone. The sensation that would have led the way had disappeared.

My breath came in short, quick gasps. Dizzy, I lowered my head and clung to my knees.

No, no, this had not happened. Once more, a vision tried to tell me something, to *show* me something, and I had been prevented from going after it.

How the heck would I find out what it was now?

7

———

"NADINE."

I turned and found Cheryl crossing the street to where I stood on the sidewalk outside the university café.

"Nad, how are you?"

"Good, I think," I mumbled, unsure of what to say. I glanced at my watch. I had six minutes before my shift started.

"You know, I was thinking about what happened at the bookstore the other day. You never explained to me what that was," she said, then hesitated, probably expecting I would snap at her and refuse to elaborate. Cheryl had seen me zone out a few times, and I always pretended nothing happened. "Should I be worried?"

"It's nothing." I forced a smile. "You don't need to worry about these episodes. Probably low blood sugar."

"Come on." Cheryl placed a hand on my back and pushed me into the café. Inside, she sat at her usual spot. "Tell me the truth, how are you?"

"I'm fine." I stepped toward the door that led to the back.

"Nadine," Cheryl called after me.

I guess after years as a therapist, Cheryl had learned a few tricks about how to know when someone was lying.

I took a deep breath before turning back to glance at her.

"About your *episode*, I may know someone who can help. I have his card right here." She opened her purse and rummaged through the contents.

I shook my head. "It's nothing, Cheryl. Don't worry. I don't need any help."

She extended the card. "Just take it, in case you change your mind."

I pushed it away and gave her my back, ashamed for not being able to break through whatever held me back and trust my friend.

My gaze ended up outside the café where a large black raven perched on a tree branch. It had a scar over one eye. With goose bumps running up my spine, I ran to the back of the café.

FOR THE FOURTH CONSECUTIVE DAY, I VISITED NYU's NORTH GATE before the start of my classes, hoping the feeling would come back. Nothing. I dared to cross the street the last two times, but that had not helped either. Perhaps the weird tug inside me hadn't meant anything.

I was about to head back inside the campus when a taxi passed me with a number painted on its side: 816. The light radiating from the number eight was strong and pure.

I approached the guard at the gate. "Do you see anything unusual about that cab? About its number?" I asked, pointing toward the passing taxi.

Jim, the same guard who saw me speak with Micah the other day, shook his head. "No, ma'am. What should I see?"

"Nothing," I answered quickly. "I think my eyes are tired."

Should I give in and admit I was hallucinating? I could always open up to Cheryl and accept the card she offered the other day.

Focused on my dilemma, I walked on not paying attention to anything. The sudden sound of cawing startled me. I fought against the urge to look up. I didn't want to see the raven. I didn't want to think it was following me. I told myself it was a harmless black bird, lost and hungry.

I didn't realize I had been running until I entered the building and rested against a wall, wheezing and shaking.

"Did you see a ghost?" Micah's voice startled me.

"What are you doing here?" The hallway was crowded and many students stared at me. I tried to compose myself as girls gawked at Micah and glared at me.

He leaned on the wall, hands inside his leather jacket. His face was a mask with a sly grin, but his black eyes seemed pained.

"Just came to say hi."

"Hi," I snapped. "Now bye." I walked past him, not wanting to give him a chance to ruin my day. The other two times I had talked to him, he made me forget about everything else. About Victor. I couldn't allow his charm to overtake me over so easily.

"Hey." Micah grabbed my arm and pulled me back until I was right before him. "Why the rush?" he asked, his delicious vanilla and sandalwood scent washing over me.

The endless black pools of his pupils met me.

"I have class," I breathed, feeling dizzy.

"I'll let you go." He released my arm, but then extended his hand. "But could you hold my hand first?"

I stared at his palm turned toward me. "Why?" I looked up, and the pain I thought I saw in his eyes grew clear.

"Please," he muttered through gritted teeth.

"All right." I didn't know what holding his hand would do, but I wouldn't be a brat if he was in pain.

As I was about to slip my palm in his, getting ready to feel the shock that came with it, Raisa showed up beside me.

"Nad, you didn't introduce me to your friend," she said, flipping her hair and smiling like a model. With anguished eyes, he glanced at me and let his hand fall to his side. "So?" She bumped her shoulder against mine.

"Raisa, Micah." I beckoned from her to him. "Micah, this is Raisa, my roommate." Our moment already forgotten, he turned toward Raisa with a wide and perfect smile.

Raisa let out a dreamy sigh.

"Nice to meet you, Raisa."

"Nice to meet you too." She giggled. "How come I've never seen you before?"

"I'm new in town." It seemed he had pressed a button that was labeled "pain off, charm on."

I intruded before Raisa let her boldness take over and invited him out. For some reason, I was afraid of hearing Micah's answer to her request. "We should be going or we'll be late." I pushed her, trying to pry her from the gorgeous Israeli model standing before us.

"Bye, Micah," Raisa said in a singsong tone. I kept pushing her down the hall.

"Bye, girls." I didn't bother turning around to look at him.

"What a hunk," she exclaimed once we were inside the classroom. "How come you never told me about him?"

I rolled my eyes as I took my usual seat in the back. "I just met him."

"Yeah, and? Come on! No girl would meet a guy like him and not report to her best friend."

That was the thing Raisa didn't understand. She was a good friend, but I wasn't sure I had any best friends. I didn't feel comfortable talking about my classes, my grades, or my family. I didn't like to gossip and get together to talk about hot guys—and I certainly wasn't going to confess my visions. I just wanted to be alone with my visions of Victor. Besides, if she knew how crazy I was, she wouldn't want me to be her best friend.

Raisa's friends walked into the classroom and ran to us, huge smiles wreathing their faces.

"You guys won't believe who we saw yesterday," Martha said, taking her seat beside Raisa.

"Who?" Raisa asked.

"The blond guy from the club." Martha clapped her hands together.

"Folks," the instructor called. He waited until the class settled, then spoke in a somber tone. "The university has been informed of some disturbing news, and students will be dismissed from school for today." General ovation took over, but with raised hands, the instructor managed to shut everyone up. "This isn't for fun, people. Early this morning, the body of a student was found outside campus, near Madison Square. It seems the girl was assaulted, raped, and then killed."

Like me, the whole class gasped. My stomach hurt as if I'd been punched.

Someone asked, "What was her name?"

"I think most of you knew her." The instructor swallowed hard. "The victim was Sarah Cunnings."

Oh my God. Nausea swirled in my stomach. Sarah had been at the café the other day. I had just spoken to her.

More students asked questions, including where she'd been found and when and where her funeral would be, but I seemed to have lost my voice.

The professor continued talking about Sarah's death and her family's arrangements for her funeral.

"That's it," he finished. "You may go now. And please be careful."

He left, followed by my classmates, who all exited silently.

I remained glued to my chair for a few seconds longer, trying to make sense of the news.

In my backpack, my cell phone vibrated. Shaking off the awful images in my mind, I picked it up. Having missed the call, I listened to the voice message.

"Who was it?" Raisa asked from behind me. I hadn't registered she'd stayed.

"The hospital. They lost my resume and want me to go there and give them a new copy."

"What time does your shift start?"

I was still baffled, my mind moving in slow motion. It took me a moment to think it through, to figure out what time it was now and what time my shift started.

"After this class." I looked at my wristwatch again. "In about forty minutes."

"So you're going to the hospital right now?"

"I think so."

"I'm going with you."

"You don't need to."

"Are you kidding? After what happened to Sarah? I'm not leaving you alone."

I flinched. I had already forgotten about Sarah. I felt sick. "Guess my mind is somewhere else."

"I'll go, but we have to get a cab."

The cab dropped us off right at Langone's main door.

"It won't take long, right?" Raisa asked, crossing her arms. I did the same, wishing I had a thicker jacket. "Your shift starts soon."

"I know."

For some reason, my head snapped to the right, just as a

silver car drove around a corner. It approached the hospital and advanced toward the garage, right beside the hospital's main door. When the car was close enough, I realized it was a gray Audi A3.

I froze. It couldn't be.

The vehicle cruised to the garage's entrance. Its dark windows prevented me from seeing the driver. Paralyzed, I watched it proceed to the end of the first level—where there were a few empty spots—and park near an employee-only entrance.

The driver opened the door and stepped out.

My breath caught in my throat. My heart skipped a few precious beats. Raisa stood beside me and I clutched her arm, steadying my wobbling knees.

"Hey! That's the guy I told you about," she said. "The one at the club last week. Martha and Susan told me his name. It's—"

"Victor."

$$8$$

Victor Gianni, with his honey-colored hair, entrancing sea-green eyes, imposing figure, and his impeccable posture, stood next to his car. In my world, the real world. Not in a vision.

"How do you know his name?" Raisa asked.

Unable to find my voice, I shrugged. Besides, how could I answer that I had dreamed about him for the last nine months. And, until now, I had no idea he actually existed.

Nonetheless, there he was.

I squinted, analyzing him. His physical appearance, the car, and the setting were known to me, and yet *he* seemed different.

In my dreams, he was buoyant and romantic. He smiled and winked and spun me around imaginary ballrooms and danced with me in the middle of the street. He was my Prince Charming, born to make me happy, be my best friend, and some day, be my lover.

All in all, he was a very different guy from the one standing before me in the real world. The in-the-flesh Victor wore a worried crease on his forehead. He seemed to carry the weight of the world on his shoulders. I wanted to reach out, to comfort him, to help him. With blue jeans, a stark white polo, and brown boat shoes, he looked more like a mama's boy than Romeo.

He spun and his gaze swept across the garage—across me—but his glance didn't linger on me for more than one second. I gasped as pain stabbed my chest. He didn't know me.

He turned his attention to his car. From the backseat, he fished out a brown jacket, which he folded over his arm. He retrieved a card from the pocket and used it to open the hospital access door.

That was when my legs regained energy and I ran like crazy. I forgot about Raisa, about my job, about everything. I dashed toward that door. I couldn't let him get away. I had to find out why he didn't know who I was.

I almost didn't reach the door in time, but a nurse stepped outside and propped it open. I inched my way inside Langone.

In the cold atrium, I found myself disoriented. Too many people, too many corridors and doors, and an intense smell of anesthetics that made me nauseous. He was nowhere to be seen. My breath came in short gasps as I searched for him.

This was too much. The dizziness and the anxiety took over. I found a staircase, sat on the lower step, and put my head between my knees.

"Are you okay, miss?" a woman asked me. Moving cautiously so I wouldn't puke, I lifted my head and saw a chubby nurse with a kind smile. "You're very pale."

"I'm fine," I lied. I knew too well I wouldn't be all right until I found Victor.

"Are you here alone?" she asked, patting my shoulder.

I shook my head. "I came with my friend."

"Do you need help getting to your friend?"

"No, I just need a few minutes alone." I tried smiling, though I was sure it didn't look good.

"Well, if you need anything, the nurses' station is right over there, at the end of the hall." She pointed to her right.

I nodded, and when she walked away, I returned my forehead to my knees.

Oh my God. My head spun, and there was no way I could think this through rationally. Desperate tears filled my eyes as I considered the possibility I was really losing my mind, and I wondered whether I should get up and head toward the psychiatric ward. My mind now played tricks while I was awake. No visions needed anymore. How much of this could I take? I didn't want to find out.

"There you are." Raisa sat beside me. "What the hell was that?"

I shrugged, not sure what to tell her.

My cell phone rang. It was Adam. Reluctantly, I took the call, only to listen to him ream me out.

"You're twelve minutes late," he yelled. "Drag your butt here right now, or I'll tell our manager about the freak things you do."

"I'll be right there," I mumbled, disconnecting before he could scream even less pleasant words.

My mind whirled with confusion as Raisa and I left through the same door. I had hallucinated—no way was Victor real. Nonetheless, in the garage, I realized two things. First, his car was still parked there, so I had not imagined that. Second, Raisa was beside with me and she had seen him and confirmed his name.

Still I felt heartless, soulless. Victor didn't know me.

At the café, the minutes dragged on forever. I couldn't concentrate on any task. I prayed for Cheryl to show up and help distract my busy mind, but that didn't happen.

Three hours passed, but with three more to go I couldn't take anymore. Pretending to be sick, I asked to go home. When my boss let me leave, I ran to the nearest campus gate and took a cab back to the hospital.

My hands sweated, and my whole body shook when I entered the garage. I was afraid Victor's car wouldn't be there anymore.

What now? I had felt compelled to check if his car was still there, but now that I found it was, what next? I hadn't thought my actions through, and now I was outside the hospital in the cold and dark. God, what was happening to me? Was I losing all reason?

The need to know if the man I'd seen was Victor prevented me from going home. I hid along a wall where people would not see me while I kept an eye on his car. And I waited.

To pass the time, I got out a book and tried to read. After rereading the same paragraph six times, I gave up and stashed it inside my tote. Next, I tried playing a silly game on my phone but kept messing it up. Then I hummed some songs I liked.

Cramps shot up my legs at the same time that damned bird cawed from outside the garage. I left my hideout and stepped onto the sidewalk, ignoring the fact it had become night while I was standing watch in the garage—not that the darkness was much different from daytime, but there were more sinister individuals haunting the night. Trying to find the raven and keeping an eye out for the bats, I looked around.

The raven flew toward me from out of nowhere. I yelped and fell on my butt.

"Stupid winged thing," I cursed under my breath. I got up and looked around to see if it would charge again.

The bird was nowhere I could see.

"Damn it," someone muttered from behind me.

The hairs on my arms stood on end. I knew that voice —Victor.

It was him. It was Victor. God, he was here. I ran toward him but halted when I saw him crawling to his car, one of his hands over his chest, panting as if breathing hurt too much. I watched frozen.

He seemed unaware of my presence. Groaning, he kept crawling to his car until he was a few feet from the door. He collapsed on the cement floor, and his whole body shook.

That was when I snapped out of my trance and ran the rest of the way to him, fear and worry heightening my adrenaline.

"Oh my God, Victor, what's happening?" I asked, hearing the tears in my voice. "Please, talk to me. What is happening?" I knelt beside him.

"Leave me alone," he croaked, trying to push me away. As if the gesture could lessen the pain, he pressed his eyelids together. "Just go away."

"I won't." I bent over him. As gently as I could I touched his face to try to steady him, but when my skin touched his a warm shock passed from me to him. He took a deep breath. His body stopped jerking.

As if suddenly filled with renewed energy, he surged to his feet and retreated several feet. I remained kneeling on the cement.

"I told you to leave," he snapped.

I flinched. Not in all the months of dreaming about him had I thought Victor would ever snap at me.

"You seemed to be in pain, Victor. I couldn't just leave," I said, finally standing.

"How do you know my name?" he asked, groping at his jeans. He then pulled out his wallet, glanced at it, and stashed it inside his back pocket once more. "What did you do?" He touched his face, where my hands had been a second ago.

"What do you mean? What did I do?" I asked, more confused by the minute.

"Tell me how you know my name." He glanced down and I followed his gaze. His hands still shook. He hid them behind his back. "Have you been following me?"

"You don't know me?" My voice, barely audible, sounded both hurt and hopeful.

He tilted his head. "Nope," he said, then turned toward his car again.

"Wait," I called as he opened the door. "Don't go. Please, ju—"

"Gotta go." He cut me off. A second later, he was inside his car and backing up.

Unable to move or breathe, I watched Victor leave the garage —leave me—as if I were some revolting parasite.

9

———

I CRIED MYSELF TO SLEEP.

Raisa noticed I wasn't well and didn't force any information out of me. Even if she managed to make me talk, would she have understood?

My alarm clock blared early the next morning, warning me it was time to get dressed and go to class. I didn't. Instead I went to the hospital. Perhaps I was just deluding myself, but I had to try again. I couldn't let Victor, a real flesh and bone Victor, escape so easily. Besides I knew too much about him, and I could use the information to find him.

At least I had an excuse to go there since, with all that had happened, I had forgotten about taking my resume in when they had asked for it the previous day.

Once at the hospital, I checked in with the receptionist and handed her my resume. Taking advantage of the moment, I asked to visit Bianca Gianni, Victor's Italian grandmother. The receptionist confirmed my suspicion that his grandma was real too. She asked if I was a family friend. I lied, saying that I was, otherwise she wouldn't have told me that Mrs. Gianni had been taken for an examination but should be back to her room on the eighth floor in about an hour.

So everything Victor had told me in my visions was real? Why? I figured I didn't have time to waste mulling over that. I took an elevator to the eighth floor to wait for him there. He was bound to show up at some point, and I didn't care if I missed my classes or my job to speak with him again.

On the eighth floor, I dismissed the wooden number shining brightly on the wall and walked down the corridor looking for Mrs. Gianni's room. It wasn't far.

I raked through my mind, trying to recall another episode in my life when I had been this nervous. Besides my brother's funeral, no memories came.

To steady the trembling of my body, I leaned against the white wall, letting the anesthetic smell impregnated in the corridor fill my lungs. Maybe the drugs would help calm me. They didn't. I tucked my sweaty hands inside the pockets of my hoodie—another ineffective attempt to calm my senses.

Expecting to see Victor with each door that opened, each new footstep that drew closer, each new voice that crossed the corridor caused my breath to catch. I knew he would have to pass through this place sooner or later. I had to have patience.

Not much time had passed, when I saw an old lady with white hair and bluish-green eyes being brought in by a nurse in a wheelchair. I had never seen or spoken to his grandmother in my visions, but he had showed me pictures of his family, and those eyes were enough proof that this woman was his grandmother.

I was shaking again. Holy hell, there she was. She was real. Like Victor was real. Everything I knew about him was real. I still couldn't believe it.

I heard a heavy sigh and turned toward it. It was Victor. He was leaving the elevator down the hall and coming toward his grandma's room. He had seen me and didn't seem happy about it.

He wore faded jeans, a T-shirt, and a thin jacket. Too casual. I shook my head. The fact that my dream Victor and this real Victor were exactly the same physically, while their clothing styles and posture were the opposite of each other still boggled my mind.

He came to a stop before me. "You again." There was disdain in his tone. I cringed.

"How are you?" I managed to ask and immediately felt silly. I had planted myself here in this hallway for over an hour waiting for him, and when he finally arrived I didn't know what to say. Though I really did want to know how he was. The last time I had seen him in the flesh, he'd been jerking on the floor of the hospital's garage, in pain. "What was that ... ah ... before ...?" I trailed off, hoping he would understand what I was referring to.

He shrugged, his sea-green eyes still staring at me with suspicion. "I don't know. By the way, how do you know my name?"

I twirled a lock of my hair around my index finger as I considered my answer. I wanted to answer him. I wanted to be honest, but he would never believe me.

As if my answer would pop out of the walls, I scanned the hallway.

At the end of the corridor, a nurse left a room and entered another.

"The nurse," I almost shouted, hoping he wouldn't notice my sudden lie. I avoided his inquisitive eyes. "I heard a nurse calling you earlier that day."

His deadpan expression hid his thoughts and didn't let me know if he was buying it or not.

"What did you do to me last night?" he asked, crossing his

arms. God, I hated how his voice and his posture were so guarded and mistrustful. I wasn't used to it.

"What do you mean?"

"When you touched me, the shock and the pain went away. How did you do that?"

"I don't know." This time I wasn't lying. I really didn't know. He frowned, clearly still suspicious. "Seriously, I have no idea."

His shoulders stiffened. "What are you doing here? What do you want?"

My eyes widened as I retreated a few steps, trying to avoid his toxic tone.

Yes, he looked like my Victor—the same voice, the same hair, the same face, the same mouth that had offered me smiles and rendered me breathless many, many times. I wanted to touch him, to embrace him, to tell him everything was going to be okay. Maybe if I touched him he would remember me, and he would *want* to touch me too.

I came closer to him, looking deeply into those wary green eyes, my fingers itching to stroke his skin, to feel it smoldering under my caress. But I didn't. He was like my Victor, but he *wasn't* my Victor. The Victor from my visions would never speak to me like this. He would never snap at me. No, no. My Victor loved my company, loved to hear me sing, loved to embrace me and inhale my scent.

"I'm sorry," I whispered, my voice croaking under the heavy pressure inside my chest.

Then I walked away.

At first, each step was heavy and slow, but as forlorn tears spilled over and shook my body my pace increased until I was running. I ran as if the strides could erase the agony slowly consuming me.

How could I have been so blind? How could I have believed Victor truly existed and that he loved me? Why had I tortured myself by looking for him? I knew the answers to these questions. If I could make one wish, I would ask for my dream Victor to be real. When I'd seen a guy that could be his identical twin, I thought my soul's wish had been fulfilled.

It had been too good to be true. Nobody could be so lucky. Still, I couldn't believe I found a guy that *looked* like my Victor—but he would *never* be *my* Victor.

I HAD TO STRETCH THE NOT-FEELING-WELL LIE FOR A FEW MORE days with work since I didn't have any strength to get up from my bed. Adam was livid for having to fill in for me, while Raisa and Olivia were left worrying.

On Friday, after I spent three days in bed barely eating or speaking, the girls called Cheryl.

"I heard you've been hiding in here since Tuesday," she stated. My face was buried in my pillow, but I felt the bed wobble as she sat next to me. "You're not eating, you're not going to class or work, and you aren't speaking to your friends."

Through the pillow, I smelled them. Cinnamon rolls—my favorite snack.

"That's not fair," I mumbled.

Cheryl chuckled. "I'm not above using all weapons available to me."

Grunting, I turned to her and instantly saw giant-sized cinnamon rolls on a plate beside her. They were still hot, with extra sugar icing. Exactly the way I liked. And the fact I was starving added to the temptation.

"God, you're playing dirty," I kidded. My first joke and half-smile in nearly five days.

She passed me the plate. "I'm glad you decided to talk to me."

We sat in silence while I ate. It wasn't an awkward silence though.

"Thanks," I said after I devoured three rolls. I was feeling better and cozier. I figured it was Cheryl's presence, her sure self and kind smile.

"You're welcome." She offered me a mug of coffee I had missed earlier. "So, what is this all about?"

Where to start? Or, a better question, would I even tell her? Here I was, in the privacy of my room, with a woman who was both a friend who wanted to help and a psychologist. I could take advantage of this opportunity and open up for the first time ever. But was I brave enough? I wasn't sure.

I decided to give it a shot and opened my mouth to let the words come out naturally.

"I-I ..." I stuttered, not ready to confess how insane I was out loud. I tried another route, not far from the truth. "I met a guy." I swallowed hard. "I feel very, very attracted to him, but he has been sort of rude to me. He hasn't let me get close."

"Hmm. All of this because of a guy?" She smiled. "Tell me about him."

I stood and smiled. "He's gorgeous. Perfect. His hair is dark blond, and he is very tall. And his body ..."

Cheryl chuckled. "It's easy to see when you are nervous or excited." She pointed to my hair. "You start doing that thing with your hair and don't even notice it."

I looked down at my hand near my shoulder, where my finger was entwined in a strand of my hair. I hid my hands behind my back, holding them together to stop my nervous habit and to steady their trembling. Still smiling, she beckoned for me to continue.

I took a deep breath and plunged on. "Well, I just feel this pull, this incredible need to be near him. I talked to him on Tuesday."

She seemed surprised. "How was it?"

My brows contracted. "He was rude actually. And that's why I've been hiding in here. Maybe my reaction was a little childish."

"Oh, Nadine, maybe it wasn't childish at all. How do you feel about him? Strongly?"

I thought about it for two seconds before answering, "Yes, very much."

"I'm no godmother from a fairy tale, but I think love is worth it. If you feel like you should be with him, then don't give up. Go after him. Show him you're a great girl. Show him what he's missing." Cheryl sounded like a motivational speaker.

At her tone, a reluctant smile appeared on my face. "Cheryl, I've never heard you speak like that before."

"Well, I believe that when you think you found the one, you shouldn't give up easily."

I had always wondered if she'd ever been in love. I started whirling my hair again, but stopped a second later. I had to stop with this habit. "And you, Cheryl? You're talking like you know the feeling, but I've never seen you with a guy and never heard you speak of anyone special."

Her silver eyes became dull. "I lost the love of my life many years ago."

"Oh my God! I'm so sorry."

"I've never told anyone. I don't think I'm ready to go looking for another romance. The truth is I don't think I'll ever be ready to love again."

I reached for her hand and squeezed it. "I think I understand." If Victor kept rejecting me, I knew I'd become lonely and bitter fast.

"The past is past." She perked up. "Now, we must do something about your case."

I chuckled at her renewed spirit. "What do you suggest?"

"Find out where he will be, what he will do. Be there, stare at him, practice some hair flipping and lashes batting. Ask some pointers to Raisa. I'm sure she knows all about those. Nadine, you have to try."

My chest still ached from Victor-not-Victor's rejection, but what Cheryl said was true. I had to try. I truly felt like he was the one for me—at least the one from my dreams—and until I was convinced this Victor was not the one I thought he was, or he remembered who I was, I wouldn't give up.

10

Somehow Adam found out I was feeling better and, after talking to our manager, informed me I was to work double shifts on Saturday and Sunday to compensate for the days I'd missed during the week.

As a result, when I arrived home Saturday night and was invited by Raisa to go to the club with her, I had to refuse. I felt exhausted and useless. There was no way I could go out, even if there was a possibility of the real Victor being there. As it was, I found out on Sunday he'd been at the club with two classmates.

"He's totally hot, but Nad, please, he has this permanent I'm-mad-with-the-world look." Raisa also told me a few girls tried to talk to him, and he turned them down. "I think he was rude to them." Then she mentioned how his stance was stoic and detracting at the same time. "He doesn't look like a bad boy. He just looks antisocial and annoyed."

So, I wasn't the only one he mistreated or the only one who noticed how his posture shouted "back off." That was sort of a relief.

When the hospital called me to schedule an interview, my hands started sweating. There was a big chance I would run into Victor there. Despite the fact I wanted to see him and talk to him, I didn't know if I was ready to face him just yet. But there was nothing I could do. I needed this job. I agreed on an interview time, right after my shift was over on Monday evening.

Destiny or not, I literally bumped into Victor's grandma when I left the human resources office after my interview.

"I'm so sorry, ma'am." I grabbed her arm to steady her. Bianca Gianni was old and fragile, with a neat white bun and gentle wrinkles adorning her still beautiful face. Sadly, she was alone. No Victor.

"I'm fine, dear," she said, her parched tone revealing how sick she really was. But she found the energy to smile at me. She wasn't as tall as her grandson, but she was still much taller than me. "I was close to the walls and doors. You know, in case I trip." She chuckled, and I grinned.

Hmm. Ideas sprouted in my mind. "Do you need any help getting somewhere?"

"No, no, dear. I'm just stretching my legs. I get tired of spending most of my day in these damned hospital beds." Her dull laugh became a couple of dried coughs. "I apologize for my inappropriate words."

"No need to apologize." I stepped back, letting her pass me and get on with her walk. If what my vision Victor had told me was right, she stumbled over her feet all the time, and I would be there to offer her my arm for support.

Not even ten seconds later, Bianca did trip and when I offered assistance she accepted it.

"There aren't many nice young ladies around anymore," she said with a gentle smile.

"You know," I said, prepared to use bribery to find out what I wanted to know while we strolled through the hospital's sterilized corridors. I had a chance to prove if all I knew about the

Gianni family was right. "I was on my way to the cafeteria to buy a cocoa cappuccino. Would you like one?"

Her green eyes brightened. "I would love one," she exclaimed, then lowered her voice. "My grandson would kill me if he knew I had one. You see, I shouldn't eat chocolate or drink coffee. And certainly not both at once."

I chuckled at the old lady's enthusiasm. I loved the fact that during one of my visions, Victor had commented how it was hard to keep his grandmother away from chocolate, and coffee, and other things she shouldn't consume in excess.

My heart rate rocketed. Oh God, it was all true!

"I won't tell him if you don't," I whispered, and she eagerly agreed, looking like a child who was about to get a new toy.

After getting cocoa cappuccinos, Bianca and I sat at one of the cozy internal gardens the hospital had built after the darkness had taken over. By then, we had formally introduced ourselves, and she had told me about her illness—like in my visions, she had stomach cancer.

"I don't think I have much time left," she confessed, seated by my side on one of the wooden benches. She had on a heavy wool coat, but she looked cold. I considered getting her inside, but she seemed so relaxed next to the living plants. "I try to be strong, you know. I have to. Otherwise I don't know what will become of my grandson."

To keep her talking, I pretended I didn't know what she meant. I asked questions I knew the answers to just to make sure we were talking about the same Victor. "Where are his parents?"

"Oh, they died when Victor was thirteen, dear." Her voice was strained. "My husband, my son, and his wife were in a store that was robbed. The criminal became nervous and shot everyone."

I nodded, recalling when he had told me the same story. "I'm so sorry."

I was going to ask more, but a shadow fell over me. I glanced back and found Victor glaring at me.

"Grandma." His tone was dangerously low. "What are you doing outside? And with a stranger?"

"She isn't a stranger," Bianca said. "Her name is Nadine, and she's a nice young woman. She's in the NYU pre-health program and just had an interview for a position within the hospital." His grandma sounded like she was trying to sell him on me. I didn't like it. And, from what I could see, neither did Victor. She turned to me. "I apologize for his behavior."

"You don't need to apologize for me," he retorted. "I'll apologize when I think it's necessary."

"Then at least be polite," she chided him. I guessed this was a regular situation, seeing as she had raised him since his parents' deaths.

He puffed up but remained quiet.

"I'm sorry," I muttered, smiling feebly at Bianca. "It was nice meeting you."

"Oh, it was nice to meet you too, dear." She reached out and patted my face. "If you ever come around again, I wouldn't mind your visit."

My weak smile widened, but it was short lived since Victor's glare made my whole being wilt.

Afraid of answering, I just nodded. "Goodbye," I said.

I stalked away, wanting distance from this rude, cruel Victor whose sharp voice I could hear behind me. He reproached his grandma for talking to me and trusting a stranger. Even as tears brimmed in my eyes, I hummed to myself to mute his offensive words. How could the two Victors look so alike yet be so different?

THE NEXT DAY I LEFT MY APARTMENT IN A HURRY, NEARLY LATE FOR work. Ugh, I had never been this disorganized before. I was usually the most punctual, organized, and responsible person. Now I was a jumble of messy thoughts and goals. I just wanted to get on with my life, to make it to the end of a normal day like a normal person with normal problems.

When Micah stepped in front of me, I realized my normal day would have to wait. The air swept out of my lungs. With thoughts of Victor consuming my energy, I had forgotten about Micah and how gorgeous he was.

Like some dark stallion, he was dressed in all black, except for the T-shirt, which was white. Black pants, boots, and leather jacket. Added to that combination was his endless ebony eyes, jet black hair, full lips, and tanned skin. I wondered if he was real at all. Like Victor, he was too handsome to be true. Perhaps he was another trick of my mind, another hallucination sent to haunt me and make my legs tremble.

"What do you want?" I asked, walking past him. Why did I become irritable every time he was near me?

"What? Can't I just want to see you?" With his long strides, it didn't take him more than three seconds to catch up with me.

"Last time I checked, no," I snapped. Poor guy, I was releasing my anger and frustration on him. Was it because I was mad real-life Victor wouldn't give me the attention Micah did? Mad because I wanted the attention to come from Victor, not Micah?

Micah grinned slyly. "Come on, you must know you're beautiful enough to make a guy want to see you again."

I skidded to a stop. "What? Is that a joke?"

He stepped toward me, closing the gap between us, and ran his fingers over my cheek, taking my breath away. An ice-cold shock came with his touch, but it was much fainter this time. I shivered and realized he was taking advantage of my vulnerability to make contact with my skin.

I pulled away. "Back off!"

He was laughing, but, oh God, he was so sexy when he laughed. "Sorry. Couldn't resist."

"I knew it." I stomped on. "You're after my touch."

He fell into step with me easily. "Will you stop running from me?"

I didn't answer him. Instead, I asked, "Why do you need to touch me?" I kept my gaze fixed ahead.

"I've told you. You're too beautiful to resist."

"Cut the crap." I halted and faced him. "If you're not gonna give me real answers, then leave me alone."

"Well." He raised his hand as if he were going to touch my face again, but gave up and buried his hand inside the pocket of his jacket. "I just wanted to see you."

My heart skipped a beat. "No. You want my touch."

He leaned closer, his intoxicating scent making me dizzy, and whispered, "That wasn't the only reason."

My throat was suddenly dry. My pulse accelerated. It was impossible to resist him. "Here." I extended my hand, curiosity corroding my stomach. I wanted to find out if the touch of our hands would bring that bizarre effect again.

For a second, his black eyes shone with surprise. But soon eagerness took over, and he clasped my hand. The icy shock that returned with the contact made me gasp. I watched him close his eyes and tilt his head back. I was hallucinating again, wasn't I? How could a person touch another and—I don't know—gain energy from it? Drink from it? Feel better because of it?

I hadn't thought of this before. Victor said my touch made his pain go away. Was this what happened to Micah, too?

He released my hand. "Thank you."

"What does it help you with?" I asked, the wheels in my

mind starting to function. "Pain? Is that it? You feel constant pain, and my touch relieves it?"

His eyes bugged. "I—" He closed his mouth. "How did you know?"

"Why didn't you tell me?" I resumed walking toward the café, Micah by my side. No more stomping now that he'd told me the truth.

He shrugged, his hands inside his pockets. "You would think I'm crazy."

I laughed out loud. "Oh no. That's not even close to craziness in my dictionary."

He smiled at me. A true smile. "You should laugh more." Then he sighed, returning to his somber mood. "Not just pain," he continued. "Your touch also helps with queasiness."

"Are you sick?" I touched his arm, worried.

He glanced at my hand on his arm and showed me his sly grin. Self-conscious and flushing, I pulled my hand back.

"I don't think I'm sick. If I was, wouldn't I feel aches and nausea all the time? It comes and goes without reason. And there are times it's so intense, I can't get up."

So that was what had happened with Victor. He had crumpled to the ground because of this intense pain. But what was it? How could both of them feel the same thing? And why did one feel cold and the other felt hot?

Now I was super curious. "Does something trigger it?"

"Not that I have noticed."

"Who else besides me can relieve your pain?"

"No one. I've never thought it was possible to lessen the aches." His smile widened, and he halted then continued, "Until I met you."

I stared into his eyes, hypnotized. "What?"

"We're here." He motioned behind me.

I turned around. The heat of embarrassment flushed my

cheeks. We had arrived at the café, and I hadn't noticed. Should I invite him in? I wanted to. He was a charming guy who actually wanted to talk to me. Dreamy.

A knock on the glass behind me snapped me out of it. Adam. He pointed to his wristwatch and glared.

"Well, see you later," Micah said. He took my hand and kissed my palm, his eyes on mine the whole time.

I felt hot again. "See you," I muttered. He released my hand, bowed, and started walking away.

I stood there, watching his perfect form grow smaller and smaller, my mind so lost.

Another knock on the glass made me jump. I didn't even turn to see Adam glaring at me. I entered the café, my mind divided between warm thoughts of Micah and cold moments with Victor.

"I HAVE AN APPOINTMENT WITH MY ADVISOR NOW," I TOLD RAISA after we left class. I hated summer semester. I was taking only three classes, but because of the intense workload, they seemed like eight. "I'll meet you at home after my shift?"

"Yup," she answered, returning to the gossiping Martha and Susan.

Shaking my head, I hurried toward the science building. Despite the craziness going on with my life, exams were coming up and I needed to study. Besides, keeping my mind busy helped a little in stopping my pervasive worry that I was a lunatic.

I was about to knock on the door of my advisor's office when it opened and Victor emerged, startling me. He looked amazing in faded jeans and a dark blue NYU sweatshirt—sending my heart into overdrive—even if the look was too casual to match the Victor of my visions.

With my hand over my chest, trying to slow down my sudden irregular breathing pattern, I whispered, "What are you doing here?"

Frowning, he closed the door behind him. "It's none of your business."

Ouch. Okay, so maybe that was going too far. I opened my mouth to yell at him, frustrated with his constant cold shoulder, when I realized his green eyes were staring at me not only in anger but also in pain. "You're hurting again, aren't you?"

"Excuse me," he muttered between gritted teeth. He pushed past me and marched away.

"Wait." I followed him, keeping up with his fast pace and hoping the few students walking by didn't notice our quarrel. "I can help. I think."

"Just leave me alone." His voice was strained, and he put his hand over his chest. "I need to go."

"No," I said, stepping right in front of him and preventing him from bolting.

With labored breathing, he leaned against the wall beside us. "Get out of my way," he groaned. "I need to go now."

I reached for him and he shoved my arm back, but this time I wasn't going to let him boss me around. "Stop it. Let me help you before you pass out."

Before I could reach for him again, he sank down to the cold floor, panting and trembling, his skin paler than usual.

Kneeling in front of him, I picked up his hand. His eyes went wide as a warm jolt built up behind my fingers and spread from my skin to his. Seconds later, his breathing was back to normal. His pulse had evened out. Slowly, he stood, smoothed his jeans, and ran a hand through his messy golden hair.

"Wh-what did you do?"

I shrugged. "I don't know what it is. I just know what it does."

"What are you?" He folded his arms, hands tucked in his armpits. "Are you some kind of witch? A druid?"

I couldn't help laughing. "Really? Do you believe in that stuff?"

"Well, not really. But I don't have another explanation for what you just did."

"Welcome to the club. I have no idea how it works or what exactly it is."

"But you knew my pain would go away if you touched me." It wasn't a question.

"I thought it would. You were the one who told me it had happened before."

"I did," he muttered.

With wary eyes, he kept staring at me. I wouldn't get anywhere with him like this. He seemed ready to bolt. I wouldn't be the one clinging to him and begging for him to listen to me. Besides, what could I tell him? That I knew all about him, and he wasn't precisely as great as I wanted him to be? Crazy, huh?

I couldn't believe I was about to walk away from him, but I knew I had to. I needed to test him, play hard-to-get, and see what his reaction would be. Besides, I remembered my meeting with my advisor.

"Well, I guess I need to get going." I gestured toward the door of my advisor's office a few feet behind us.

He frowned. "Yeah, right."

I wanted to say goodbye, tell him to look for me every time he felt unwell, give him my cell phone number, and much more. But I didn't.

After taking a deep breath, I turned and left.

BRIGHT SUNLIGHT BLINDED ME FOR A MOMENT. WHEN MY EYES adjusted, I found myself once again on the crystal path, facing the omnipotent crystal palace. It had changed though. Dark clouds surrounded the tallest towers, and its shine wasn't clear anymore—now it was a dull purple.

I followed the path, wondering what I would see this time.

Unafraid, I entered the palace. I doubted whoever was inside could see me. This vision felt like one of the ghostly type, similar to how it had felt the last time I'd been here, an eerie crawl in my skin and the sensation I was swimming among clouds.

I wasn't afraid of being found, but I became scared and anxious once I saw the interior. The crystal thrones were still there but some were broken. The reflecting pool was almost empty, and the flowerbeds among the thrones held dead stems that added to the putrid stench filling the space.

I recognized Imha, with her too-long flowing black hair, sprawled over Levi's throne, holding one of those poisonous sticks in one hand and her purple topped stave in the other. Behind her huge viscid, winged creatures stood nearby, their heads bent low, apparently waiting for her to do something.

Shortly she stood up and, spinning the dart on her fingers, strode menacingly toward the nasty creatures.

"You dare come back without her?" Her voice was thin and cruel. A chill ran down my spine.

The creatures shrieked. I guessed they weren't capable of speaking.

"It isn't entirely their fault," Omi said, entering the room. Like before, he looked filthy and crass with his scruffy brown hair and goatee. His red-orbed stave shone brightly on his hand. "She's smart and doesn't remain in the same place for too long." He halted before Imha and bowed.

Who the hell were they talking about? Who was *she*?

"I don't care!" Imha bellowed. The palace shook. "She's been hiding for thirty years! How is that possible?" Omi opened his mouth to speak, but she charged him, the dart in her hand poised to strike. Her stark stare gave me goose bumps.

"I don't want to hear any more excuses," she hissed. "Find her and kill her. Aren't you the god of war? Prove it! Bring on the worst war the world has ever seen. Cause her to surrender. She won't stand that. After all, she *is* the goddess of love and family. She can't bear humans suffering."

Imha let go of Omi and retreated.

"Why is she so important to you?" he asked. "She's gone, and I doubt she wants to come back. Besides, the last time I confronted her, she seemed weaker. She's no threat."

"She's planning something." She sat back down on Levi's throne. "I can feel it."

He shrugged. "If you say so."

"What are you waiting for?" she snapped, spitting rage with her words. "Go! Go find her! Kill her. Bring me her scepter."

Omi bowed and left as Imha laughed—a hysterical laughter that made the hairs on my arms stand on end.

That was when the palace walls started melting and fading, along with everything else, taking away the surroundings and replacing them with my familiar room.

I was seated in my lilac armchair, quaking and dizzy, my biology book on my lap. I sucked in ragged breaths.

Holy hell, what was that? Gods wanting to kill other gods? My head was spinning, and I couldn't think clearly.

What had been the meaning of that vision? If it had any meaning at all. I snapped the biology book shut. I was getting tired of this. I had to do something, to look for help. It was diffi-cult for me to accept, but if I were hallucinating, it would be better for me and everyone around me if I sought assistance.

I stood, picked up my cell phone, and called Cheryl. She cared about me. She'd help. The phone rang, but nobody answered. I left a message for her to call me as soon as she could, then I got out my laptop to shoot her an email.

I was surprised to find one already sent by her in my inbox.

Hi, Nad. I had to go to Chicago to meet with some associates. I'll be back soon. BTW, if you ever change your mind about talking to someone about your episodes, I left a business card in your nightstand drawer. Take care, XOXO. Cher.

I blew out a breath, disappointed. Cheryl traveled all the time, going to Chicago, Philadelphia, Los Angeles, and other major cities, but she always took my calls or answered my emails. I knew I shouldn't take her email personally, but I felt even more alone now than I had before.

My cell phone rang, and the caller ID identified Raisa. I took the call and heard her excited voice come over the line. "You have to come here right now! Olivia and I are at Washington Square. Victor is here with his friends."

Against my wishes, my heart throbbed and my stomach knotted.

"The square is being set up for the carnival on Saturday," Raisa continued. "Some are helping and some are watching." She giggled, and I already understood what her part in it was.

I glanced toward my unopened drawer, where the card of someone who could help me with my insanity awaited me. Well, the card wouldn't go anywhere. Victor, however, wouldn't stay at the square for too long.

"Be right there," I told her, excitement bubbling inside me. I disconnected, went to my closet to change into more suitable clothing, then left my apartment to see the man of my dreams.

12

———

I found Olivia and Raisa at the park, seated on a wooden bench, observing the commotion going on around them.

"You clean up nicely," Raisa teased me.

I flushed and stuck my tongue out at her. I'd tried not to go overboard since we were only hanging out at the park. I'd chosen tight dark blue jeans, a thin white sweater, and matching beige boots and purse. Plus, I had combed my hair until it shone and applied black mascara to accentuate my dark green eyes.

I sat beside them. "What did I miss?"

"Nothing much," Olivia answered. "The graduate students are running around like crazy setting up the stands and organizing the games. We're laughing and gossiping."

I rolled my eyes.

"He was there a few minutes ago." Raisa pointed toward a white stand not too far from where we were. "I think it's where you can donate blood."

I nodded and remained quiet, my hands pressed hard against my thighs to stop their trembling from spreading through my whole body.

The girls fell into easy conversation—and gossip—while I scanned the surroundings looking for Victor.

Twenty minutes later there was still no sign of him.

"I guess he isn't coming back," I said, my spirit sinking. I turned to the girls. "Thanks, though, for calling me."

"It's okay, Nad." Raisa patted my hand. "We know you would have done the same for us."

I smiled. "Yeah, I sure would."

"I'm glad to know that," Olivia said. "But you shouldn't move. He's back, and he just saw you." I froze. My heart flipped as she watched something past my shoulder with a smile. "Don't turn yet. Keep talking to us as if you didn't know he was here."

"Okay," I whispered, feeling my palms sweating. "At least tell me what he's doing."

"Staring at you," Raisa said, pretending to scan around nonchalantly.

"He is?"

Olivia nodded. "Yeah. I think he's trying to focus on helping out, but every few seconds he glances at you."

"Oh God." I was shaking. Raisa held my hand. "What do I do? Should I wave if our eyes meet?" I felt like I was thirteen again. Getting mushy over a guy. But this was Victor. Or at least the real-world equivalent of Victor.

"I dunno." Olivia stood. "How is it when you two meet?"

"Good question. It is weird," I said, hoping to deviate from the topic. "We've never had an actual conversation. Mostly, we snap at each other."

"Really?" Her brows moved up. "'Cause the way he's looking at you, I would say he's at least curious about you."

Curious might be the right word. After all, I could weirdly lessen his pain and dizzy spells with a simple touch. But curiosity wasn't good enough.

"Maybe I shouldn't have come."

"No, stay here." Olivia held her hand out to stop me. "I'm gonna go buy coffee for us. At least stay until I get back so Raisa won't be alone."

Raisa turned her hazel eyes to me, batting her lashes, and I laughed. I was crazy about coffee.

"All right," I agreed, watching as Olivia rushed to the nearest coffee shop. "What's he doing now?"

"Carrying and opening boxes." Raisa smiled. "He just looked at you again."

"Oh God," I turned, relaxing against the back of the bench and looking for Victor.

There he was, with a utility knife in his hand, opening a large box. His head was lowered and his messy hair fell over his face. I was used to the Victor with non-messy hair, but I had to admit, the hair-over-the-eyes look was totally hot. In fact, he looked handsome in jeans, a burgundy polo, and a brown suede jacket.

And yet, he was oblivious to the many girls staring at him, crazy to have his attention—me included.

Raisa broke through my thoughts. "You're doing that thing again."

"What?"

"The thing with your hair." She pointed her chin to me and, looking down, I found my index finger coiling a strand of my hair.

"Oh," I muttered, untangling my finger and crossing my arms. Raisa laughed.

When I glanced at him, he was staring at me. My heart fluttered, but he averted his eyes. I felt like dying.

"I told you I shouldn't have come." I stood, feeling hurt tears surging up.

"Don't be silly. Sit down and enjoy the view."

"I don't think I should." I was ready to argue, but Olivia was coming with three steaming foam cups.

"So, what happened in my absence?" she asked, handing us our coffees. I tasted mine, pleased it was mochaccino, my favorite.

"He looked away from her when she looked at him," Raisa related.

"Really?" Olivia put a hand on her hip. "What a fool."

"Well, girls, I think I'm out." I raised my cup toward Olivia. "Thanks for the coffee."

"Stay, Nad," said. "We're going to grab a bite somewhere later. Come with us."

"I need to study." It wasn't a lie.

"It's okay, Raisa," Olivia said. "If Nad thinks she needs to study, then let her go."

Raisa raised her brows. "Why? She'll get an A or a B+ even if she doesn't study."

I rolled my eyes. "I'm off. Bye."

They waved goodbye, and I walked back home, feeling even worse than before. Why did I have to come here? Why did the girls call me? I sighed. They were doing what any friend would. I was the one with such bad luck, or karma.

I was one block away from my building, at the exact same place Micah had saved me from the bats, when *his* voice called me.

"Nadine!"

With wide eyes, I spun around and found Victor running in my direction. Then, on instinct, I scanned our surroundings, making sure the bats weren't hiding. I waited, and he came to a halt in front of me.

"H-hi," I stuttered.

"Hey." He ran his hand through his messy hair. I guessed that without the mousse or whatever kept dream-Victor's hair intact he did that a lot. He kept glancing around. I wanted to ask what he needed, but I held my tongue.

A cold breeze blew and I hugged myself. I had gone out without a jacket, hoping the tight sweater I had put on would emphasize my thin waist, but now I regretted my decision.

What did he want? Was he going to be nice for once, or start one of our arguments? "Can I help you with anything? I mean, you didn't come all this way to compliment my singing."

Once more, he ran his hand over his hair. It seemed so soft and shiny I wanted to touch it too.

"Well," he said, then paused and looked around. "I wanted to ask for your touch," he said in a rush of words. I raised my eyebrows in surprise. "I've been feeling rather nauseous since morning, and the pain has been building for the last hour. Do you mind?"

My hand was already extended toward him. He hesitated for a second then gripped it tight. The warmth wasn't as strong as before, but it burned my skin, nonetheless. Like Micah, he tilted his head back, drinking in whatever it was I passed to him.

With a loud sigh, he let go of my hand.

"Are you better now?"

"Yes," he said, frowning. "The nausea and the pain are gone. Thank you."

Then why was he scowling? "You're welcome."

Victor cleared his throat. "I should get going."

Ouch. What now? I was a disposable object? "Yes, of course." I tried to hide the hurt in my voice, but didn't think I was successful.

"Good night," he said before marching back the way he had come.

Guess I had been used.

13

———

THE DAY AFTER THE BIOLOGY EXAM, I WAS IN THE CHEMISTRY LAB, working on a project that was due in a few days. I didn't think I'd failed the test, but I was certain I could have done better if Victor hadn't been taking up ninety-nine percent of my mind. I moved to put away my experiment but bumped the edge of the desk and dropped the beaker. Acrid smoke irritated my eyes, and the scent of burning rubber clawed at my lungs.

I gasped and clutched the lab bench. The antiseptic-white walls of the lab loomed, threatening to close in on me. I gagged, then coughed, then berated myself. I couldn't let things slip out of control. I had to get good grades—no, *perfect* grades—if I ever wanted to go to med school and provide a better future for my parents and my siblings.

But I wasn't able to concentrate on anything.

I began tidying the mess I had made when *his* voice startled me.

"Can I come in?" Victor asked.

I turned, conscious I wore gloves and goggles and my hair was pulled up in a messy bun. I yanked off the goggles.

"As far as I know, the lab isn't mine."

Beautifully clad in jeans and a black sweater, he stepped into the classroom.

"But you're the only one in here." He halted across from the table where I was working.

Hoping he didn't notice the accident that had occurred before his arrival, I continued cleaning up the mess while we both remained silent. The silence was killing me. What was he doing here? Why was he looking for me?

I glared at him. "What do you want?"

"What do you think?" he asked. That was when I realized his hands were trembling.

"God," I muttered, taking off my gloves and offering him my hands. "Why didn't you say anything before?"

He shrugged, placing his hands over mine. The warmth spread. He gasped and the quivering eased.

Once it was done, he pulled his hands back and placed them inside his pockets. "Thanks."

"You're welcome."

And he walked away. Just like that.

My legs gave out, and I found a stool to sit down before I fainted from breathing the toxic substance I'd been working with. Or because of my response to him.

Oh my God! I was just an object to him. A thing he could use whenever he wasn't feeling well. I felt like a recyclable soda can he used up and then threw away.

A tiny explosion forced me to return my attention to the lab and my project. Shit. I cleaned up the mess and, fighting tears, went back to work.

Then, after a light pang in my chest, warmth and tingles filled my body, as the room revolved in darkness, and I wasn't in the lab anymore.

I was in a forest, among many tall and thick trees, in almost absolute darkness. The heavy smell of moss and wet leaves engulfed me.

I jumped back when a spot of light came from my right. I saw a cloaked figure approaching, her arm extended, her palm facing up, a bright pink flame hovering over it.

She stopped right beside me, but didn't seem to see me. I was in one of the ghost type visions. I leaned to look at her face from under the cloak, but that wasn't necessary. Ceris. She looked sideways, her piercing and unforgettable blue eyes searching around, anxious and fretful. After making sure she was alone, Ceris ran and I darted after her.

We ran fast—it wasn't easy to keep up with her—dodging trees and roots and small animals.

I concentrated on her wondering why I was seeing her and what she was doing in the middle of a forest. The questions distracted me from the fear building inside my chest. The total darkness and the sounds of wild animals didn't help.

After a great distance, she slowed and, suddenly after passing a few more trees, we entered a clearing. A wooden cottage stood in the center. Light emerged from its few windows and smoke came from its chimney.

Appearing relieved, Ceris marched to the door.

Before she could knock, it opened.

In the tiny living room were three identical women. They had no wrinkles or age marks, long silver hair, knowing gray eyes, and translucent, pale skin. Even though I couldn't tell their age, I knew they were old. Very, very old. They wore simple white clothing. One was seated on a ragged brown love seat, knitting a red scarf. A second sat on a pillow on a faded beige rug and read an old book with torn pages. And the third was knelt before the fireplace, stirring a rusted kettle placed over it. None of them appeared to have noticed Ceris's presence.

As the goddess and I stepped in, the door closed—by itself—and the silver-haired women kept on with what they were doing.

Ceris took off her black cloak, letting her white-blond hair flow freely behind her.

She placed herself among the three women. "I need your help."

After what seemed an eternity, the one knitting spoke. "We cannot help you anymore."

The one reading added, "We already altered too much of the future to help you."

"He needs her. I may not know how she does it, but he would have died without her," Ceris yelled, her eyes wide.

"Yes," the third one said. The way they kept to their activities and did not look at Ceris was disturbing. "He would have died without her. However, you did not think of her, did you?"

"No, you did not," the one knitting said. "What do you think will happen to her once this all is done?"

She shrugged. "I promised her life to you. After the deal is done, she won't matter anymore."

"Oh, won't she?" The one reading stood up and her gray eyes glowed. "How do you know she won't matter?"

"I don't care about her life. Not after the deal is complete," Ceris snarled. "She will be all yours then."

"Yes, but until then, she is yours," the one at the fireplace said, also standing. "Until then, her life is the most precious possession you have."

The one knitting joined the other two in front of Ceris. "Take good care of her." She smiled, and it was almost evil.

That was when the three pairs of gray eyes met mine. My stomach revolved and I gasped. They were looking at me, directly at me, during a vision where I was supposed to be a ghost.

I came back from the vision still seated at the lab's stool, acid dripping over the table. The acid fizzed and popped, melting the wood and making a huge hole.

"Shit," I cursed under my breath and jumped down, frantically trying to clean up my most recent mess.

But I couldn't. My hands shook so badly, I only made a bigger disaster. First, a cold visit from Victor, then a vision I couldn't understand and scared the hell out of me. It was too much.

I needed help. Immediately. I needed Cheryl. After months of avoiding telling her about the visions, it was time to come clean. She was a psychologist, and even if I did need a psychiatrist, she could at least explain to me what was going on. She could give me reassurance while some colleague of hers helped me. Then, I would be okay.

My breath ragged, I pulled out my phone and called Cheryl. No answer. I left a quick voice message, hoping she would hear it soon and call me back.

Sighing, I glanced at the mess over the lab table. I didn't have any strength left to clean—or try to clean—anymore. I grabbed my stuff and left, pausing only at the monitor's office to pay him to clean the mess for me.

I ran home with plans to drug myself to sleep so I wouldn't have to think about the damned gods and goddesses that kept haunting my visions.

***

AFTER I'D CHANGED MY OUTFIT FOUR TIMES, RAISA DRAGGED ME out of my closet.

"You look beautiful. Now let's go," she said, opening the door for me. Already in the hallway, Olivia stuck her head in to add her urging.

Before leaving our apartment, I stopped by the mirror. I wore skin-tight jeans, a loose pink crochet sweater with a white, cropped sports top underneath, and pink pumps. I had pulled my hair back in a ponytail, leaving a few messy strands adorning my face and had applied makeup—just enough to accentuate my eyes and my high cheekbones. Perfect for the fundraiser carnival organized by the university.

"He'll fall in love with you tonight," Olivia said.

I rolled my eyes, but felt a smile creeping over my face. Maybe Victor wouldn't fall in love with me, but I was hoping to be attractive enough to get his attention. Maybe get him to like me a little.

We were still down the street from the carnival, but I already could see the colorful lanterns—red, yellow, green, blue, pink— that had been raised atop decorated but temporary poles. Their soft glow illuminated the whole park, casting lively shadows on the grayish stone floor. Each concession stand matched the color of the lantern placed directly in front of it. I gasped, amazed with the beauty. The real New York had never looked this good.

I scanned my surroundings, taking everything in. Students and their relatives and friends strolled around with wide smiles on their faces, talking animatedly, holding large cotton candies or tasty-looking caramel apples. Long lines formed in each of the many game stands. A round stage had been set up in the center of the park, and a local band was playing cheerful songs.

I took a deep breath, relishing the smell of sweets and tangy beverages that formed a thick, invisible cloud of scent over the place. On days like this, it was almost easy to pretend the world was safe, joyful, and fair, and the people who lived in it were decent, happy, and well cared for. My heart squeezed a little, secretly wishing it could be true.

"He doesn't sing as well as we do," Olivia said, gesturing toward the skinny lead singer on stage. I nodded, laughing.

"Let's go grab a hot dog." Raisa pulled my hand, jumping up and down. "I'm starving."

"I vote we go for a hamburger or a pizza," Olivia objected. "There are fewer people in those lines."

"And I want a cotton candy first," I said as my stomach growled.

The girls and I parted ways to get what we each wanted, and agreed to meet again near the kissing booth. Raisa wanted to see who were the girls giving kisses out and the guys who would pay for them.

I nibbled my cotton candy, ambling to our meeting point, my mind distracted by the real world and mundane things, when I saw Victor. I froze. He was headed toward the booth he had helped set up. I couldn't pretend he didn't look handsome in dark jeans and a long-sleeved white shirt.

But beside his looks and his sexy do-not-get-close stance, I was disappointed in him. I was starting to think he knew I would never say no to healing him, but that didn't mean I enjoyed being used.

Adding to my frustration was the reality that my visions scared me. They made no sense, and they weren't about Victor anymore. In the back of my mind I could see the answer: It was time to seek professional help. But what if I was hospitalized or interned in a clinic? I'd risk not graduating. If I didn't graduate and get a good job, there wouldn't be anyone else to help my family, to provide a better future for them. Could I do that to them? I would rather call Cheryl, ask for her help, and see if there was a way to cure me of this insanity without being locked away in an asylum. But I couldn't find her, and she hadn't returned my calls.

"Nice view," Olivia said from behind me, rescuing me from my thoughts. "He's really cute."

"Yes, he is." Trying to forget about him, I turned to her and saw she was frowning while munching her pizza. "What is it?"

"I have a terrible headache." She rubbed her temple with her free hand. "Even ibuprofen and paracetamol aren't working anymore."

An idea popped into my head. "Let me try something." I offered her my hand and, frowning even more, she put hers over mine.

Nothing happened. At least, I didn't feel any shock or jolt or warmth or cold. I tried thinking about healing her, taking away her pain, but I didn't feel my energy being passed into her. When I saw her suspicious gaze examining me as if I were crazy, I pulled my hand from hers.

"What were you trying to do?" she asked. I shrugged and she laughed. "You've been watching too much TV. The spiritual healers in TV series aren't your style."

I forced a smile. "They aren't, right?"

But my mind was elsewhere. I was starting to believe I couldn't distinguish reality from visions anymore. How could I heal Victor and Micah and not heal Olivia?

A guy sauntered past us with a sweatshirt from NYU's football team. The number displayed on his sweatshirt was eighty-six. And sure enough, the eight glowed like a beacon.

My pulse rose. Oh God, please, I didn't want to be crazy.

I turned around and started walking away. Connecting with Victor didn't matter anymore. Not if I was losing my mind. Even if there was a special connection between real Victor and me the way there was in my visions, if I was mentally ill, I shouldn't be trying to connect with anyone. Besides, the only connection we had in reality was my healing touch. That wasn't something we could build a relationship on—me crazy and him using me. I'd had enough.

"Hey, Nad, where you going?" Raisa asked when I darted past her.

I stopped just long enough to answer. "Home. I'm not feeling well." I resumed my walk before she could say anything that would change my mind.

Then a loud caw came from above. My palms dampened. I looked up and saw the raven flying against the dark sky. The scar confirmed it was the same one. Oh no. Not the damn black bird too.

I pressed forward, hoping to get out of the crowd before frantic tears spilled out of my eyes.

Every few steps, I glanced up to keep tabs on the bird's location, wishing it would stay around the carnival to prove it wasn't following me.

I was almost out of the crowd when Victor appeared by my side. "You don't seem well."

"And what do you care?" I snapped before resuming my frenzied stride.

He caught up with me. "What's the matter?"

I halted again, and my breath caught when I looked deeply into his wonderful sea-green eyes. They weren't as unfriendly as before. For a second, I could pretend he was my Victor, the one I loved. But just for one second. I shook my head, wishing there was a switch where I could turn "me" off sometimes.

"Do you need my touch?" I asked, a hostile end to my words.

"No."

"Good." I turned. And practically ran over Micah. "Hi," I whispered, aware I sounded like a breathless teenage girl.

With his black eyes shadowed by a scowling brow, he said, "Hello." His frown deepened as he glanced from me to Victor. Then, he gave a brief nod to Victor, who nodded back.

"Is everything all right?" Micah asked as he stepped closer to me.

"Yes," I said. "I was just leaving. Going home."

"I'll walk you." He offered me his arm without taking his glaring eyes from Victor's.

With all my strength I tried not to, but I glanced at Victor. As if he had felt it, his gaze briefly met mine, much softer than the scowl he'd offered Micah.

I forced myself to keep going. "Sure." I linked my arm with Micah's, turned away from Victor, and left without saying goodbye.

Only after we had walked about a block did Micah seem to relax.

"Who is that guy?"

"Just ... a guy." I glanced up at him. He seemed more relaxed, but not his normal confident self. "What is it?"

He kicked a pebble on the pavement. "Nothing."

He seemed worried or frustrated by something, but I decided it was better not to press him for answers. Instead I remained quiet the rest of the way, occasionally humming the last song I'd heard at the carnival.

"Well," I said when we got close to my building. "Thanks for walking me."

He shook his head and flashed one of his dazzling smiles. He was recovering. Definitely. "Thank you for the company." He bowed.

I curled a lock of my hair. "See you soon?"

"Hmm, I'm leaving."

"What?" my voice broke, revealing my discontent.

He grinned and approached me. Oh God. His serious eyes bore into mine. "Something came up. I need to go abroad."

"For how long?"

"I don't know."

"So, you need my touch?" The hole in my soul called "disappointment" grew. Didn't they all need my touch? That was probably the only thing I was good for. Once more, I felt used.

"I don't need it, but I would like to have it. Like recharging batteries, you know?"

"Yup," I snapped, my temper rising. I extended my hand to him. "A goodbye gift."

As soon as his hands covered mine, the cold jolt spread from my skin to his. I watched as he boosted his energy and sent away all his pain.

Then it was done, and he pulled back.

Micah glanced at his cell phone. "It's time for me to go."

Anxiety hit me. I might feel used, but I didn't want anyone suffering. Not if I could do something about it. Even if that meant putting my needs last. "What are you going to do if it happens again?"

"What I did all these years. Grit my teeth and endure it." He bowed, retreating. "Take care, Nadine." His melodious voice wrapped around me.

"You too," I whispered, unable to move.

I watched as he strode to his bike, about half a block down the street, and left in a cloud of exhaust fumes.

14

My plan was to remain in bed until the world ended, or until Cheryl called back or came over and forced me out of my bed. If that didn't happen, I would wait until the girls called 911 to take me to a psychiatric hospital where I would spend the rest of my life.

But on Monday morning, Adam called, yelling at me that I was late for work. What a familiar refrain. Then my mother called, saying how she was proud of me, of my plans for the future, of the person I was. If only she knew. But it was the hospital's call that finally forced me get up. I had been chosen for the position of Patient Care Technician, and they wanted me to go there that afternoon to sign the contract.

Finally something good in my life. Perhaps it was a sign that not everything was lost, and I shouldn't let the craziness in my life take over. A sign to let me know I would get through this. I would be a great doctor, and I would have money to provide a better life for my family.

I knew what could happen in the hospital, who I might meet there, but I tried to ignore that thought. I entered the clinic in the early afternoon and was escorted to human resources where

I signed my contract. Suddenly, I felt almost hopeful, if not happy. The pay was much better than working at the café, and it would look much nicer on my resume. Plus, I'd be able to help people.

With a satisfied smile, I left the room and was heading out when I heard two nurses talking.

"She just died?" one of them asked as they walked past me.

"An hour ago," the other one said. "Her grandson is in shock, poor young man."

My heart squeezed. Oh no.

I was barely thinking when I ran to the elevator and went straight to the eighth floor. I didn't know for sure who the nurses were talking about, but I had a pretty good guess. I didn't stop to consider maybe Victor wouldn't be in his grandma's room anymore and kept running until I was at the door. I stopped, panting, and leaned against the doorframe.

As he stared at the empty bed, he looked like a statue in a crumpled T-shirt and jeans, hair messier than usual, and eyes bright with unshed tears.

I wasn't sure if he had seen me yet, and I wasn't sure what to do. One thing I was sure of though: I wasn't going to leave him even if he was utterly rude to me.

"She told me to say goodbye to you," he whispered, and my heart stopped for a second. He glanced at me. "Can you believe it? She barely knew you, but she said she had this intense feeling you're a great young woman." I couldn't identify the tone of his voice. Jealousy? Rage? Sadness?

"That was kind of her." I took a few steps into the room. His eyes stayed on mine. "I'm so sorry."

He nodded, dropping his head. A loud sob escaped his tightly clamped lips.

I couldn't take Victor—mine or not—in this state. Acting on pure instinct, I closed the gap between us and pulled him into my arms. For a second he was resistant, and I thought he would push me away. He didn't. Slowly he turned into me, passed his arms around my back, and quietly wept, his head buried in my neck, his whole body trembling against mine.

My hands held him firmly, like they had done so many times in my dreams. He felt exactly the same under my touch. His body felt the same pressed against mine. He was *Victor*. Oh, I was so confused.

I had met Bianca Gianni only once, but I had heard so much about her in the last ten months I considered her a close friend, or at least the loved one of my loved one.

To calm him, I did what I always had done in my visions. I sang his favorite song—at least it was my dream Victor's favorite song. It was an old song, but my dream Victor liked only oldies. Carefully maintaining my low soprano, I sang *Walk On* by U2, while slightly swaying and rubbing small circles on his back. His sobs slowed, and his chest stopped quivering.

"I'm alone," he whispered in my ear.

"I know this might sound rather senseless to you now, but you're not alone," I assured him. Risking him running from me I continued, "You've got me."

He didn't run. It might have been my imagination or longing, but I thought his arms tightened slightly around me. I resumed singing.

Near the end of the song, a nurse entered and cleared her throat. At once, he jumped back and gave his full attention to her, practically ignoring me, but I could easily see he wasn't absorbing a word she said. He was too affected to think things through.

So I stepped in and talked to her. Before I knew it, I was planning Bianca's funeral and cremation, earning nods from Victor. It had been Bianca's wish to be cremated and because she had no friends or family besides Victor, there would be no reception or gathering. Her funeral would be quick and simple.

In silence, we left the hospital. I walked next to him to the parking garage.

At his car, he stopped. "I can give you a ride home."

"O-okay," I said, surprised. I thought that, once we were out of the hospital he would push me away and be rude to me as usual.

The ride was quiet and tense. I could feel how depressed he was, how desolate. And there wasn't much I could other than offering my shoulder to him.

And that was exactly what I did.

Once he stopped his car in front of my building, I turned to him. "Are you all right? I mean, not all right, really ... you know what I mean."

His eyes fixed on mine, he nodded. "I'm okay. Still have a lot to process and a lot to do, but I'll be okay."

I took a long breath, trying to be brave for my next words. "You ... hm, you should come up with me. I can make you something to eat. I mean ... you shouldn't be alone right now."

He seemed to consider it for a moment. "Thank you for the offer, but I'll be fine." His voice was almost back to his usual harsh tone. Ouch.

I nodded. "Okay, then." I hesitated, then pointed to the building behind me. "If you need anything, you know where to find me."

"Thanks," he said.

A little hurt, for whoever knew what, I opened the door and turned away from him.

"Nadine?" he called.

Holding my breath, I pivoted back to him. "Yes?"

"Thanks," he repeated, the shine in his eyes unusually

gentle. "For being there with me and talked to the nurse and all that. I mean it."

I offered him a small smile. "Sure."

Then, without another word, I exited his car and closed the door.

Victor peeled away before I made inside my building and, like a stupid, heartsick girl, I stared after him until he turned the next corner and disappeared from my sight.

15

———

APART FROM THE GRAY SKIES, THE SCENE WAS BREATHTAKING.
Standing at the edge of a precipice, I had a clear view of the
town below, among many hills and mountains. The many
European style houses, few parks and squares, and almost no
tall buildings created an inviting mosaic. At the center of the
town, a large angel fountain marked where eight roads met.

Water splashed behind me, and as I turned around, I saw
several gorgeous women dancing and singing along the shore of
a blue lake. Some played harps and others blew in flutes. The
women, clad in skimpy white dresses, had long hair adorned by
flowers with pale, shiny skin, cherry-red lip, and their eyes
shone like torches. They were beautiful in a ghostly way.

The lake before me was blue and clean. The scent of fresh
water and wild flowers was intense, and I welcomed it.

I approached them, certain I was in an observation-only
vision. That was when I saw a thick black cloud coming toward
them from the opposite direction. With it came the flapping of
many huge wings. My blood froze in my veins. Oh no.

From among the cloud, Omi, dressed in his usual crumpled
white suit, came forward, holding his stave. Instantly the women

dropped everything they were doing and stood together, facing the imposing god. I stayed close to them.

"Oh mighty Omi, to what do we owe your visit?" one of the women asked, bowing.

"Where is she?" His skittish gaze scanned the surroundings. "I can feel her aura lingering here. Where is she now? Answer me, nymphs!"

"Who are you talking about, my Lord?" another one asked, also bowing.

"Do not elude me," Omi snarled. "You know exactly who I am talking about, and you are going to tell me what she was doing here and where she is now!" He raised his hand and the black cloud behind him advanced a little, the sound of ruffling wings increasing. The women gasped, taking a few steps back. "Where is the goddess of love and family and beauty?"

"We don't know, my Lord," a blue-haired nymph answered.

He pointed his stave at them. "I can sense her aura!"

Another nymph curtsied and said, "Yes, my Lord, she stopped by here, but we don't know what she was doing or where she went."

"Lies," Omi yelled. With a wicked grin splitting his face, he raised his stave. "One more chance to tell me her location."

"But, my Lord, we don't know!" One of the nymphs fell on her knees. "Please, believe us."

Another one stepped forward. "It's true, my Lord. The goddess came here, but she didn't speak to us. We know nothing about her."

Omi grunted. "Is that your final answer?"

"Yes, mighty god," the blue-haired one answered.

With an enraged cry, he swept his arm down. At the cue, the black cloud parted, revealing the foul creatures within, the same ones I had seen at the crystal palace during a previous vision.

The winged monsters dove down at the town, their strident

shrieks and stench made my skin crawl. But Omi wasn't done. From the orb of his scepter, he cast a red bolt and threw it at the nymphs, who waited for their deaths, standing like statues and holding hands. The bolt hit them and set them on fire. Gasping, I retreated a couple of steps. I wanted to help them, to save them from his fury, but I was only a ghost here.

In seconds the fire consumed them, and they turned into black shadows that dissipated into the gray skies.

In my shock, I almost didn't see Omi sauntering to the edge of the precipice. With trepidation, I walked to the edge too, making sure I kept a good distance from him.

I peered down at the scene below. The cloud and the monsters were destroying the city. Men, women, and children screamed and shouted. My heart hammered a punishing beat, and I had a hard time breathing. When I thought it couldn't get any worse, he cast new red bolts and hurled them into the city. The town exploded into flames. My legs gave out, and I fell to the ground. Red mixed with black until black took over.

"Nadine?" Raisa stood before me. "Talk to me," she yelled, jerking my shoulders.

I glanced around. I was in my room. My tote was over my shoulder, and I wore regular day clothes. All right, I was safe in my world. This was the first vision I'd had in a while, and not one that I'd ever care to have again. A chill crept up my spine. I didn't want to think about what I'd seen with the nymphs and that town. Goose bumps ran up my arms. God, Omi was a beast. I was glad he only lived in my dreams.

But having a vision reminded me of Victor. I hadn't seen him in my visions in ages, and hadn't heard from the real-world Victor for more than ten days now. But who was counting?

"What?" I asked.

"You were screaming, for Pete's sake!" Her eyes glowed with

concern. "You're scaring me, Nadine. I think these episodes, or whatever you have, are going too far."

"I'm fine," I said, walking past her. After not hearing from Cheryl, I didn't feel confident seeking out the specialist she'd recommended. I didn't think I could handle finding out if I was permanently insane by myself. I needed Cheryl, but she apparently didn't need me.

A glance at my wristwatch informed me I would be late for my shift if I didn't start moving. Thankfully, this was the last day I would be working at the café, and I was finally done with summer semester.

I turned to leave, but Raisa stepped in my way. "You're not fine. You were yelling and panting."

"Raisa, let me go. I'll be late."

"Damn your job. You're quitting in a day anyway."

"Yes, but I have a contract to fulfill, and it says I have to work until the end of the day. So if you'll excuse me, I really need to go."

She crossed her arms. "Fine. But be prepared. We're going to talk about this later."

I rolled my eyes. "As you wish."

Unnecessarily, I slammed the door when I left our apartment.

To try to alleviate the anxiety and the rage I was feeling, I jogged to the café, glad I preferred wearing ballet flats instead of high heels like Raisa. When the cawing over me began, I increased my pace. I tried to ignore it but I glanced up. The scarred raven circled the sky right above me.

Inside the campus, I ran past a temporary stand selling flowers. There was a phone number painted in red at the side of the stand. The three number eights that composed the telephone number shone and pulsed, as if calling to me.

When I entered the café, I was panting and flushed. Adam

shot me a glare from across the counter. I did my best to ignore him, and after leaving my things in the back and grabbing my apron, I went to work.

All the coffee I drank during my shift didn't help with my anxiety and my shaking. I had to keep my hands and mouth and mind occupied at all times or I would have a meltdown—scream, pull out my hair, and who knew what else.

Near the end of my shift, when I was finally starting to calm down, Victor entered the café.

He glanced at me, his intense stare pulling out my soul. I forgot how to breathe. Averting his gaze, he picked a table at a corner next to the large glass window that looked over the park outside.

Oh, I knew exactly what would please him. I walked up to him, tucking my order tab in my apron pocket. "A tall mochaccino and double fudge doughnut?"

His eyes went wide. He smiled. "That will do."

I whirled around, pressing a hand to my chest. After picking up his order, I went back to serve him. Luckily for me, the café was quiet, and when he gestured to the chair across the table, I sat down.

Twirling my hair around my finger, I blurted out, "Are you all right? You've been gone for over a week, and I kept thinking you would have one of those attacks and I wouldn't be able to help." His gaze was fixed on me, and I flushed realizing I had confirmed for both of us that I cared about him.

After swallowing a bite of doughnut, he answered, "I was looking for a clean river, lake, or sea nearby. My grandma wanted her ashes sprinkled over clean water. But I couldn't find any. I'm guessing I'll have to go overseas for that."

"If you're thinking about going overseas, maybe you should go to Italy and look for clean water there. I think your grandma would be happy about that."

His brow creased. "She would."

"You missed your classes last week then?"

"I'll begin at the med school in the fall. For now, I'm only with the res—"

"The research team, yeah, I know. You should have come to the research team almost a year ago, but you didn't because of your grandma. When the doctors told you to transfer her here, you contacted the school and transferred here too." Realizing what I had done, I put a hand over my mouth.

He almost dropped the mug he was drinking from, his eyes fixed on mine. "How do you know that? Not even my grandma knew that."

Now the damage was done. Might as well keep going. "I know that too. She argued with you and gave you a hard time until you accepted coming, even if it meant leaving her behind. But you couldn't leave her. She was the only family you had left."

"How?" His gaze searched mine for answers, and I could see the lines of suspicion in his forehead. "How did you know my name? My favorite song? My favorite coffee drink?"

"I know everything about you, or almost everything."

"Could you elaborate on that?" His tone was more brittle, like we were back to the snapping-at-me phase.

"Well. I don't know. I don't want you to think I'm crazy."

He seemed to consider his next words. "It depends. If you classify being able to heal my aches and nausea as craziness, then we're both crazy and the rest doesn't matter, does it?"

It made sense. After all, what did I have to lose? After taking a deep breath, I confessed, "Since I came to New York, almost eleven months ago, I've been having visions about you. Visions, not dreams. I'm fully awake when they happen. And during these visions we talk for hours. You tell me about yourself. We spend a lot of time together."

"Are you sure it's me?"

I laughed. "Want to put it to the test?"

"It's a possibility." He sipped from his mug, his expression still wary.

"Just answer true or false to my questions."

He shrugged. "Okay."

"Your favorite color is white."

"True."

"Your favorite food is five-cheese homemade lasagna."

"True."

"Your father and his parents were born in Italy. They came to the U.S. when your father was still a toddler."

"True."

"You keep a photo of your parents and yourself under your pillow and a smaller one in your wallet."

"True."

"You have a crescent moon shaped scar on your knee from falling out of a tree when you were seven."

His eyebrows went to his hairline. "True."

"You should have been with your parents during the assault that killed them, but you got distracted in an electronics store across the street. Your best friend, Jason, was killed in a car accident, and you should have been with him. You were on your way to Lauren's house when a tornado formed, but she had just called and asked you to run an errand for her, which caused you to be late and miss it. And you feel like you should have died with them."

Some time passed before he answered, "True."

"The last time you slept with a girl was almost a year ago, and you only did it because you were super drunk, which doesn't happen often."

With reddening cheeks, he held up his hands. "All right, all right." He was visibly shaken by my knowledge. "Give me a minute. I need to process all this." I started to get up, but he held my wrist, the warm shock startling me. Was he in need of my touch? "I didn't mean it like that. You don't need to leave."

"No, it's fine." I pulled my arm from his grip. Perhaps, I also needed a minute. "I should check on the customers."

I left him just as Adam was coming toward me with fuming eyes. I wasn't up to listen to his complaints. I raised my hand to prevent him from speaking and hurried to the back, where the strong smell of coffee beans wrapped around me. I started pacing.

Oh my God! So it was true. Everything! The facts the Victor from my dream had told me, the in-the-flesh Victor had just confirmed. Oh, I knew many more facts and was certain they were all true too. How could it be? Did it mean my other recently bizarre visions about Imha and Omi and Ceris were true too? But they weren't real, were they? Of course not.

Making me jump, Adam showed up at the back door with an indifferent look on his face. "Your friend is calling for you."

"Th-thanks." Like an idiot, I stopped by the restroom and in front of the mirror made sure my hair and my clothes looked okay. What was I doing?

Shaking my head, I went back work. For more than ten minutes, I waited tables and served coffee. When everyone at the café seemed content, I returned to Victor and sat in the same chair as before.

"So," he said, running a hand over his disheveled golden hair. "What other embarrassing facts do you know about me?"

I shrugged. "I don't know. Probably a few more." I realized I was still twining my hair and stopped, then put my hands under my butt and sat on them. "Aren't you mad at me?"

"These visions you have—can you control them?"

"No."

"Then I have no right to be mad at you." He placed his

elbows on the table and rested his chin on his hand. "But I confess, none of this makes sense. Your visions and my pains. You see, I had a checkup three months ago when the pains intensified. I'm as healthy as a person can be."

"I know. I feel like I'm losing my mind. In fact, there are days I'm certain I'm going to end up in a psychiatric hospital for the rest of my life."

His eyes met mine, and the air was sucked out of me.

"Well," he said, "losing your mind or not, I'm grateful for you. The pain had grown so bad, I'm sure I would be dead by now if it weren't for you."

I froze. That struck a chord within me, but I couldn't put my finger on where I had heard that before.

As if pulled by a string, my head turned toward the TV near the ceiling on the opposite corner of the cafe. The reporters delivered news: in Australia, hundreds of dolphins had been found dead on the beach; in Argentina, sick people robbed drugstores at gunpoint; in a public park in the Netherlands, a terrorist blew himself and a bunch of families apart; and in Russia, a pack of giant bats attacked and killed a group of teenagers.

What blew my mind away was what came next. The reporters showed aerial images of a small town in Switzerland, totally destroyed. Everything was either black or still on fire. There were no survivors because, as the reporter at the site said, it had happened too fast. And, while hovering over the town, they showed the images of the mountains around it and the precipice with the lake, now polluted. It was the precipice where I had stood in my vision.

My stomach lurched. I shot up and ran to the bathroom in the back, where I threw up what little food I had eaten today. My body went limp, and I fell on the floor shuddering.

After a few minutes, a knock startled me. My mind didn't connect the dots, and I couldn't find my voice to answer.

"Nadine, are you okay?" Victor asked.

What was he doing here? I tried sitting up and speaking to him, but my body wouldn't cooperate. I wanted to tell him the door was unlocked, but he'd figured that out because a second later he knelt beside me.

"What happened? Nadine?" His strong hands gripped my shoulders, and he helped me sit up against the wall. "Talk to me."

I was dizzy, wasn't I, seeing his eyes shining with worry?

A few violent tremors ran up my body, and I felt like crying. I gathered all the strength I had left and said, "I saw that." My voice was clogged with emotion. "I saw what was happening on TV in a vision right before I came to work." I didn't realize I had been crying until the tears blurred my vision. Victor wiped my cheeks, his touch sending a warm, relaxing jolt to my skin. "I never thought it would be true. It was just a vision."

"I wasn't just a vision."

"You were." I wanted to shout, though I could only whisper. "Until two months ago, you were just a vision. I never thought you could be real." The walls were closing in on me. "Oh God, I can't take this."

My backbone lost its strength, but he held me in place. "Come on, I'll get you home." He caught me in his arms as if I were a weightless, ragged doll.

His sweet scent wrapped around me and, for a few moments, I forgot everything else. Why was he carrying me? Where was he taking me?

When he deposited me in my bed, I wondered how we had gotten here and why I didn't remember any of it. He sat beside me.

"I think we should call a doctor." I heard Raisa's frantic voice, though my sight was still hazy and I couldn't pinpoint her location.

"She just needs some rest," he said. Then, he passed a cool glass to me. "Drink this. It'll calm you."

All I wanted was to calm down. I gulped the sour contents of the glass and lay back on my pillow, the whirling wind in my mind gradually slowing.

"She doesn't seem well," Raisa protested.

"Let's give her some peace and quiet," Victor said. His weight left my mattress.

I wanted to pull him back, but I didn't think I could move my arms. I heard Raisa make some further comments, but then the voices went away and I was left alone in the dark.

16

I woke up with a throbbing headache.

I got out of my bed and saw I was wearing only my tee and undies. Why wasn't I wearing my pajamas, or even my jeans? I couldn't think through the headache. In my bathroom, I found some ibuprofen. While there, I decided to brush my teeth and take a shower.

The warm water running over my skin helped with the pain and I relaxed, enjoying the clean water.

Clean water. Darkness. Pointy teeth. Large wings. Crumbling walls. Red bolts. Fire. Smoke. Burnt smell.

The events rushed back into my mind, making me dizzy. Gasping, I almost fell on the slippery floor, but managed to steady myself. I left the shower, wrapped in a towel, and searched my room for my cell phone or wristwatch. I settled for my alarm clock and was shocked to find it was eleven at night.

Wait. Had I dreamed it? About Victor being at the café, the news, being carried home?

I shoved on a pair of jeans, a black sweater, and flat black boots and went to the living room, hoping to see him there. The apartment was empty and dark. Not even Raisa was home. Her bedroom door was open and the lights were off.

On the kitchen countertop, I found a note in Raisa's handwriting:

Went out with Olivia.

Victor has your keys. He said he will be back soon.

Call if you need anything.

My mind was in hyper mode. I needed something to do. I couldn't even go out since my keys were with Victor.

I sat on the sofa and tuned the TV to a cable news channel. I had to know more about what had happened to that small town.

More bad news: the potable water crisis, the energy crisis, the agriculture crisis, the *everything* crisis! I wondered how long it would take for the world to end.

Then, updated news about the burnt town in Switzerland. The people working the case had no explanations or clues as to how the firestorm had happened and how it—whatever it was— had been able to devastate an entire town in a couple of minutes. The images were shocking. The fire had been extinguished, leaving everything black. The camera zoomed out, and there it was, the precipice where I had been.

My stomach turned and nausea surged up. Oh God. How could it be?

I ran to the kitchen. I gulped down a large glass of water, trying to push the nausea back down. It helped a little.

Back in my room, I picked up my cell phone and called Cheryl. To hell with the hour. I hadn't talked to her in more than three weeks and I needed her right now, even if it was almost midnight. I needed her to listen to me, to calm me down, to tell me I was not insane and that therapy would be sufficient to treat my visions and hallucinations. The call went directly to her voicemail.

A noise from the living room made me forget about Cheryl. My heart fluttered. "Victor?" I called, rushing to the other room.

I made it to the doorway before I bumped into a solid figure that loomed over me. I stumbled and would have fallen back if strong hands hadn't steadied me by my elbows. Micah's sandalwood scent hit me before I could see him.

His sly smile played with my soul. "Hello there."

"What are you doing here?" I pulled my arms from his hold. "When did you get back? Wait, how did you get in?"

"Darling, I would love to answer all your questions, but we don't have time." His eyes expressed urgency even if his debonair tone didn't. "We have to go."

I stepped back. "Why?"

"All right," he said, coming closer. "If you're gonna play hard to get, then at least give me some of your goodness before the game."

He extended his jarring hand.

Oh God. I held his hand in mine. The cold shock startled me, both from the contrast with the warmth that came with Victor's touch and from the strength of Micah's grip. With closed eyes, Micah moaned, as if my touch were the essence of his life.

"How long have you been in pain?"

"A few days." He pulled his hand back. "Thanks." He walked into my room and headed toward my closet.

Frowning, I followed him and found him pulling out a suitcase. He opened it. "What are you doing?"

"What does it look like?"

"Micah." I pulled his arm, trying in vain to make him look at me. "Stop with the freakiness. And stop messing with my stuff. Tell me what the hell you're doing?"

He turned to me. "We gotta leave. Now."

I laughed. "Okay, okay. If you're trying to scare me, I'll pretend I'm scared, then you can stop the sh—" His hand shot out to my throat, and he pinned me to the wall. I gagged. The enraged shine of his deep black eyes sent shivers up my spine.

"If you want to live, do as I say," he snarled. His cool breath against my skin made my insides melt from pure terror. "You have five minutes to pack, and then we are out of here." He released me and marched out of the closet.

I fell on the floor, my hand on my throat, as I sucked in desperate gulps of fresh air.

Holy hell. My mind spun. I peeked out of the closet. He wasn't in my room. Quivering hard and stifling sobs, I crawled out of my room and grabbed my cell phone. My wish was to call Victor, but I didn't have his number, and I didn't think he wanted to be my rescuer. Instead, I pressed the speed dial to call Raisa. I hoped she would pick up her phone, wherever she was.

On the first ring, the phone was snatched from my hand.

Micah threw it against the wall. "Damn it! Why can't you listen to me?"

I tried to keep my distance from him, but the shaking of my body made it hard to walk backward, especially since my mind had shut down. I kept bumping and stumbling over the furniture.

"What do you want?" I cried, trying to recall where I had left my purse with my pepper spray.

"I want to get out of here," he yelled, coming closer. After another puff, he went back to my closet and threw random clothes inside the suitcase. "Behave, or I'll have to use force again."

I was already on tiptoes, reaching for the room's door. I was halfway through the living room when I heard him behind me. "Damn it, woman!"

I darted to the door. He ran much faster than I did and got to me as I was turning the knob. Where I would have gone, I have no idea. I just wanted to get away from him.

More sobs made their way out of me as he dragged me back into my room.

A stabbing pain took over my chest, warmth dispersed through my body, the tingles crawling over my skin. The room spun into darkness.

A vision.

A younger Micah wandered with an older couple in what looked like a marketplace. The air was cool but humid, almost stifling. Improvised stands stretched through the crowded streets, with vendors selling fruits, grains, fabrics, shoes, jewelry, and anything and everything else. Nobody seemed to care about the dark sky and the dangers that came with it.

Like the older Micah, this younger version was dressed in black, but without the leather jacket. His hair was cut shorter, the same style as the tall man beside him. They had the same pose, the same wide set of shoulders. The man was, without a doubt, Micah's father. Beside them, with long brown curls and the same deep black eyes, a woman observed and touched colorful veils hanging from one of the stands, then she stepped closer, linked arms with his father, and smiled up at him. Micah's mother.

His parents seemed content with each other as they sauntered around and looked at the things that interested them.

I accompanied them, trying to understand their foreign words, or at least interpret their body language.

Suddenly, people around them started shouting words that sounded like curses. Micah looked around. He was taller than most, so he gazed over the heads of others, probably seeking the source of the commotion. He stiffened, and I was curious about what he saw.

Without wasting a second, he grabbed his parents' arms and pulled them toward a stand to hide, as many others were doing.

But, out from the path they had chosen, emerged a man

wearing a brown robe and a white turban and holding an automatic rifle. The man shouted something. Micah pulled his mother behind him and retreated, hands in the air. His family moved back until they were in the middle of the street, together with other scared people who also held hands up. Six men in robes and turbans surrounded them, pointing their rifles at their heads.

One of the armed men shouted hurried words. I guessed orders or instructions. Shuddering, the trapped ones—there were at least twenty—took off jewelry and expensive pieces of clothing, then handed them over, along with wallets and money, to the men with the guns.

Micah's mother held on to her necklace, trying to hide it, but the man closest to her saw it and advanced toward her, brandishing his gun in her face. I gasped, wishing I could pull her out of there. Micah and his father reacted and tried to reason with the man who shouted at her.

Chaos erupted. More people saw that as a distraction. With the probable intention of stopping the attackers, men and a few women lunged at the armed males, who started firing random shots. Micah ducked, pulling his mother with him, but she flopped like jelly in his arms, blood spilling from her mouth. With tears brimming in his eyes, he searched for her wound and found not one, but four. He choked out a sob as his father dropped beside him, a bullet in his forehead.

The color drained from his skin, and Micah stared at his parents, frozen, until one of the armed men pointed his weapon at his head.

Yelling like a dying animal, he lunged at the man who, unprepared, tumbled back, cracking his head on the stone floor. He stilled. Micah took the rifle and stood, the evil shine in his eyes startling me. He turned to the other men and started shooting. He immediately took three out with shots. The other two charged him, causing him to lose the rifle and fight hand-to-hand.

But there was something going on with Micah. His eyes shone, the rage spread through his features, and he didn't seem in control of himself.

He punched and kicked the men until they lay on the ground with the others, bleeding and motionless.

The people watching drew back, now scared of him, but he didn't notice. He knelt beside his parents' bodies and, with tenderness, reached under the neckline of his mother's dress, taking the delicate golden necklace she had been trying to hide. With a sob, he fastened the jewelry around his neck, then the mask of emotion that had covered his face fell and he began to cry.

"Nadine!"

I could hear Micah calling my name. I blinked several times, then my gaze focused. We were back in my living room, and he held my arm with too much force, his eyes wary and too close to mine. "What was that?"

My legs gave out. I wanted to sit on the floor, but he held me in place.

I reached under the neck of his shirt and found the necklace. I gaped, not believing it was true. "You killed the men who killed your parents," I whispered, feeling my hands trembling under his grip.

He frowned and shook his head. "How can you possibly know that?" he asked, venom woven through his words. "You know what, we need to go. We'll talk later."

He dragged me to my room, letting me sit on the floor while he rummaged through my things, putting them into the suitcase. I wasn't really paying attention. My mind was a big muddled mess—a tangled jungle—and I couldn't assimilate what was real and what wasn't.

Where was my phone? I had to call Cheryl and demand she come pick me up. I wanted to go to the hospital. I needed to be admitted. I needed to be sedated. I needed Cheryl. Oh, that was right. My phone had been smashed against a wall and was in pieces on the floor.

Micah came out of my bathroom, carrying a few bottles of moisturizer and shampoo and other stuff. He threw the things into the suitcase on my bed and turned to me. "You don't look okay."

"I'm not okay," I whispered. "Why would I be okay?" I asked. "Have you seen Raisa? I need to ask her something."

"What are you talking about?"

I shrugged, my mind spinning. "I don't know."

Shaking his head, he opened my nightstand drawer and, I guessed looking for more important stuff, rifled through it. He pulled out a piece of paper. "Is this important?"

My head pounded. My thoughts slowed. Was the card important? I raked my mind, trying to make my brain work. A hint of memory fluttered.

"Cheryl gave it to me," I muttered. I watched, mindless, as he threw it, along with other things he took from the drawer, inside my suitcase.

After what seemed like forever, he closed the suitcase, grabbed it, and pulled me up by my arm.

"Let's go." He tugged me to the living room.

The front door opened before we reached it. Victor stood in the doorway.

I extricated myself from Micah and ran to him. "Victor," I whispered his name like a prayer. "Please, help me."

His sea-green eyes set on Micah, his pose defensive, but he let me approach, and even embraced me when I bumped into him.

"What happened?" he asked, his tone soft and gentle.

The tears came back to my eyes. I needed to get away from Micah, who'd obviously gone crazy, but I needed to get away from the visions more. I needed to get away from everything. "Take me to the hospital, please. I need a psychiatrist. It's urgent."

"What?" he asked, frowning.

"God damn it!" Micah cursed, gritting his teeth. "You're worse than her." He pointed to Victor. "Two beacons, now three, together."

"Excuse me?" Victor asked, putting himself between Micah and me.

"All right," Micah said. "You too, then. We gotta go. Now!"

"What are you talking about?" Victor asked, switching his pose to menacing. "And what are you doing in here?"

"No time to explain, people." Micah's tone rose. "Let's go."

"I'm not going anywhere." Victor grounded himself. "Neither is Nadine."

Micah raised one eyebrow. "Oh yeah? Tell that to your friends." He went to the window and pulled the thick beige curtains away. Huge bats hovered around the window, baring their teeth and staring straight at us.

"Oh God," I whispered. "Is that why you were forcing me to leave?" Micah gave me an inscrutable look. Maybe he'd been trying to help me, not kidnap me. "B-but you can repel them." I wiped away my tears. Regaining the strength in my legs, I walked a few steps toward Micah. "You can repel them."

"True, but I'll bet they're rethinking their priorities. I would say killing you two would be at the top."

"Why?" Victor came to stand beside me. "Why kill us? And how can you repel them?"

"Enough," Micah shouted. "Come on, pretty boy, we gotta go. Questions come later."

"I'm not going anywhere with you," Victor repeated.

Snickering, Micah hurried past us. "Oh no?" He left the apartment.

Instantly, the bats advanced, breaking the windows and chasing after us. I yelled and ran with Victor to the hallway where Micah waited, leaning against the wall.

Victor closed the door behind us, and we ran to the elevator.

Micah followed us, my suitcase in his hand. "Are you done playing?" he asked, entering the elevator with us. "Can we go now?"

I was trembling, and when I spoke, my voice was too. "What are you trying to prove?"

"That we need to leave before they reconsider the fear they feel for me and attack the three of us," he explained.

"And why do they want to attack us?" Victor asked, as the elevator door opened at the first floor.

"That's a good question I don't have an answer for," Micah said, stepping out of the elevator.

A quick sequence of images rushed in my mind. The bats flying in. The outside door at the garage downstairs. Victor's car parked on the other side of the street.

On impulse, I pulled Micah back inside the elevator as the front glass broke and shrieks exploded in the lobby. I pressed the close-doors button and watched as the bats flew in and advanced toward us, my finger already on the garage button.

Micah turned to me. "What was that?"

"Just ..." I shook my head, not sure what to tell them. Instead, I glanced at Victor. "Your car is parked around the corner, right?"

"Yes, right beside the garage gates. How do you know?"

I lowered my gaze. "I'm not sure." The elevator doors opened again to the underground garage, and I beckoned for them to follow me. "Victor, do you still have my keys?"

"Here." He extended them to me as we rushed to the end of the garage.

I grabbed the keys and found the one I wanted. "I'm not sure how it's going to be, if the bats will know we're on the other side of the building already, but I think we should run to the car." My stomach revolted just imagining being out there with the bats.

"Wait." Micah raised his hand. "I won't leave my bike out there alone."

I faced him. "What do you want to do? Run there?"

Micah crossed his arms. "Well, not run, but you could drop me right in front of it. Hopefully, the bats will stay away from me."

"And then what?" Victor asked, his tone irritated.

"Drive west and drive fast," Micah said, pulling his phone from his pocket. "I'll follow you. Give me your number so we can contact each other."

"You broke my cell phone," I said, regaining some of my confidence.

He glanced at me with his trademark smile. "Yeah, sorry about that." He nodded at Victor. "Give me yours." They exchanged numbers. "On three," Micah said as I unlocked the door and we got ready to bolt. "Ready. THREE."

We left the building and ran together to Victor's car. We made it inside just as the winged things rounded the corner, their shrieks gelling my soul. I shuddered.

Victor started the car and drove to the front of the building, the bats hovering above us.

Micah leaned close to the door. "About fifty miles west of here, there is a big and colorful gas station. Meet me there."

"There are dozens of gas stations on the road," I yelled.

"Not that many anymore. Besides, it has giant neon signs and many colored lamps." He bowed at me. "No way of missing it."

He opened and closed the car door, and ran to his bike.

A bat closed in on him and I inhaled sharply. Micah turned to face it and, slowly, it retreated.

"How can he do that?" Victor gaped as Micah hopped on his bike.

"I don't know," I whispered, equally amazed.

Two bats bumped into the car and Victor sprang into action, taking off and driving into the unknown.

17

———

The silence inside the car was killing me, but I wasn't going to be the one to crack. As far as I knew, my mind was too messed up for me to say anything coherent.

I kept replaying everything that had happened in the last month. I'd met Micah, found a real-life but different Victor, lost contact with Cheryl, and lost the visions of dream Victor. Freaky gods appeared in my visions instead, and I'd watched both the destruction of a town in Switzerland and a part of Micah's past in visions. Plus the shining number eight everywhere I looked.

I would give anything to crawl inside a cave and have a vision, a long and permanent vision, where Victor, the dream Victor, and I lived happily ever after. Instead, I was now on the road, on the run. My heart squeezed tight, hurting. My hands shook every time I thought about the things that were happening to me, and I didn't understand. I was scared and alone. I took a deep breath. If only I could go home and forget about it all.

However, I was buried too deep in this mess. I had to find out what was happening. Why bats were coming for me, why there were two guys I could heal with my touch, how I could heal them ... and so many other things that made my head throb.

I sent a text message to Raisa and Olivia from Victor's phone, telling them bats had entered our building, they should stay with friends for a while and be careful upon returning there, and I was going to spend a few days away with Victor. I could already see them imagining I was on a romantic getaway. If only.

After forty minutes of silent driving, he finally spoke. "Do you trust that guy?" He eyed Micah on his bike through the rearview mirror.

I sighed, staring out at the dark exterior. Besides the road and what the car's headlights illuminated, not much else was discernible. It was like life was nonexistent. Here and there, we would pass another car or see some houses or RVs along the road. Victor sat in the driver's seat next to me, but I'd never felt so alone.

"I don't know who to trust. Can I trust you?"

"Good point," he said. After a couple of minutes, he tried again, "How did you meet him?"

"Micah saved me from a bat attack two months ago. He appeared and the bats went away."

"Just like that?"

I turned to him. "Just like that. Didn't you see how the bats reacted around him back there?"

"I did. But I needed to make sure you saw it too."

I chuckled, a hollow, sad sound. "I know the feeling of doubting yourself, but I don't know what is happening or why. Sometimes I think I'm losing my mind. I should face this and do what I should have done a long time ago." Tears burned my eyes. "See a psychiatrist and ask for help. I don't know what is real or what isn't anymore."

"Oh, this is real, trust me." He glanced at me; one side of his mouth curled up.

How familiar that half-smile was. I whispered, "You sound like the Victor in my visions. How do I know I'm not hallucinating right now?"

He didn't answer me. After a while he asked, "How is the Victor in your visions?"

I couldn't help but smile. "Well." I shifted my weight, turning to face him directly so I could analyze him. "He's an exact copy of you, physically, I mean. Except the hair. His hair is a little shorter, and it's never messy. You dress more casually than he does too."

He kept his eyes on the road, and I kept my eyes on him. It was still hard to believe they weren't one and the same. "He's kind, funny, confident, elegant. He loves to dance, and we can talk for hours about anything." Oh, I missed him. And that thought made me realize something. "When did you move to New York?"

"About seven weeks ago."

Almost two months ago. That was when the first non-Victor vision occurred. "You know, since actually having met you, I haven't had visions about the other you. Just about other unrelated events."

"Like what?"

"Like the town in Switzerland that was burned to the ground in seconds. I saw it happening."

"Did you see how it happened?"

"Yes," I whispered.

"What was it?"

I turned away. "You wouldn't believe me."

"Try me."

But I didn't say anything because I was gawking at the gas station that was coming into sight ahead of us.

"Holy hell," I whispered.

How bizarre. The gas station had colossal green neon signs with the name of the place, Al's Corner, spread along the road, plus several tall posts with stadium-type lights around the perimeter. I bet the place didn't cast a single shadow. The owner must be afraid of the dark.

"This is the most bizarre thing I've ever seen," Victor muttered, startling me. Once more, he seemed like my Victor by saying what I was thinking.

He brought the car to a stop in a large parking lot alongside a diner that was as bright as the rest of the gas station. Micah parked beside us a few seconds later, revving the engine of his bike before letting it die.

As he circled his car, Victor cursed and kicked the air. "Look at this." He pointed to the largest and densest scratch on the side of his car, right under a cracked window. He turned to Micah, who stood leaning against his bike with a sly grin. "This is your fault. You're going to pay for this."

"It's not my fault the bats want your blood," Micah said, shrugging.

"And why do they want his blood?" I asked. I crossed my arms and quickly scanned the place. It was almost empty except for one customer and two attendants inside the diner.

"Not only his," Micah said. "Yours too. And mine, but for some reason, they prefer not to come too close to me."

"What else do you know?" I asked.

"Not much more," he said. "Since my parents died, I've been experiencing certain things. Weird things. One of them is the ability to feel when a person has a different and strong aura. And the three of us have strong, unusual auras."

"Three beacons," I whispered.

"Yes, our auras together become like beacons, calling the bats and whatever else," Micah said.

Victor gave him a sidelong look. "Do you expect me to believe this shit?"

"Believe what you want," Micah snapped. "I'm just telling you what I know."

"And the pain?" I asked, interrupting them before the bickering increased. "Did it start after your parents' deaths too?"

"Nope." He shook his head. "It started a few days earlier."

"Wait." Victor raised his hand as if he was asking for a time out. "You also have pain?"

Micah's brow creased. "What do you mean, *also*?"

I answered before Victor could. "You two both have pain. And, so far, I've been able to take it away with my touch. For both of you."

Both guys gaped at each other.

Micah stepped closer to Victor. "Back to your question: Do I expect you to believe all that? Hell yeah! If you're like me, the aches you feel are inexplicable, and yet you won't believe the bats want to chew on us specifically?" He snickered. "If you didn't believe, why did you come?"

"You want to know why I'm here?" Victor asked, clenching his fists. "I'm here because she"—he pointed at me—"has visions about me. She knows everything about me, and I just met her. I gotta figure that out. Besides, she's the only one that can lessen the ache."

Well, that hurt. Deep down, in the darkest corners of my soul, I'd hoped he'd say he came because he wanted to be with me. I was so naïve. Of course he was here for himself. Why else would *this* Victor do anything?

"Visions?" Micah turned to me. "What visions?"

"Like the one I had where I saw when your parents died." I stared at my feet, afraid of his reaction. "I've been having visions of Victor for quite some time. Though, this past month or so, my visions have become more delusional, less ... ah ... personal."

With his typical smile, Micah said, "You won't try to tell me the visions about him"—he nodded toward Victor—"weren't delusional, will you?"

I almost laughed, as if it didn't hurt to be here and believe I was in the craziest vision ever.

"If you only made us come here to tell us bats are after us, can I go home now?" Victor asked.

"If you want to die, be my guest," Micah said, flinging a hand toward the road that led back to the highway.

"You make no sense," Victor muttered, turning his back to us.

"Can't you see something is going on here?" Micah asked, his voice strained. "I've been wandering Earth for the last four years, looking for people who could explain things to me, people who were like me. And I found you two. I couldn't believe it when you healed me." He stared into my eyes, so grateful and so hopeful, he took my breath away. "And then you." He pointed at Victor, who turned to listen. "Your aura is comparable to mine, but it's also different. I can't explain. And you feel the pain and the dizziness like I do."

Victor shrugged. "That doesn't explain things."

"No, it doesn't," Micah said. "But aren't you wondering why we are the way we are?"

Wait. "You left," I said, turning to Micah. "You said you had something to do abroad. What was it?"

"I followed the lead of a strong aura," he confessed, regret and rage filling his features. "But it was a trap. Someone wanted me away from here. From you." He stared at me, sending chills up my spine. Away from me? "I was attacked, but I managed to escape."

"Attacked?" I advanced toward him, my hands rising to search him, to see if he was okay, but I caught myself before getting too near. I cleared my throat. "By whom?"

"I don't know!" He raised his hands in exasperation. "I couldn't get a good look at them, but one thing I do know—whatever it was, it didn't feel human."

"What?" A hysterical laugh was stifled in Victor's question. "You're kidding, right?"

"All right, Nadine." Micah offered his hand. "Leave this damn skeptic behind and let's try to save ourselves."

Leave Victor behind? Even if he wasn't exactly my Victor? I looked between them, my mouth open, words absent. "We can't just leave him behind."

"What if I want to be left behind?" Victor asked, his eyes raging.

"But—"

I didn't need to continue. Putting his hands to his temple, he gritted his teeth as the enigmatic pain assaulted him. He started shaking, and his breathing became erratic. He fell on his knees and lowered his head, gripping his chest like he could take the pain away with his hand.

But it wasn't his touch that could take the pain away. It was *mine*.

I knelt beside him, my hands on his face. Instantly, warmth from my palms spread through his smooth skin, saving him from losing consciousness. Victor inhaled and his cheeks flushed; he stared at me, his eyes revealing the frustration that consumed him.

"You may find a way of surviving the bats and other creatures that might come for you," Micah said. "But you won't survive that."

"He's right," I whispered, trying to put all my charm and hope into my eyes to move him into agreeing. "We don't know what's happening, but you need my touch. We should stay together until we find out more about it."

Either my charm worked, or the relief from the pain was too

attractive.

Victor nodded and stood up with me. "What now?" he asked, eyeing Micah.

"Now? I don't know." Micah shrugged. "We keep moving? I try to sense someone else like us?"

My stomach growled. "How about we eat something while we think," I suggested, glancing at my wristwatch. It was almost three in the morning, and I had barely finished my snack the previous evening.

"I'm in," he said, offering me his arm.

I felt the urge to glance at Victor, but instead, linked my arm with Micah's, turning toward the diner.

There was a colorful neon sign on the window, advertising snacks and drinks and listing prices. Each letter or number was a different color. There were two number eights among the listed prices, and it was a relief to see they were not glowing or sparkling or anything else weird.

"That's new," I said, frowning.

"What?" Micah asked, following my gaze and examining the sign.

"The eights aren't shining," I said. The fives were pink, the ones were blue, and the eights were lit by white neon light. "No more than the other numbers."

Micah chuckled. "Of course they aren't. The two eights are burned out."

What?

The eights were shining after all.

We took a table near the window. Micah sat by my side, and Victor sat across the table from us. The waitress came soon after, and we ordered a mochaccino and a cinnamon roll for me, a Pepsi and a chocolate doughnut for Victor, and beer and French fries for Micah.

Victor turned to me. "What was that about the number

eight?"

I sighed, considering if I should tell them. Well, I was up to my neck in things I didn't understand. Telling them one more bizarre thing couldn't hurt. "Since my visions started, every number eight I see shines. In magazines, painted on walls, in books, on shirts, wherever. It's like they have a white backlight."

"Do you know what it means?" Micah asked.

"I wish," I muttered.

Victor tapped his fingers on the table. "Forget glowing numbers. We have to think about what to do. We can't just wander around trying to find whoever can help us. If that's the case, then I would rather go home until Micah senses someone. Or something."

God, his pessimism and rudeness was starting to irritate me.

"Are you always this much of a naysayer?" I asked, narrowing my eyes at him.

"Most of the time, I'm worse," he snapped, leaning closer.

"All right, children," Micah chided. "We do have to think about what to do. I'm certain we shouldn't remain in one place for too long though. Together, our auras are intense flares for anyone who might be after us."

Anyone? Besides the bats, who could be after us? Even so, I wanted to know why the bats were after us.

Their voices grew dim and the world around me swirled. I closed my eyes against the rushing dizziness and saw in my mind's eye a large, beige-colored stone room. Multiple white flags popped out on top of stone pillars, lit candles spread throughout the perimeter, and an altar stood at the back, where a poster I couldn't clearly see was on display. Descending the altar stairs, a blond man, about average height and dressed in white robes, appeared before me. From his pocket he pulled out a card. I looked closer. In his hand, he held the same card Micah had picked up from the drawer in my room.

"Nadine?" I heard Victor call me. "Are you okay?"

The vision faded and I returned back to the diner, panting. I frowned, confused at the worry in his tone.

"What did you see?" Micah asked.

I sighed. "I know who can help us."

18

WE LEFT MICAH'S BIKE WITH THE OWNER OF THE GAS STATION, chained to a thick column, much to his chagrin. Then, we drove for three hours to find a decent motel. I was thankful when we finally found one because I almost died from the intensity of their scents inside the car, unable to decide which one tantalized me more.

The bedroom given to us had two full beds. I took one, Victor took the other, and Micah was able to get an old mattress from the receptionist to sleep on the floor.

Five hours later, the guys and I were up and inside an old department store, buying clothes and other necessary stuff for them, since they hadn't brought anything. After loading up, we went back to driving and eating our snacks inside Victor's car.

We were headed south on I-95, to Jacksonville, Florida. The business card indicated we would find Morgan Holt, whoever he was, there. Our plan was to drive until evening, stop to rest for a few hours, and then keep going in the morning. If everything went as planned, we would arrive there by noon the following day.

The outside was scary. Even sort of protected inside the car, knowing bats and everything else was out there made me feel like crawling into a corner and crying. It worsened whenever we passed a destroyed town or had to stop and find an alternative route because of broken roads or bridges.

I rode shotgun, while Micah was spread out on the backseat, whistling without rhythm with songs playing on the radio.

My mind was somewhere else. Where exactly, I wasn't sure. Every time I closed my eyes, the events of the past days, months, flashed before me. I was tired of thinking about it. The more I thought about the occurrences, trying to reason them out, the more my head hurt.

Distracted with the dark and lifeless outside view, I began singing with the songs playing from the car's stereo—mostly rock and alternative and only a few pop songs. I had sung about ten songs before I noticed Micah leaning toward the front, gawking at me.

"What?" I pulled my hands from the dashboard where I had been playing an imaginary piano without noticing. I flushed.

"I had no idea you could sing like that," he said. The heat in my cheeks increased.

"That's amazing," Victor said, glancing at me with a gentle smile tugging at his lips. Oh, my heart.

"It is," Micah exclaimed. He did sound impressed. "Let me ask, why are you in the health program? You have the talent and the looks to succeed in showbiz."

I frowned. Did he think I was beautiful? It wasn't the first time he'd implied it.

"It's a long story," I said.

He offered me one of his trademark smiles before leaning back, relaxing on the backseat, and putting his clasped hands behind his head. "It's a long trip. Humor us."

I received a quick, but reassuring, sidelong glance from Victor. It was enough to make me talk. "I have to take care of my family. My father's a farmer, my mom's a teacher, and I have two brothers and one sister, all younger. Because of the farm crisis, life's been tough." My throat closed up and I swallowed.

In the rearview mirror, Micah caught my eye, then nodded.

"Before the other three were born, there was another boy. Because conditions were so bad, he ... he died." Tears brimmed in my eyes. But I wanted to go on. "Things got a little better after that, but I decided to follow a route that would give me enough money to help my family. By the time the oldest of my brothers leaves high school, I'll be a doctor. I'll be able to pay for his college tuition. And I want to provide an early retirement for my parents."

"How are you paying for your tuition now?" Victor asked, eyes on the road.

"A discount due to need, and a scholarship because of my SAT scores. The rest I pay for from my salary."

"I don't understand." Micah leaned forward again. "In show-biz, you can make much more than a doctor ever would."

"That's if I succeeded." I turned sideways to look at him. "I can't waste time and money trying. Nobody becomes a star and rich overnight. Especially nowadays. Haven't you noticed there are less and less artists performing out there? Besides, not everyone can be a classic, chic singer. I'm so not gonna walk on a stage wearing only a bikini and wiggle my butt for the camera like most pop singers do these days to get more fans. That's not my style. But I'm fine. It was my option. I like medicine, and I like helping others."

"You say that now," Micah said. "When you're older and tired of hearing grandpas complain about bladder control problems and teenagers crying because of acute acne, you'll regret your decision."

His vision of my future brought some humor to the situation. I chuckled. "Sorry, but I won't change my mind."

Micah shrugged. "Suit yourself." He lay down in the back-seat, eyes closed.

Taking advantage of the silence, I glanced at Victor. "Are you okay?"

"Yeah, why?" he asked, suspicious.

Always on the defensive. "Just asking. Driving for too many hours might not be pleasant." He smiled, but his eyes were still on the road. "If you need to stop to stretch your legs or grab a coffee to keep you awake, we won't mind."

"I mind," Micah said from the backseat.

I turned to him. "Shut up. Nobody's talking to you." When I glanced back at Victor, he was truly smiling. "Okay?" I asked in a helpless, gentle tone. I felt stupid.

"Okay," he said, losing the smile and focusing on the road.

I sank down into the seat, turning up the volume and singing along, pretending everything was right in the world.

I was in a dark, chilly, tiny room with stone walls and no windows. My arms ached. I looked up and, illuminated by a thin strip of moonlight, I saw my wrists wrapped by metal chains. My clothes hung in tatters and when I moved, my back scratched painfully against a rough wall.

What was this? Where was I?

Imha walked into the room, her head high, holding her stave. A black cloud followed her. I flinched. Well, that answered my mental questions and put a clamp on my spinning mind.

"Hello, Nadine," she said, an evil smile over her red lips. "How are you?"

My face went cold. I was interacting in this vision. Oh my God!

Approaching me, Imha tsked. "It is polite to answer questions addressed to you. Didn't your mother teach you good manners? You don't want me to call my friends, do you?" she asked, still smiling. "Be a nice girl and tell me everything I want to know."

I grimaced, then finally finding my voice, I asked, "What do you want to know?"

Imha laughed, like an evil queen in a fairy tale, sending goose bumps over my skin. "You know what I want. I've already asked you many, many times. Tell me everything, and I will end your suffering."

"Will you release me if I tell you?" I asked, trying to gain time and find out as much as I could about this vision while I tried to figure out how to go back to the present.

She laughed again. "After all you did, dear? No, no. But, if you tell me, I promise your death will be quick and clean." Imha came closer until her face was inches from mine, her eyes sparkling with pure vice. "On the other hand, if you keep up with this silence game, I promise you, you will regret ever being born." She kissed my cheek. Her lips were icy, and under it, my skin crackled, drying out. The withering spread, sending searing pain through my face until it reached my throat, making me gasp and choke.

The realization I could die hit me. I tried inhaling the air that would save me, but it was in vain. The parching spread down to my lungs and chest. The world spun and the room became even darker. Blood trickled from my wrists as I struggled against the cuffs, and my legs went numb.

Imha sent a purple bolt from her stave to my chest. The bolt hurt as if it had opened my flesh and crushed my organs. I tried to yell but couldn't. However, a few seconds later—although it seemed like decades—the power of the bolt spread and the drying feeling left me. I took a deep breath, not caring that my whole body weight dangled from my bloody wrists. I didn't have any strength left, not even to look at Imha while she laughed.

"And that is just the beginning," she said, sauntering toward the dungeon door. With her back to me, she added, "I'll give you a while longer. Choose wisely."

She left. The door closed behind her, leaving me in total darkness. Despite myself, I cried.

A harsh jerk of my shoulders pulled me out of the vision. I blinked several times before being able to discern Micah's face close to mine, his deep black eyes holding a hint of worry. Beside him stood Victor with the same worry spread over his features. Micah awkwardly held a towel around my naked, dripping-wet body.

My mind worked to figure out what had happened. It had been late night when we'd stopped in Fayetteville, North Carolina, to eat something and to sleep. We'd found a motel and, though I protested, we stayed in one room again. As Micah had said, it was safer to stay together in case something happened.

The last thing I remembered before being in the dungeon was taking a hot and relaxing shower. That must have been when the vision had come to me.

Super self-conscious of my unclothed state, I flushed as I pulled Micah's hand away and tightened the towel around myself.

"What are you doing in here?" I snapped, crossing my arms over my chest as if my folded arms would help hide my body.

"You were screaming like a mad chicken," Micah said.

"We called to you, but you didn't answer," Victor added, avoiding my gaze.

"So we forced our way in." Micah pointed to the door behind them where I saw the broken lock.

I stepped out of the tub, found a robe hanging beside the sink, and put it on over the now soaked towel.

"I must say though," he said, staring at me with his sly smile, "you would look good in a bikini. Much better than many famous singers."

I rolled my eyes, the heat growing intense in my cheeks.

Finally looking at me, Victor asked, "What happened?" His soft tone sent a shiver through me.

My first instinct was to glance at my wrists, to see if they were all right.

"It was a vision, wasn't it?" Micah asked, examining my eyes.

"Yes," I muttered, a knot in my throat. I was about to fall, but the guys held my arms and pulled me into the bedroom, helping me sit down on the bed.

Seated beside me, Victor held my arms to stop them from shaking. "What did you see?"

"I have a better idea," Micah said, sitting on the other bed, facing us. "Why don't you tell us about *all* your visions? I don't know what you usually see."

I closed my eyes and shook my head. I wanted to tell them about my visions, but I wasn't sure I felt comfortable sharing them. Besides, they added to my fears of insanity and the confusion inside my head.

"Please," Victor asked. His eyes were gentle. "You said after meeting me, you had other visions you didn't understand. Tell us."

How could I deny him? After a deep breath, I related my past visions, all of them.

"It was horrible," I said, stifling a sob. "I felt it all."

"Do you think these visions are related?" Micah asked, getting up and pacing before me. "Are they showing you what is happening, or maybe what has happened?"

I noticed he was thinking out loud, but I had to add, "I wasn't tortured in the past, if that's what you are asking." And I certainly hoped not to be tortured in the future.

"True, true," he said, a thought line carved into his forehead. After a while, he turned to me. "I hope this Morgan guy understands about your visions too."

I nodded, agreeing with him. I hoped Cheryl had been right to give me the guy's card. I couldn't take much more of this terror.

19

Around six in the morning, we were already on the road. This time I welcomed the intoxicating mix of the guys' scents to daze me. It was a little easier than dealing with the images that loomed behind my closed eyes.

Near Jacksonville, the cities and towns weren't only dirty and deserted, they seemed destroyed or in ruins. My stomach tightened. Jacksonville wasn't much different. Houses stood without roofs, buildings with broken windows and doors, trees had fallen in the middle of the streets, and parks were littered with shattered benches and destroyed playgrounds. In short, it was a mess, like the rest of the country.

When Victor stopped the car in a large abandoned parking lot, I gaped. "It can't be here."

He checked the business card once more. "Well, that's the address."

Before us, a low building that reminded me of a manufacturing plant stood alone—or half-stood, since most of its windows and roof and some of the walls were in ruins.

"There's no one in there," I said, eyeing Micah from the rearview mirror. "Is there?"

Furrowing his brows, he nodded. "Someone's there. Let's go." He opened the back door and jumped out of the car.

Before following him, I scanned the area. Even in the daytime it was dark, and the street lamps were like the nearby buildings: broken. I didn't want to run into any bats even if Micah could repel them.

Tugging my jacket closer, I left the car with Victor right behind me. I glanced skyward. At least it wasn't too chilly down here.

Side by side, the guys and I walked to what seemed the main door of the rundown building. When we entered, I saw the interior was as devastated as the exterior, at least in the first room. Micah jumped over chunks of wood and what was left of cushioned seats, and reached a door in the back. Different from the others, this door was whole and clean.

Before opening it, he waited for Victor and me to approach. Together, we entered a tidy reception room complete with a desk in front of another door, chairs, a sofa, and a blaring TV.

A receptionist greeted us. "How can I help you?" She wore a fake smile. Her red hair definitely came from a bottle, and her chubby cheeks were nothing compared to her belly. She was wearing a black mini dress, three sizes too small. The heavy cloud of perfume she wore couldn't cover up her strong, too sweet stench. I almost threw up.

"We're here to see Morgan Holt," I said, stepping closer to her.

"Do you have an appointment with him?" she asked, her fake smile wavering.

"No."

"Then you'll have to come back another day." She grabbed an organizer from her desk. "We can schedule a date now. Tell me what this is about."

Yeah, right. "It's urgent, ma'am. Could you please call him?"

"Everyone's problems are urgent," she snapped.

Before I could snap back at her, a young black guy came out of the door I wanted to enter. He was dressed in a white robe.

"Miriam," he started, but stopped when he saw us. "May I help you?"

"I need to see Morgan Holt," I said, turning my back to the receptionist and throwing some charm at the young man. I flipped my hair and batted my lashes, hoping my green eyes would do the trick—all things that I had seen Raisa doing before. She would be proud of me.

He smiled at me. "Do you have an appointment?"

Oh, here we go again. I stepped closer to him, moving my shoulders as if I were uncertain of what to do. "I don't. But, you see, I need to see him. My friends and I came from New York to talk to him."

"New York. Really?" he asked, still smiling. "I love New York, though I haven't been there in five years." He showed me the door, beckoning for me to come with him. "How is the city?" he asked as we crossed the door's threshold.

While we walked, he told me his name was Carl and he was one of Morgan's assistants, though I still had no idea what they did.

About fifty feet down the corridor there was a large staircase. Carl led us down the stairs to the basement.

"You flirt," Micah whispered in my ear when Carl was busy opening another door for us. Sure, I was flirting a little, but I would use every trick I had—or thought I could have—to figure out what was going on with my visions and with Micah, Victor, and me. I shrugged and waved him off just as Carl turned back to me.

We entered a large room with many cushioned chairs along the wall.

"Wait here, please," he said, walking toward the white double doors in the back of the room.

Frowning, Micah came to stand right beside me, staring at the doors.

Before Carl had taken a few steps, the doors opened and a blond man in white robes came out, staring straight at Micah.

"Morgan Holt," I whispered, recognizing the man from my vision. He looked older in real life, about fifty-something, with highlighted blond hair down to his shoulders, and big, round brown eyes. Not too tall, but slim.

"By the gods, you three are like fireworks," Morgan said, sounding much younger than he seemed. As if in disbelief, he gaped at us. "Who are you?"

"Hi, Mr. Holt, we—"

"Mr. Holt is my father," he said. "I'm just Morgan. And you are?"

"Nadine. And this is Victor and Micah." I motioned toward them, then tried again. "Morgan, we need your help."

"Why would ones like you need my help?" he asked. There was a musical accent to his speech I could not pinpoint, but his definition of us was what caught my attention.

"Ones like us?" I asked. "What are we?"

"You tell me," he said, raising his arms in exasperation. "I've never felt auras like yours."

"Yeah, see,"—I curled my hair around my finger—"we don't understand this aura thing."

Morgan raised an eyebrow, examining us. I felt like a monkey in a cage getting ready for an experiment. "All right, come to my office." He led us to a side door into his tiny and cramped office.

He beckoned toward one of the only two chairs, indicating I should sit, while he took the second one. Before I sat I glanced back, making sure the guys were with me. And my breath was knocked out of me. Looking like seductive perfume ad models, Victor and Micah leaned against the wall. Victor stuffed his hands into his jeans pockets, and Micah crossed his arms over his black leather jacket. Good God.

Trying to focus, I turned back to face Morgan. "Thanks for receiving us."

"Don't thank me yet." Morgan propped his legs on his desk. "I'm just curious about your auras."

"As are we," I said.

"You talk as if you can't sense them."

"I can't, but he can." I pointed to Micah, who nodded to confirm it.

"I see." Morgan squinted, studying us. "And why are you here?"

"We need your help." Suddenly I felt like a guilty woman getting ready to confess a crime. My chest tightened as the ridiculousness of the situation hit me. I almost laughed out loud. "Things we don't understand have been happening, and someone said you could help us."

"Do you know who I am?" he asked, getting up. "What I do?" I shook my head, embarrassed. Tsking, Morgan turned to the wall behind him and, from the floor, grabbed what look like a rolled rug. "I'm a priest. A priest of a forgotten creed." He unrolled the rug and hung it on screws on the wall.

When he retreated, I gasped.

I think he was about to explain the drawing but noticed my reaction and waited. I stood and walked toward it.

It was the throne room of the crystal palace, showing the thrones lined up and the gods and goddesses elegantly seated on them, holding their staves. Levi was in the middle, Ceris on his right, Mitrus on his left, then Imha and Omi and the others I didn't know. Under them there was a large symbol.

"I know them." I ran my fingers over the drawing.

"You do?" Morgan asked, his eyes wary.

"This is Levi, Ceris, Mitrus, Imha, and Omi." While saying their names, I pointed to each respective figure. "I don't know the others' names."

With wide eyes, he said, "The others aren't as important. They aren't lesser gods either, but the ones that make the big decisions are the ones you named. How do you know them?"

I glanced at Victor and Micah, scared of revealing my secret to a stranger. I swallowed and said, "I have visions about them."

Morgan's big round eyes became even wider. "You do?" He sounded excited. "Do your visions become real?"

"Well, I kept seeing this guy in my visions, and he told me everything about himself. Then, I met him in person." I pointed at Victor. "He didn't know me, but I know all about him. And there was the episode of the burned town in Switzerland. I saw it happening. It was Omi. He threatened the nymphs on a lake nearby. The nymphs didn't give him the information he sought, so he killed them and wiped out the city."

"Really?" Morgan's eyes gleamed in awe. "You do know what they are patrons of?"

I glanced back at the beautiful drawing in the rug. "I'm not sure."

"Well, Levi is the god of life, balance, and spirit. Ceris is the goddess of love, family, home, and beauty. Omi is the god of war. Mitrus is the god of death, the underworld, and the dead. Imha is the goddess of chaos and discord. And the others"—he pointed at them in the drawing—"are the god of the sun and the day, the goddess of the moon and the night, the goddess of nature and seasons, the goddess of entertainment and arts, and the god of magic."

Intrigued by its familiarity, I stared at the symbol on the lower part of the rug. I squinted, examining it. It was white, like it was made of crystal, and composed of a thick circle and, in the center, the sign of infinity, which started shining when I set my eyes on it.

"Did you see that?" I asked, pointing to the symbol.

"See what?" Morgan asked.

But I didn't answer. I tilted my head and saw it clearly; the infinity sign was the number eight lying sideways.

I stumbled back, my breathing coming in little snatches of air. "I've seen this symbol as long as I've had visions."

"This is the creed's symbol," he explained. "The pantheon's name is Everlasting Circle. We believe our gods are the true and only gods who exist. The others—Egyptians, Greeks, Celts, Mayans, and even the Christian God—are all based on the Everlasting Circle. However, with the appearance of other religions and myths, the Everlasting Circle was forgotten."

"But why do I have visions about it?"

"If your visions are about the past, present, and future ..." Morgan paused, reaching to a smaller rolled rug under his desk. He opened it over his desk. I gasped again.

The rug contained a drawing of three identical women with silver hair and gray eyes, wearing simple white dresses.

"I saw them with Ceris," I whispered. "Who are they?"

"They are the Fates. Their names are Mani, Nay, and Lavni. Or, the past, the present, and the future, respectively. And, if what I'm suspecting is true, you have the Destiny Gift, a rare gift from them. In fact, I thought it was only a legend, or an idea."

"What? Why?"

Morgan smile widened. "I have no idea, but this is exciting!"

"I'm not excited," I almost shouted, then retreated to my guys. "I'm confused."

"So," Micah spoke up. "You're saying the things she sees are true?"

"Probably." Morgan shrugged.

Oh God, so now what? Imha would torture me until I died to

tell her something I didn't even know. I would rather die now, without any suffering.

"But why would I have these visions?" I sat down on the chair so the world would stop spinning around me.

"A warning?" Morgan rolled the smaller rug up again. "Did you know your aura isn't as strong as theirs?" He pointed to Victor and Micah.

"What do you mean?" Victor asked, finally speaking since we had arrived. He stood behind my chair.

"Your aura." Morgan looked at Victor. "And his." He pointed at Micah. "Are inexplicable. I've never heard of auras like yours. Now yours," he said, looking at me, "it's strong, stronger than all I have seen, but it's nothing compared to theirs. So, perhaps, your aura shines because of your gift." He looked at the guys again. "Now I wonder why your auras are so much stronger."

I closed my eyes, feeling a headache coming. "Still, it doesn't explain why I would have this gift, or whatever this is."

Morgan sat in his chair. "Like I said, perhaps the Fates want to warn you of something that's to come. Or maybe something that happened they need you to look into."

"But what?" The strength drained from me. I was so tired of thinking about this, of trying to put the puzzle pieces together.

"Why don't you tell me about your visions—which ones seemed more vivid?" Morgan asked.

I held a laugh back. "All of them." I told him about the first vision of the gods, the one about Levi and Mitrus disappearing after a fight, since it was the first vision I'd had out of the dream Victor pattern, but Morgan didn't let me continue with the others. He paced in his tiny office.

"By the Everlast, so it is true," he exclaimed.

"By the Everlast ...?" I whispered, not following.

Morgan waved me off. "It's an expression, associated with my creed." He clasped his hands together. "We call the crystal palace you described the Clarity Castle. And that object they used to kill each other, it's not a spike. Those are evil objects they aren't allowed to make." He laughed, sounding giddy. "Don't you see? Your vision shows what happened thirty years ago. That's why the world is in chaos. My acolytes and I have been saying Imha took over, but we weren't sure about it. We have been praying for Levi to regain control and balance the world once again, though we had no idea what happened to him. "This"—he pointed at me, and I assumed he meant my vision—"explains the darkness, the chaos, the evil that took over the world." Morgan's face was blanketed by worry and realization. "I can't believe he's dead. It can't be. Imha will destroy this world if she stays in power. What else do you know?"

I gulped, kind of embarrassed about being in the spotlight. "I think Ceris is hiding, and Imha and Omi are hunting her."

"Of course, with her lover out of the picture, she would be next," Morgan mused, resuming his pacing. "And I would bet my life Ceris is trying to find a way to bring Levi back."

"What do we do in the meantime?" Victor asked, startling me. Not that I could ever forget his strong presence and his delicious scent, but he was so quiet and stoic sometimes, it was hard to think he had any emotion or interest left.

Morgan tapped his fingers on his desk. "I'm trying to think. There must be a reason Nadine is having these visions. I just can't figure it out."

Neither could I. And my life just might depend on finding the answer.

20

Carl came in and reminded Morgan he needed to attend the next rite. Morgan invited us to observe the ceremony, and we agreed. He didn't seem to have any new ideas about what my visions meant, and I thought maybe we could learn something from attending one of his religious functions.

We entered the same room I had seen Morgan in during my previous vision—the large high-ceiling beige stone room, with side pillars that held white flags. The Everlasting Circle symbol was painted on each of those flags. There were candles around the perimeter of the room and an altar in the back. The poster I hadn't been able to see during the vision now burned my eyes. It was another drawing of the gods, with the symbol behind them.

While he rushed around the room and prepared the rite, Victor, Micah, and I observed him.

"You don't believe in the crap he's been telling us, do you?" Victor asked in low tones.

I turned to him, and responding in a voice equally low, I said, "Do you have any other explanation for what is happening?"

"No, but come on." His eyes were doubtful. "Gods and Fates and gifts? How can he prove any of this?"

"Do you have proof the Christian God exists?" I rolled my eyes at Micah, who snickered beside us. So far, I had believed in the Christian God, but now, everything and anything seemed plausible—or doubtful.

Victor remained quiet.

"His aura is strong too," Micah said, his gaze following each of Morgan's moves. "And he has the gift of sight."

"Okay," I said. "Explain something to me. Everyone has an aura, right?"

"Yes," Micah answered.

"But these auras are different?"

He nodded. "Yes. There are good auras, weak auras, bad auras, and special auras. Ours are the latter."

"Special how?" I asked.

He shrugged. "Just special. They feel different. Purer, stronger. Like Morgan said, Victor's and mine are much stronger than yours, though."

"This mess is so insane," Victor muttered.

I ignored Micah and stepped closer to Victor, hoping my eyes could express my feelings. "I don't know what to believe; I don't know who to trust. But here we are, and trust me, I've been debating whether I'm not in a vision right now. This isn't easy for any of us. Unfortunately, it's all we've got so far."

I could see I hadn't convinced him, but how could I convince him of something I wasn't completely convinced of myself?

Morgan called our attention and directed us to stand under the altar.

The rite started.

With white chalk, he drew the Everlasting Circle symbol on the floor and chanted. The words in the chant asked Levi to come back, to be resurrected, and bring light to the darkness.

Whatever else he said or did, I didn't catch.

I felt the usual stab, the warmth running inside my body, the prickle over my skin. The darkness took over, and I wasn't there anymore. I was on top of a steep, red rock, looking at many other red rocks. It reminded me of the Grand Canyon, though I was sure it wasn't the exact same place.

"We are near the Grand Canyon." A woman's voice came from behind me. I turned to see who it was, then gasped when I saw the identical Fates. They continued, speaking together, and said, "It's called Cathedral Rock."

"This is where you need to go," one of them said.

"Don't scare the girl off, Lavni," another said. It was confusing. Even if they decided to formally introduce themselves, I would never know who was who. She continued, "But you have to hurry, my child."

"Otherwise, the world won't have a chance," the third one said.

"Excuse me?" My head spun.

They approached and pointed toward the horizon. "The world can't survive in the chaos it is in."

"To have a chance of avoiding the end, you and your friends need to come here," Lavni said.

"What is so special about this place?" I asked, looking around. All I saw were red rocks.

"Ask Morgan. He knows," one said with a knowing smile.

They waved their hands and the horizon changed. The darkness of the sky descended, winged creatures advanced, and lightning struck.

"If they catch you before you arrive, it will be the end." I heard the Fates' voices, though they weren't by my side anymore. "The world will be at war with the darkness. And the darkness will win."

Images flashed before me on the vast horizon: the Eiffel Tower in Paris and the Cristo Redentor in Brazil crumbled to the ground, winged monsters devoured people in parks, huge waves brought gigantic sea creatures up to die on beaches, fireballs hurled from the skies burned the ground, children yelled and ran from schools as earthquakes destroyed everything. All the while, Imha stood on the side, observing and laughing with pleasure.

My stomach churned, and I fell on my butt.

Micah and Victor knelt by my side. Morgan stood close behind. I scanned the area, realizing I was back from the vision and we were alone in the beige stone room.

"What did you see?" Micah asked, leaning closer, his cool breath washing over my skin. I inhaled deeply, hoping his sweet scent would numb my senses, and I could just stay down and not care about anything else. "Nadine, talk to me."

"Nadine." It was Victor, his voice holding a gentle tone. "Say something."

I didn't want to say anything. All I wanted was to close my eyes and forget about gods and Fates and visions and auras.

But I didn't. I could feel within my soul my vision was true. "What is so special about Cathedral Rock?" I asked Morgan in a clear and loud tone, masking my fear and my frustration.

He pressed his hands together. "Cathedral Rock is a gateway to the Clarity Castle."

***

"That is, if the stories are true," Morgan said from the backseat of Victor's car. We had left Jacksonville and were now on the road toward Sedona, Arizona. To Cathedral Rock.

"Which one of our stories has not been true?" Micah asked, eyeing his backseat partner.

Morgan threw his hands up. "Man, I'm on your side. That's why I'm coming with you, isn't it?" He sounded more like an excited young man than a fifty-year-old priest.

"How long to Sedona?" Micah asked while I stifled a laugh. I just hoped he didn't kill Morgan before we got there.

Victor glanced at the dashboard. "Thirty hours, according to the GPS."

Morgan leaned forward. "We need to make a stop in Wichita."

"Kansas?" I asked, looking back at them, and saw Morgan nod. "Why?"

"I know a priest there. Last week, on the phone, he mentioned he was studying the gateways," he explained. "We might need his guidance."

"Again, why?" I asked.

"Because the gateway is a place of strong power, and it isn't out there for everyone to see," Morgan said. "It's hidden somewhere among those rocks, and I know nothing about what to look for. My friend does."

I turned to our driver, hoping he wouldn't snap again for having to take us even farther. With a sidelong glance, Victor nodded.

"All right, boys," I said. "We're going to Kansas."

21

———

IT WAS ALMOST MIDNIGHT WHEN WE STOPPED AT A HOTEL PAST Birmingham, Alabama.

This time we got two rooms, and Micah called dibs on sleeping with me. In the hallway, after bidding goodnight to the others, I caught Victor's gaze lingering on me. I saw something there, something I couldn't quite grasp. Was he jealous? No. Worried? That wasn't it either.

Inside our room, Micah threw himself at one of the beds, tossing me one of his trademark smiles. "So, darling, will you join me?" He patted the empty space beside him.

I rolled my eyes and rummaged through my things. "Why are you in this?"

He sat up straight. "What do you mean?"

"Why are you here? Why are you coming with us and helping us?"

"I thought it was pretty obvious. Because of you, darling." He winked and I rolled my eyes again. "Okay, seriously, I don't know." His tone became quieter. "There are a few moments when I believe that whatever is happening to us has something to do with the darkness surrounding the world."

"What do you mean?"

"I don't know." He shrugged. "The bats and the feelings make me think the darkness is involved in our problems, I guess. But this world doesn't bother me. I even like the dark. What I don't like are these pains and the impression I'm missing something, that I'm still missing some part of me."

It made sense. Though how could he not care that the world was drowning in darkness and every living creature was in the path of death?

The image of his possessed face as he killed his parents' killer flashed before my eyes.

I approached him and, careful with my words and tone, said, "What happened when you killed those men?" At his raised eyebrow, I hurried on. "I mean, in the vision, you looked ... not yourself."

"One more question to which I don't know the answer. Like you said, I wasn't myself. The sight of my parents dead beside me was too much. I was out of control."

Like when he had attacked me in my closet and almost strangled me. I don't know if he could also read minds, but he looked up at me, regret flickering in his black eyes. "I'm sorry about the way I acted at your apartment. I was trying to get you out of there, safe and sound, and you were making it so hard. I don't know what came over me." His eyes were focused on mine, causing my breath to catch. "I'm sorry."

I nodded. "It's okay," I whispered before disappearing into the bathroom. Besides dying for a shower, I needed to get away from the temptation of lying with him in that bed.

When I went back to the room, the temptation grew. Micah wore only jeans, which left his chest and chiseled muscles apparent. His tattoos sucked me in. He had a coiled snake on his left shoulder, four lines of Hebrew writing over his chest, and tribal drawings to the side of his abdomen, which spread onto his back.

I averted my gaze, my cheeks growing hot.

"Hi, darling," he said, deliberately provoking me.

I stopped in front of the mirror to comb my hair. "It's not that warm in here."

"I know." He chuckled, adding to my irritation. "I need your touch and thought being shirtless would make the deal more attractive. Plus, you would want me more."

With my jaw practically on the ground, I turned to him. "Want you *more*? Are you insane?"

"No." He sat at edge of the bed near me. That was when I saw his hands shaking. "Could you come here and help me?" he asked, his tone nicer but more urgent.

Disregarding his gigantic ego, I walked the few steps to him and extended my hand. Even if I wasn't tempted, he needed me to become healthier. He grabbed my hand and, with one corner of his lips curling up, he pulled me closer, resting my palm on his brawny chest.

The cold shock spread from my skin to his before I could protest. For a moment, I forgot I was touching his body and relished the refreshing sensation that came with my healing ability. It was like a relieving twinkling sensation crawling under my skin, taking me over. Pressing my hand with his, he moaned, eyes shut and head tilted back.

The cold diminished slowly, until it was gone. Still holding my hand to his chest, he opened his eyes and looked straight at me—through me.

"Are you better?" My voice broke, my breathing uneven.

Nodding, he gripped my other wrist. He pulled me until I was standing between his legs, less than two inches from him. His gaze never left mine as he stood, brushing his body against mine. My heart skipped a beat.

He leaned into me, but I pulled back. He put his hand behind my neck. "You want this," he whispered, his breath mixing with his scent, poisoning my mind.

"No," I said, putting my arms against his chest to push him back. Who was I kidding? He was super hot and into me at this exact moment. Of course I wanted this. But, would I still think I wanted this when I saw Victor the next day? Until I met Micah, the Victor in my visions had been the only guy in my life.

Micah pulled me to him and leaned down. He wasn't as subtle or gentle or slow as Victor was in my dreams. He was direct and rough and damned sexy. His lips brushed against mine, but a knock on the door made me jump back.

He grunted. "Who is it?"

"It's me," Victor said.

My eyes went wide, and I ran to the door and propped it open. Victor sloped against the doorframe, his face white and his breathing irregular.

"Oh God, what is it?" I reached to him, passing my arm around his waist and helping him in.

"Pain," he whispered between gritted teeth. I helped him sit on the bed.

Micah stood before the window, still shirtless, fuming and pacing, not looking back.

"Did I interrupt something?" Victor raised his eyebrows, glancing from Micah to me.

"No," I exclaimed, hoping I wasn't blushing.

Victor extended his hand to me. "Please, could you help me?"

Without answering, I took his hand in mine and almost fell on my knees when the warmth took over me, sending strong feelings to my core. God, he was so weak!

In the depths of healing, I heard Micah murmur, "I'm gonna take a walk."

Victor ended up taking more of my energy than I realized. After the healing, I plopped down on the bed beside him, sleepy.

"Thank you," he whispered, glancing sideways at me. "Does it hurt you?"

"No." At least, I didn't feel anything. "I'm just a little tired."

He looked around. "Where's Micah?"

"I think he left." I stood up and walked to the window. A minute ago, I had been in Micah's arms, ready to kiss him. A shiver ran up my spine. God, Micah was impossibly hot and dangerously sexy. If only my heart didn't belong to Victor—the Victor from my visions. I glanced at the guy before me, wishing he was the one he would never be.

After a few tense moments, he spoke, "Tell me more about your visions." His voice was low and unsure. "About me in your visions."

I leaned against the cold glass window. "Why do you want to know?"

"I was wondering how different your Victor is from me." He glanced up at me, his sea-green gaze sweeping into my soul. "Was he a good friend? Or more?"

"Well, I'm not certain." I wanted to hold his stare, even if it made me dizzy and confused. How could I talk about him to him? "We were best friends, companions, buddies. And we also acted like boyfriend and girlfriend, most of the time. I mean, we were jealous of each other's past. I burned inside the few times we talked about your former girlfriends." I saw his lips twitching as if they wanted to curl up in a smile, but it never came. "We kissed a little, but we never made out. So, I'm guessing we weren't more, like you asked."

"Do you like him?" he asked. When I frowned, he rephrased, "Do you love him?" I averted my gaze and didn't answer, but I guess my silence was the answer. "I'm sorry," he whispered.

I glanced back at him. "For what?"

"For not being the one you wanted me to be. It would have been nice to be the one you hoped for. It would be nice to have a friend again, to have someone to care about."

What to say to that? I compelled myself to be still and keep my mouth shut.

Unfortunately, unlike Micah and my dream Victor, he didn't seem one bit into me. I wouldn't be the one falling on my knees and begging for his love. With his stoic and reserved personality, I would look like a clown, or worse, desperate. All I needed was to run to him and cry on his lap. That would be fantastic.

I glanced at the alarm clock beside him. "It's getting late," I said, willing my voice to sound firm and strong.

"Yeah, right." He stood and walked to the door, where he paused and looked back at me. He had to make my pulse race even more? How unfair. "Good night."

"Good night."

Once he was gone, I threw myself on one of the beds, hugged the pillow, and forced myself to think about ponies and cute puppies so I wouldn't cry.

God, these three men—two real and one fictitious—were going to kill me.

22

———

THE AIR INSIDE VICTOR'S CAR WAS HEAVY AND TENSE WHEN WE got on the road again the next day. A few times, Morgan tried to initiate a light conversation, but none of us gave him much attention. We only stopped twice for gas and to stock up on food we could eat in the car since our plan was to arrive in Wichita later that evening. We'd meet Brock, the other priest, sleep a little, and head to Cathedral Rock the next morning.

During each stop, I thought I was going to have a heart attack. We saw sinister figures. Everyone looked scared and wary, surrounded by poverty and destruction. Each gas station and store was protected with gates and metal doors. It was a pain to get in, and almost as hard to get out.

The clouds grew darker and thicker as we approached the city. Morgan had contacted his friend, Brock, and arranged to meet him in the pub of a local motel. As we drove up, I noticed that despite the rest of the city being dark as night and dirty as a trash bin, the motel was quite nice and well illuminated, and had the security system—cameras and alarms on each corner. We parked and got out, stretching our legs. At the reception desk, a girl in a pink mini dress, who looked more like a hooker than a receptionist, batted her lashes at Micah as she gave him keys for two rooms. I didn't know I had such rage within me—only Victor and Micah had ever awakened such feelings in me.

With unwelcome jealousy surging through me, I hoped my long nails scratched Micah's hand as I took one of the keys. "This is my room. If you three don't want to share one, then ask for another one." I walked away, assuming the guys would follow. If I'd heard the receptionist correctly, their room was on the second floor, while mine was on the first. Very far away. I needed space.

"What did you do to her?" I heard Victor ask Micah. But if Micah answered, I didn't hear it.

"We meet in one hour at the pub," Morgan yelled at my back.

I waved them off and hurried to my room. Enough of the guys—I wanted to be alone.

A SERIES OF IMAGES FLASHED BEFORE MY EYES. THE GIRL DYING right in front of me, burned by the acid rain. The attack from the bats on the street. My experiment on the chemistry lab spilling and burning through the table. And old woman dying and leaving her grandson alone. Sarah screaming while a hooded man chased her. The bats invading my apartment. The gods throwing Black Thorns at each other. Imha torturing me.

"Nadine!"

I sat up in bed and sucked in a sharp breath. A book fell from my legs to the floor.

What?

A knock echoed on the closed door. "Nadine? Are you there?" Victor called.

Shaking the numbness from my mind, I turned the lamp on

the nightstand beside me on, jumped off the bed, and rushed to the door.

I threw it open and found Victor standing outside, all dressed up in neat jeans and a button up shirt.

He frowned at me. "You were sleeping?"

Was it that obvious? I ran a hand over my hair, trying to comb it with my fingers. "I must have fallen asleep while I was reading." I glanced to my wristwatch. "Holy shit, I'm late."

"Yeah, that's why I'm here. To check on you."

Of course. Why else would Victor come see me.

I stepped back. "I'll need a few minutes to get ready."

He advanced into the room with me and closed the door. "Okay."

I stared at him. Didn't he get the hint. "And you're gonna stay there."

"To make sure you don't fall sleep again."

I rolled my eyes. I was up and moving. It was obvious I wouldn't fall asleep again, but I wouldn't argue with him about that. Instead, I gave him my back and went to my bag over the second bed and started looking for something more suitable to wear in a pub.

Thank God Micah was the one who packed my bag, because he had grabbed about four dressy outfits. I pulled out a dark teal halter dress with a short hemline and a wrap-up silver stiletto.

"Hell no," Victor said from behind me.

I turned around and found him closer than I expected him to be. "Excuse me?"

"I just came from the pub and let me tell you, the public in there, which is ninety percent male, doesn't look too respectful. You're not wearing that to go there."

I gaped at him. I couldn't believe his audacity. Who did he think he was telling me what I could or couldn't wear. Now I was determined to pamper myself up, just to irritate him.

"You don't get a say in it." He snatched the dress from my hand. I exhaled out loud. "What the hell? Give me my dress."

He leaned closer, his blue-green eyes too close. His lips ... too close. "Not a chance."

Anger filled my core and, with closed fists, I pushed him. "What the hell, Victor? Why are you acting like that?"

"Like I have a common sense?"

I snorted. "Common sense? No, not even close. That's more like—" I shut my mouth.

He narrowed his eyes at me. "Like what? Say it."

"No." I retreated a step.

Stubborn, Victor reached out to me and grabbed my wrist. "No, now say it."

"Nope."

He growled. "Nadine ..."

"Let me go." I jerked my arm, but his hold was firm. "Victor, let me go."

His eyes gained a different gleam, one I was sure wasn't real. Then he took a large step toward. I backed up, until my legs hit the bed and I had nowhere to go.

Victor loomed over me. "I won't," he said in low voice. "I don't want to."

He wrapped his arms around my waist, pulled me against him, and covered my mouth with his.

God, I had dreamed of this moment so, so many times. Yet, this Victor wasn't my Victor, was he? In truth, right at this moment, I didn't care. Despite the anger I felt a second ago, all I wanted now was to kiss him back.

And I did. His mouth was sweeter than I could have hoped for, his tender lips eagerly moving against mine, his tongue exploring my mouth as if it were a new, rich land to be discovered. One of his hands traveled up my spine until his fingers knotted my hair. The other hand went down, cupping my hips.

Oh, and I was over him too, my hands already under his shirt, exploring his lean, hard muscles.

He pulled my hair back, making me tilt my chin up. Startled by how avid he was, I moaned. In my dreams, I had believed he would be gentle and calm. Very different from this Victor. And I loved every second of this one.

"By the way," he breathed in my ear, "you're so, so beautiful."

With his tongue, he traced a line down my neck to my collarbone. He bit it, scorching my skin, using his hands to press me against him. I felt intoxicated by his scent, by his touch, his breath.

I unbuttoned the top part of his shirt, pulled it over his head and threw it on the floor. Then, he tugged on my sweater. I closed my eyes and prepared myself for this moment. I had been naked in front of a guy only once before, and he had been too drunk to really care. This time was going to be different. With my eyes still closed, I raised my arms so Victor could pull my seater off.

A stab hurt my chest, and tingles spread over my skin.

When I opened my eyes, I wasn't in the room with Victor anymore.

I was at the pub, watching over Morgan, Micah, and Brock. What the hell? What was I doing here? A ghost-type vision *now*? Was this a sick joke? Please, I wanted to get out of here, to get back to my room, back to Victor's arms.

But I couldn't leave. An intense feeling in my gut made me approach and observe them. I pushed Victor and his sizzling touch out of my mind.

The trio discussed something, their serious conversation interrupted by a chuckle or two. However, there was something strange going on. Whenever Micah or Morgan weren't looking, Brock glanced to a corner in the back of the pub. I frowned, and because I had a feeling I was supposed to find out whatever it was, I went to the back of the pub, behind the stage. I found a corridor with dressing rooms, restrooms, and storage doors. I followed the corridor to the end to a door that led outside. I opened the door and froze.

For a moment, I couldn't register what I saw.

But I knew: demons. Dozens, maybe. Large, nasty creatures with pointed teeth and crippled bodies, slobber dripping down their slanted mouths, sharp claws where fingers should be. Bats hovered over them, silhouetted by the dark skies.

My stomach hit the floor, and nausea made me lean against the doorframe.

What were they doing here?

One of them, clasping a sharp spear, entered the back door and ran down the corridor. He met three humans who halted and opened their mouths to scream. Before they could emit a sound, the demon held his spear high and stabbed their hearts, deft and fast. Their bodies crumpled to the floor, and he stomped over them without losing his focus.

I screamed. Thankfully, I was a ghost here.

The demon stopped at the pub's door at the end of the corridor and spied from it. Brock glanced at him. Relief showed in his features, then he nodded toward Morgan and Micah.

The blood drained out of me.

"Hurry," a disembodied voice whispered.

The whole image disappeared—the demons and bats outside, the dead bodies in the corridor, Brock nodding at Morgan and Micah—gone.

"Nadine!" Victor held me in his arms, seated on the bed. The worried look he cast over my face touched me. I took a deep breath and counted while my pulse slowed and my breathing grew easier.

I couldn't believe this was happening. I couldn't believe I would have to walk away from Victor, from this amazing moment, but if my vision was right, Morgan and Micah would be attacked soon. And the demons would also come after us.

"I'm here," I answered, disentangling myself from him.

"What is it? What happened?" he asked, standing and seizing my arm, pulling me around so I would face him.

"I'm so sorry." God, why was this happening right *now*? Couldn't my visions have waited thirty minutes? I had finally gotten some response from Victor, the real Victor. He had touched me the way the vision Victor always had, and now I had to walk away from his warm, yummy body. Damn it. "You have no idea how much I want this, how much I want you, but we have to leave. Now."

"Wait, why?" He cupped my face. "You had a vision, didn't you? That's why you were so still."

I stepped out of his reach and grabbed my boots—shoes I could run in. I turned to him. "I don't know how long we have, but we're about to be attacked."

23

———

VICTOR AND I RAN FROM MY ROOM TO THE PUB AND FOUND THE guys still at the same table, drinking and talking under the smoky light.

"Where have you been, darling?" Micah asked as we approached.

I didn't have time to play his games. Demons were about to descend. We had to get the heck out of here.

"Brock, here"—I jabbed a finger in the man's direction—"is setting us up. There are monsters and bats surrounding this place, waiting for his signal to strike at us."

"Excuse me?" Brock asked, pretending to be stunned by my accusation, but I could see past his act.

Suddenly serious, Micah asked, "A vision?" When I nodded, he stood and grabbed Morgan by his arms. "Let's go."

"Wait! Where are you going?" Brock shot up. "I didn't finish telling you about the gateway yet."

Micah pivoted and punched the man, who fell over the table. "How long do we have?"

"I have no idea." I took a step back in case Micah wanted to hit someone else. I had seen how violent and scary he could be, and I didn't want to be in his way. "I only saw them preparing to attack, so I don't know when, but I know we have to hurry."

Startling me, Micah turned to Morgan and grabbed him by the collar of his shirt. "Spill it. Do you have something to do with Brock's plan? Are you helping him?"

"No!" Morgan's eyes were wide and fearful. "I swear by the love of my dear gods!"

"Why should we believe you?" Victor asked, his voice spitting the same venom as Micah's.

"I-I don't know," Morgan said.

Then I heard in my ear, over the pounding of the music and chatter of the bar crowd, "Trust him." It was the same incorporeal voice from my vision.

"Morgan is on our side," I said, pushing Micah's arm so he would release the grip on Morgan's neck.

"How do you know?" Micah asked.

Some of his anger spilled onto me. I glared at him. "Trust me, I know."

His grip didn't lessen. Morgan's skin grew purple.

"Let him go," Victor said, his tone authoritarian.

Finally, Micah released Morgan, and then turned to Victor. "Never speak to me like that again."

"Why?" Victor scowled. "Do you think I'm afraid of you?"

I saw Micah's rage surging upward, and I threw myself between them before it was too late. "Boys," I called out. "We have to go!"

This time they heard me. The three men followed me as I ran to the hotel lobby, where I stopped in front of the glass walls, motioning to the guys to stay inside with me. I didn't know if the demons and bats were out there. Yet. As fast as I could, I told them the details of my vision—the demons, the bats, the dead people in the corridor, the look that had passed between the demon and Brock. As I spoke, I glanced around and tried to locate anything or anyone suspicious. A few customers milled around the lobby, talking to themselves and hotel workers, but I saw no demons. Or bats.

"How are we going to get out of here?" I asked. Victor's car was in the parking lot, yards away. Even if we made it to the car, how would we be safe? The demons seemed fast; they could easily catch up with us and yank off the car doors, like plucking wings off a ladybug.

"I could run to the car and drive it closer to the exit," Micah suggested.

"I don't think that will work," Morgan said. "There are too many of them and too many of us. They must be tempted to risk everything to get to us. Together, we're like a beacon of power they can't resist."

"So what?" Victor asked. "We can't stand here and wait for them to attack. Besides, they must know Brock was discovered by now."

He shifted, drawing nearer to me. Warmth radiated from his body. I blinked, wishing his arms were still around me, with his perfect body touching mine, his sweet kisses intoxicating me, his inebriating scent ... I cleared my mind, then refocused. Control of the situation was slipping from our hands.

"I have an idea," Morgan said. "My aura is much weaker. I'll go outside and check it out. Perhaps they're still in the back, like Nadine saw in her vision, and we can run away before they see us."

"I don't like it," I said.

"It's all we have," Micah said.

As if we were voting, we turned to Victor. He shrugged. "I'm impartial. Though, I'd rather find a solution where none of us takes risks."

"I agree." I glanced up at him. He returned my quick look with a warm shine in his eyes. I wondered what would happen between us when we were done with this adventure—if we survived.

"We don't have time to brainstorm," Morgan argued. Then he took off.

I watched, wide-eyed, as he passed through the hotel's main door, then looked up and down the street. He seemed to see nothing alarming, but I found myself twirling my hair with both hands. Beside me, Victor squeezed my wrist, causing me to stop my nervous habit and my heart to beat even faster.

Through the glass walls, I saw Morgan give a shrug. He came back inside with an easy smile. "Nothing out there. Are you sure about your vision?"

His words felt like a punch in my stomach. I didn't like when people doubted me. I ended doubting myself too. "I-I don't know."

"Just to be sure, I'll go out again and get the car. When I pull up to the front, we leave." He motioned to Victor who fished the car keys out of his pocket and handed them over.

"Do your visions ever betray you?" Micah asked, his gaze following Morgan as he strode outside, then down the sidewalk.

I thought about Micah's question for a moment. Even if what I had seen wasn't real—my time with Victor, for example—all the things I was told or saw in my visions had come true.

"Never."

That was when Morgan started to run toward the car. I squinted and stepped closer to the door, trying to see what had triggered him to run, but stopped when I saw bats descending.

"We need to help him," I yelled, ready to sprint outside.

Micah's hand on my shoulder prevented me. "Want to get yourself killed?"

"We can't let him get hurt."

At that moment, a bat landed on Morgan's back. He fell onto

the pavement. He tried to crawl away, but another bat landed beside him.

"I'll go," Victor said.

I recoiled, watching as Morgan tried to protect his face from slashing claws.

"Don't be stupid," Micah snarled. "I'm the best one for this. I hope I still can repel them."

I didn't like the idea of any of us going out there, but I also didn't like the idea of leaving Morgan alone to serve as bat food. So, I didn't stop Micah when he ran outside.

But Morgan did. "Don't," he shouted, wrestling one of the bats that was trying to bite his neck. "It's you they want. Go!"

We didn't have time to process. The bats' attention turned to us just as the demons I'd seen in my vision rounded the corner of the hotel. They hurtled toward us and growled like gorillas, saliva streaming out of their gaping mouths and baring sharp teeth. Yellow eyes burned with pure death and desire.

I froze. Victor and Micah pulled me back, though I had no idea where we could run to, especially since Brock was coming toward us, holding a gun pointed at my face.

The guys stiffened, and my knees quivered, threatening to buckle. Brock shoved his way through the lobby, pushing the doorman to the ground. A woman saw him and screamed, shifting the attention to us.

"Turn around and step outside," Brock ordered.

"Or what?" Micah asked, clenching his fists.

"The demons won't like it, but I'll kill the girl." Brock pulled the gun's safety off.

Behind me I felt Victor move, and then a lamp flew past me, smacking Brock in the temple. His gun wobbled, and Micah jumped at Brock and punched him again. Hard.

When Brock seemed too weak to stand alone, Micah let go.

Victor grabbed me. "What now?" His arms around my shoulders tried to steady me as I shook uncontrollably. My head spun. I heard women scream and men yell, but Victor and Micah didn't seem to care that the customers and staff were freaking out around us.

Scenes flashed in my mind. The front desk, two guns under a table, a back door, a covered alley.

"We find another way out."

In four steps, I reached the front desk. I jumped over it and, from inside, opened the side "employees only" door for Victor and Micah.

A hotel employee ducked and tried to hide.

"Shut the front door," Victor ordered. The employee nodded and pressed a button that canceled the automatic opening of the front door. I doubted the barrier would hold the demons for long, but the closure would give us a few precious seconds.

From under the table, I took the guns and passed them to the guys. Micah didn't hesitate, while Victor took one with wide eyes.

Scratching sounds came from the main door.

"How can we get out of here?" Victor asked.

"Here," I said, opening a door that led farther in. I turned to the employee cowling in the corner. "Where does the alley in the back lead to?"

"A-a department store. Then a residential building." His voice cracked.

As we closed the door behind us and ran down a long corridor, a strident bell warned us the front door had been breached. The demons were now inside the hotel, hunting.

Micah opened a door labeled "Exit" and stuck out his head.

"Not that one," I said.

He quickly closed the door again. Something bumped into it —hard. I winced.

We continued down the hall until we found another exit.

Confident but holding my breath, I opened the door and stepped into a narrow, dark alley. It had a low zinc roof to protect passersby from rain, but in this case, the roof protected us from being devoured.

"What was that?" Micah asked as we ran down the slippery alley. "You knowing what to do?"

"Visions."

"Really?" He showed me a half-smile. "Interesting."

I nodded, though I wasn't sure "interesting" was the right word.

Soon the hotel was behind us and the wall of the alley gave way to a steel fence.

"This must be the residential building," Victor said, spying through the fence. I only saw a garage filled with cars. "Any more tips from here?"

"Not yet," I muttered.

A loud bump sounded on the zinc roof. We ducked and the guys pointed their guns skyward.

"Let's go," Micah whispered.

Victor and Micah grabbed me and shoved me over the fence, while the sound of demons and bats pounding against the zinc roof grew closer.

Victor was the last to cross the steel fence. He climbed over just in time to escape a claw swiping through the roof.

Micah dashed to the cars. He tried opening several doors but had no luck.

Again, images filled my mind. A blue Range Rover, a guy walking out the back door of the building, keys in hand.

I gulped, not happy with what we had to do. "Come on," I called to the guys. After a few steps toward the building, I gestured to the SUV parked a couple of spots ahead. "That car" —I pointed to the door as it was opening—"and the key is with him."

The guy stepped out of the building and froze upon seeing us.

"Sorry, pal," Micah said, charging him. They struggled, but Micah was stronger. He took the keys from the guy's hand and shoved him back inside. "Stay there if you want to live."

With the keys in hand, we ran to the SUV.

Victor grabbed my arm and shoved me in the backseat, then sat shotgun while Micah took the wheel. Behind us, more bats broke through the roof and entered the garage. From the opposite side, a guard approached, holding up his flashlight and gun.

Micah smiled and started the SUV. From one side, claws and teeth came at us, and from the other, a man with a gun pointed at our heads, and Micah was ... *smiling*?

"Hold on," he shouted, stepping on the gas.

The SUV jerked. I fumbled around and put on the seatbelt. Victor had found the garage door's remote and held it ready, even though we didn't know where the exit was yet. Guessing the way, Micah drove toward the guard, who crouched and held the gun in both hands.

"Stay low." Micah said. The guard shot at the car, bullets smacking the metal with an eerie, dull thud, loud and echoing. Another great noise behind us meant the bats had broken down the fence. "Anyone hit?" Micah asked. Unable to utter a word, I shook my head.

Instantly, Victor whipped his head back and looked at me with wide, concerned eyes. His gaze ran the length of my body and relief flooded his features once he saw I was okay.

A sense of warmth washed over me. It was comforting to see he cared.

I wanted to reach out to him, to hold his hand, to feel his skin on mine, but before I could, he turned back to help Micah look for an exit.

"There." Victor pointed to the left, past another row of cars and columns. The exit gate. He pressed the button on the remote. "Come on, come on." He looked out the back of the car at the demons I knew were approaching.

I heard the screams of a man, deep and guttural, then high-pitched and gurgling, and closed my eyes, trying not to imagine the guard being eaten alive.

Micah revved the engine. His fingers went white against the wheel. "Come on," he yelled, as if he could order the gate to speed up. I saw him looking through the rearview mirror. His eyes widened. A second later, a bump shook the car. "Hell," he cursed, accelerating.

The top of the SUV scratched against the bottom of the gate as it rose up enough for us to slip under. I was glued to the backseat. Victor leaned out of the window and pointed his gun to the back.

Following his shots, shrieks filled the air, but they soon grew fainter as we sped down the street. The creature had been hit. No others followed. We were getting away.

For now.

24

WE REMAINED SILENT FOR A WHILE AS MICAH CONTINUED TO drive into the night. The surroundings were nothing but a black blur, but I didn't hear any shrieks or ruffling of wings.

He watched via the mirrors. "Did we lose them?"

"I think so," Victor answered as he looked around, observing the exterior. He stopped when he faced me. "Are you okay?"

I held onto the back of the seat, fighting against the urge to crawl on his lap and have him hold me while telling me everything would be all right.

Instead, not trusting my voice, I nodded. If I tried to speak, I would scream or cry. God, I wanted to press "pause." I needed a break, time to breathe, to rest, to think about all that had just happened.

"Morgan?" I asked, my voice barely a whisper.

The guys didn't say anything. Victor sat back in his seat and stared at the black horizon.

Poor Morgan. He had done nothing more than be on our side and help us in any way he could, and now he was dead.

"What now?" Victor broke the silence and my unsettled thoughts. "We can't continue with our plan to go to Cathedral

Rock. Brock knew where we were going. If he was with those creatures, they know now too."

"Do you have a better idea?" Micah asked, an edge to his voice.

"Yeah. It's called remaining alive."

They bickered between them even as I heard the voice say, "Go to Cathedral Rock."

"We gotta keep with our plan," I said. I earned a shocked and upset look from Victor. It hurt, but all I could do was sigh. I could see that whatever had happened in my room back at the hotel had already been forgotten by him.

"Are you certain?" he asked, not looking at me.

"I am," I said.

"And how are we going to do this?"

"I don't know."

Micah cleared his throat as if noticing the tension in the air. "We have to get there first." His usual smile shone against the rearview mirror as the car accelerated. It should take us about fifteen hours to get to Sedona, but with his heavy foot, we might make it in half that time. I leaned forward and looked at the speedometer—almost 130 miles per hour. He would get us killed without the help of any demon.

We stopped twice to get gas and food and use the restroom. The second time we stopped, it was four in the morning. We were due to arrive at our destination in two or three more hours.

When I came back to the Rover holding a mochaccino, Victor leaned against the SUV and asked, "How are you doing?"

"Good," I answered. The heat from his gaze spread and confirmed my cheeks were growing pink. Inside, even with everything that was happening, I yearned for his touch, for his kiss.

Avoiding his eyes, I opened the back door of the SUV, putting it between us.

He leaned over the door. "We should talk about what happened ... in the hotel."

My chest ached, afraid of rejection. No, I didn't want to hear him. Not yet. What if he said it had been a mistake, and he wasn't into me? What if he said it had been a spur of the moment thing? I glanced around. Micah was buying something inside the diner, and the waitress melted before him—poor girl. I knew how she felt.

I shook my head and returned my gaze to my mochaccino. "No, it's okay. You don't need to say anything."

"Let me say what I have to say."

I brought my eyes to meet his, hoping my expression looked as courageous as I wanted to feel. "I'm not ready to hear it." I saw Micah leaving the diner. My salvation. "Forget it."

I slid into the car and closed the door.

Outside, the guys exchanged a few words before joining me in the SUV.

Micah had just pulled back onto the interstate when his cell phone rang. He answered the phone, then said, "Hey, Morgan. I thought you had become bat food."

A loud sigh of relief escaped my lips.

Micah pressed the speaker button, and we heard Morgan speaking. "I have some nasty cuts, but I'll survive."

"How did you escape?" I asked, leaning forward, wedging my shoulders between the front seats.

Morgan said, "When you guys showed up at the door, your auras offset mine and they forgot about me. I was able to get to the car, but then couldn't find you."

"Why didn't you call sooner?" Victor asked. "We could have waited for you."

"I lost my phone. I found it in a bush near where the bats first assaulted me." Morgan paused. "By the way, did you guys watch the news?"

"No," the three of us answered in unison.

"A few moments ago, the motel exploded. It looked like some fireball was hurled from above."

"Omi," I said.

"I think so too," Morgan said. "And I'm guessing he's after you three."

"We're almost to Cathedral Rock," Micah said.

"Good," Morgan said. "Don't stop. I'm on my way, but I guess I'm still a few hours behind."

"We're on it," Micah said.

We wished him good luck, and he wished us the same after asking to be called and informed of any changes.

"Morgan is alive," I whispered, resting back on my seat. At least there was one piece of good news among so many tragedies. "But Omi is after us."

THE PARKING LOT OF THE BACK O'BEYOND TRAIL SEEMED AS IF IT had been abandoned for many years. The grass surrounding the dirt lot was dead and the low wooden fence that delineated the place was cracked, brittle.

"Now for the bad part," Micah said as he examined the rotten board covered with a map of the trail. He had my bag over his shoulders. Before we left the car, he'd shoved some survival stuff into it, like extra water and power bars, and offered to carry it up the steep climb. I stared upward at the towering spires and was grateful he was playing pack mule.

I approached him. "What?"

"We have to walk almost a mile up the trail to reach Cathedral Rock." He pointed to the trailhead. "And it's steep. Not even bikes or horses can be used for this part."

"You're kidding," Victor said. "It'll take hours to reach the top."

Micah beckoned toward the trail, inviting us to follow him. "Better we start soon, then."

I turned to the trail and almost bumped into Victor. He looked down at me and my breath caught.

"Excuse me," I whispered as I walked past him.

I saw, from the corner of my eye, his hand stretching, coming toward me, but then he pulled it back and, with a sigh, followed me to the trail.

The path was marked by small piles of stone, showing us where to go. Despite the darkness from the sky and the death-defying situation, every once in a while I looked back, amazed by the gorgeous view. Even with all the darkness, I could see very far away from up here. After forty minutes, the trail became unbelievably steeper and trickier; I was thankful for the footholds carved into the stone.

I wasn't a good hiker. My palms sweated, my breathing and my pulse sped up, and occasionally dizziness and nausea over-whelmed me. It wasn't easy to keep up with the guys, and being so near Victor didn't help me. He kept looking over at me, which caused my heart to skip some precious beats.

Once, when I caught him shooting me a sidelong look, I missed a foothold and slid a few feet down the rocks on my knees. He caught me and held my arm, saving my slippery mishap from becoming a bloody accident. Under Micah's obser-vation, Victor hauled me up and, feeling my scraped knee, I bumped into him.

"Are you okay?" he asked. His hands snaked around my waist, steadying me, but I was determined to ignore his touch.

"Yes." I glanced down my leg. "Just my knee, but I think it's nothing."

"Let me see." He knelt and leaned against the steep rock.

I felt stupid as my cheeks warmed. He touched the scratch through the tear in the jeans and I winced. Victor tugged me down to sit beside him. "It's not much, but you should be more careful." He put his finger under my chin and forced me to look at him. "I know I'm distant and on the defensive sometimes, bu—"

"Sometimes?" I interrupted him without meaning to, but the words were out of my mouth before I could think.

His lips curled up in a faint smile, and I dreamed of kissing him again. "Most of the time. But that doesn't mean I don't have feelings." Hmm, I was hooked. Maybe I'd been too hasty back at the diner when I'd shut him out. "It's hard for me to—"

"Hey, pretty boy and vision girl," Micah shouted from above the rise, interrupting the words I was now dying to hear. "Pause the melodrama and drag your butts over here. We don't have much time."

He glared at us, and I noticed the mood was now dead. Victor was back on the defensive. Clearing his throat and extending his hand to me, he helped me up. However, this time he sent me ahead in case I slipped again.

I returned my attention to the trek. But I couldn't stop thinking about him. What had I learned about this Victor so far? Was he the same Victor from my dreams or not? There were times when I simply didn't know. There were times my heart beat for him the way it had for my vision Victor. Or was I imagining that too?

According to Micah, we had reached Grandmother Rock, which was the name of the saddle between two rising spires on top of Cathedral Rock. The splendid view amazed me.

"So, where to now?" Victor asked.

"No idea." Micah shrugged. "We're at the top, and I can't see anything around us. No aura, no signature. Maybe we're at the wrong place."

Victor scowled. "Yeah, that would be perfect."

Then it came. I felt it. The same vortex of spirits the tourists came here to feel. I sensed it, and it was strong. However, what I sensed wasn't the energy of spirits. It was pure energy, pure life, pure power.

Victor was about to say something, but Micah shushed him, his gaze on me.

Smiling, I closed my eyes and let the vortex wrap around me. The energy touched my skin. I gasped as its current ran through my veins, lifting me into the air. A vision took over, and I saw the place we were in. The Everlasting Circle symbol was drawn on the floor with ten circular signs I didn't recognize drawn tangent to it; each of us stepped into one of those signs.

The vortex died out and, in slow motion, I dropped down to where the center of the Everlasting Circle sign should be.

Victor stepped toward me. "What the hell was that?"

"Do tell," Micah asked, serious and unmoving. "I felt it too and, damn, it was strong."

"It's here," I whispered. "We need to draw some symbols."

"With what?" Victor asked, sounding irritated. "A red pen? Perhaps a marker?"

I glared at him. God, I hated his mood swings. At least they served to remind me he wasn't the Victor I thought he was—the Victor I wanted him to be.

"With this." Micah produced white chalk from my bag. "During the rite Morgan performed, I felt this chalk was different and ... I ended up grabbing some." He didn't seem too embarrassed for it. "I wanted to examine it better."

I grabbed the chalk from him. A shock ran through my fingers. This was the right tool to draw the symbol with. "In other circumstances, I would reprimand you for stealing."

The guys stood still, Micah smiling and Victor glaring, while I knelt down and drew the Everlasting Circle symbol and the other nine smaller signs around it. I didn't know them, but I could still see them clearly in my mind. Some had wavy lines, another had spirals, and others had hard lines, and all of them were enclosed in a circle.

When I finished, the jolt ran through my fingers once more and the lines shone a faint white light.

"That's it?" Victor asked, crossing his arms.

Pure energy flowed inside my chest and I smiled as I said, "Now, we step in."

25

———

I told Victor and Micah which sign they should step into, then said, "But wait. We have to get in the circle at the same time."

"In your vision, did you see what would happen?" Micah asked, eyeing the symbol before him. It had sharp lines, each one pointing to a different side.

I halted in front of my sign. It had curly lines. "Nope."

"Morgan said this is the gateway to the Clarity Castle," Micah said. "Perhaps it'll take us there."

And what would we do then? Declare war on Imha just like that? I hoped that if the gateway took us somewhere, it was to a place far away from her.

"I don't like this," Victor argued. I rolled my eyes. At least he was already positioned beside his assigned sign. It was composed of long, rounded lines and circles, similar to the Everlasting Circle symbol.

"Ready?" Both guys nodded. I took a deep breath and braced myself. "All right. Let's do this."

We stepped into the signs.

An immense vortex of colors and power wrapped around us.

I saw a fourth figure approaching the circle and heard the guys' grunts, then everything went gray.

I was surrounded by revolving smoke. It choked me and I gagged, nearly vomiting. Just when I began praying for it to stop, the smoke swirled into the shape of a room. A crystal room. With a crystal bed. Ceris sprawled on the bed, her body in a seductive curve. I looked around. Levi stood by the window, next to me, but obviously unaware of my presence.

"After thousands of years, you're telling me you don't love me anymore?" Ceris asked, an amused smile playing over her gorgeous features.

Levi shifted. His jaw went tight before he said, "You've changed. For many years now, you've been changing. Sometimes, I think I don't know you anymore."

Ceris laughed. "Love, you know me well. We've been together since the beginning of time."

"You've changed," he repeated.

"But you saw my changes. You were with me through them."

"But I don't like *how* you've changed." Levi turned to her, his clear eyes filled with disappointment. "You aren't the sweet, selfless, and caring woman I fell in love with. Now, everything you do is motivated by self-interest. By the Everlast, there are occasions when you're even cruel."

Ceris got up from the bed. "Cruel, love? Me?"

Levi grunted. "Don't pretend you don't know. I see it in your eyes when you're pretending."

"I've changed. So what? Everyone does."

"We are not *everyone*. Our personalities and the way we live are the main rulers of our properties. You're the patron of love, family, beauty, and marriage. But you're not living by love, family, beauty, and marriage anymore."

"A mother can fight for her family!" Ceris's melodious voice gave out to a croaked shout.

Shaking his long, golden hair, Levi walked to the door. "A mother guided by love would find less destructive ways to fight for her family."

The god left the room and Ceris wept.

The walls melted and were replaced by smoke. After a few seconds, the swirls of dark mist formed another image.

This time, I was in the crystal throne room. Ceris screamed. Imha and Omi stood still, as if paralyzed, on the other side of the room. The other gods cowered in the back. Shock crawled up my spine. I knew what I was witnessing. This was the moment right after Levi and Mitrus died.

"You!" Ceris spat out, pointing a finger at Imha. "You killed my love! You will pay for this!" Her eyes glowed red as she lunged at Imha, but she halted when the goddess of chaos pulled out a spike from behind her.

"I wouldn't move if I were you," Imha snarled. "Or you suffer the same fate as your lover."

Ceris's eyes went from red to blue to dull gray. "By the Everlast, you planned this so they would kill themselves."

Imha's hysterical laugh raised the hair on my arms and the back of my neck. "Yes, dear Ceris, I did. And, you might say this was a good plan, wasn't it?"

Ceris wobbled as if she were about to fall or faint. She reached behind her, but there was nothing to keep her up. Tears streamed down her face. "The Black Thorn. Are you insane?"

Imha tsked. "No, my friend, I'm just greedy, and I'll go to any lengths to get what I want."

"What is it you desire so much to kill for?" Ceris wiped away the tears. Her knuckles grew white from grasping her scepter so tight. To me, she seemed to be struggling not to cast a bolt at Imha.

"Power. Chaos. The world has been so calm lately." Imha's smile was intimidating. "Are you on my side?"

Gaping, Ceris turned to Omi, who remained standing, stiff and still, beside the delusional goddess. "You agreed to this? Are you on her side?"

Like the few times I had seen him, Omi's clothes were crumpled and smeared with dirt and blood, and he ambled as if he walked on the deck of a ship being tossed by waves. He turned to Ceris, half of a smile covering his thick lips. "I'm with her."

Ceris shook her head and retreated a few steps.

"Are you on my side?" Imha repeated her question, her voice resonating through the crystal walls. "I won't ask again, Ceris, so be smart."

"I'm smart. I'll never join you." With that, she cast a magic wall before her and ran to the exit.

The wall crumbled when multiple purple and red bolts hit it, but she was already gone.

"After her," Imha shouted.

Dozens of demons appeared from the shadows of the room. With piercing shrieks, they set out after the goddess of love. Giant bats flew out with the demons. One soared over my hiding spot and I looked up, suddenly seeing the creatures as I'd never seen them before. These weren't bats. Demonic faces were hidden behind a bat disguise.

Before I could see more, the scene changed.

I was inside a dark cave, and I could hear heavy rain falling outside. Ceris was beside me, kneeling before a pink bonfire. Her tears mixed with the dampness of her hair and clothes. Her pain was visible through her eyes and her shaking body.

Poor Ceris. She had lost the man she loved and now was on

the run from a powerful and mad goddess. Despite my ghost state, I reached out to her.

Everything turned to clouds again. Seconds later, the fog cleared away, and I was in a dark and noisy bar, filled with several men whose narrowed eyes glanced sideways every few seconds, who laughed and clanked loudly for nothing more than a poorly told joke.

In the corner behind me, Ceris was seated at a table across from the Fates.

"I felt it," she said, as quietly as she could with the loud sounds around them. "I felt this immense power, like an explosion of pure life." Her blue eyes were huge and gleaming. I could see a smile ready to burst out of her lips. Her hands moved as if by their own volition. "Please, please tell me."

"Tell you what, child?" one of the Fates asked.

"I've been crying for seven years," Ceris almost shouted. "Please tell me I can stop crying."

"Why were you crying, child?" another one asked.

"Stop it," she hissed, clenching her fists. "Why do you take me for stupid? You know exactly what I'm asking."

"Please, Ceris, make your question clear so we can decide if we'll answer it or not."

Ceris took a deep breath, as if getting ready to step onto a stage. "Is Levi alive?"

The Fates united their right hands and closed their eyes. A few seconds later, one of them answered, "Yes."

She put her hand over her chest, and she started panting.

Oh God, really? Levi was alive? Ceris had said she had been crying since his death—for seven years. We'd been living under the darkness for thirty. That meant this vision was one of the past. Twenty-three years had passed since this occasion. Where had Levi been this entire time? Why had they not been united?

"Where is he? Where has he been?" Ceris struggled to stay

upright. I could feel her need to bolt after Levi. If I'd learned my man still lived after all those years, I would have the same desperation.

"No, child," one of the Fates said. "He's been dead for the past seven years."

"Pardon me?" Ceris asked.

A waiter pushed his way between her and the Fates, and asked if they wanted anything. Ceris shot him an angry glare. When he backed off, she returned her focus to the other women.

"Levi was dead," another said. "What you experienced was his birth."

"Birth?" Ceris closed her eyes for a minute. "Please explain."

One of the Fates leaned closer. "Levi died when the Black Thorn pierced him. However, his soul found its way back. A few days ago, he was born into this world."

"Born? You mean, as a baby? A mortal baby?" Shock drained Ceris's face of color when the Fates nodded. "By the Everlast! What should I do now?"

One of the Fates smiled at her. "Now, you wait."

I had even forgotten I was having a vision when the scene changed. Now, I was in a playground, watching a few children play while their parents stood close by, chatting.

"They cannot see us." A voice came from behind me. I turned to see the Fates. I froze, thinking the words had been directed at me, but Ceris stood beside them, watching the children play.

"Isn't he beautiful?" She smiled, her gaze focused on a cute boy, who was yelling he was Superman. "His birthday is coming up. Six years old."

Then it hit me. Oh God, that was Levi? He looked like a regular boy, a human child.

"You shouldn't have looked for the boy, Ceris," a Fate reprimanded the goddess. "It's too dangerous."

"I couldn't stay hidden knowing he was out there unprotected. I had to find him. And, after almost six years of looking, I found him. I'm amazed at how strong his aura is. How he pulled me to him."

"Be patient, Ceris," another one said. "I can see you're anxious to help the boy. He's too young yet."

"I know," the goddess said. "I've been thinking," she started, finally turning to the Fates. "Levi is back. And Mitrus?"

The Fates kept their gazes on Levi. One said, "He will be six the same day as Levi."

"No," Ceris muttered, shaking her head. "But he is the one who caused this mess! Tell me where he is, and I'll kill him right now!"

"You know you can't. Or shouldn't. We need to restore the balance. That will only be complete if Levi and Mitrus return to us."

"And when will this happen?"

"Be patient," a Fate said.

Ceris puffed. Then her eyes bugged. "His scepter? What happened to his scepter?"

"Lost. It'll be crucial to find his scepter once he remembers who he is."

"You see, child," another Fate said, "his body is human, while his spirit is of a god. His body won't hold for too long and only the scepter will transform him into a full god again."

"What will happen to him?" Ceris asked, anxiously observing the boy as he played.

"You will see."

Something told me I knew what would happen to him, but before I could think it through, the smoke wrapped around me. When it dispersed, I found myself on a sidewalk in a town. I stood in front of a furniture store beside Ceris. It seemed nobody could see her again, since people scuttled past her—and me—without glancing or bumping into either of us.

I followed her attentive eyes. Inside the store, a couple and an old man spoke with a salesman. Then, Ceris glanced to our side toward a tall man. She approached him and whispered something in his ear. His eyes bugged, becoming glazed, as if he'd been hypnotized. He marched to the furniture retailer.

Ceris turned her back to the store. Once more following her gaze, I saw a young boy inside an electronic store across the street. He reached for the door, about to leave, but Ceris wiggled her fingers and the store's door slammed shut. The boy pushed against the door, but it didn't move. He called someone to help him. Some adult tried to open the door, but it stayed locked.

Behind us, three gunshots popped loudly. My heart lodged in my throat and I jumped. I turned to find out what had happened, but the setting altered once more.

As expected, I was again beside Ceris. This time we stood in an alley, observing a group of young men leaving a swanky club.

With his back to us, a tall guy talked animatedly to a guy with dark hair. The dark-haired guy walked around a car and invited the tall one for a ride.

Ceris wiggled her fingers in the guy's direction.

"You know what?" the dark-haired guy said. "I want to be alone. Get a ride with someone else." He got into his car and peeled out of the parking spot, leaving his tall friend to stare after him, his hands shoved in his pockets and his shoulders hunched high, as if he were perplexed. The tall guy still stared at the retreating car when, out of nowhere, a van turned the corner and hit his friend's car, which exploded upon impact.

Next to me, Ceris seemed unaffected as the giant ball of fire grew.

The tall guy staggered back, and then turned around. But

before I could see his face, the surroundings melted in smoke, placing me somewhere else yet again.

With Ceris by my side, I was in front of a cozy white house in a nice neighborhood. I wondered how such a place existed in a world like ours. As if answering my mental question, two armed guards walked past us, patrolling the streets. We were probably inside one of those closed and protected subdivisions that had become trendy since the darkness took over.

From the front door, a tall guy came out. It was dark and I couldn't see his features, but for some reason, I believed he wasn't a stranger. This had to be the guy whose friend blew up in a car, but a few years older.

He grabbed keys out of his jacket pocket and walked to the black sports car parked in the driveway. He stopped and pressed a hand to his forehead, closing his eyes, as if a headache had come over him.

Ceris pointed to him, and his cell phone rang.

"Hello," he answered, gritting his teeth.

"Hi, baby. It's me." I gaped at Ceris. She was the one speaking, but her voice was different.

The guy smiled through his pain. "Hey, hon, what's up?"

"Could you do me a favor?" Ceris asked.

"Anything," he answered.

"Pick up my prescription at the pharmacy before coming over?" she asked, sounding like someone else. "I really need it."

"All right." The guy opened the car door and slid inside. "See you in fifteen?"

"I'll be waiting," she said in her fake voice.

As the guy backed the car out of the driveway, she pivoted. The image before us switched. Now, we faced a fancy apartment building. From one of the windows on the second floor, I could see a beautiful blond girl around my age. She was dressed up and wore makeup. She kept leaning out the window, looking outside, as if waiting for someone.

A train whistle caused me to put my hands over my ears, but it wasn't a train. It was a huge tornado and it was coming for the building—fast.

My breath caught, and I was about to run to help the girl get out of the building.

Before I could take a step, the world began spinning around me, smoke coiling around me, and I found myself outside the Fates' cottage.

The door was open, and I felt compelled to peek in. Inside, Ceris took off her cloak and sat in an armchair across from the Fates.

"I need help," she started. "Levi won't make it alone. He has no idea what is happening to him."

The Fates shook their heads. One said, "You altered his future too much already. You should stay away from him before Imha senses him."

"Please!" the goddess begged. "He will die soon. His pain is increasing. His body won't hold his soul much longer. He needs help. Let me help him."

"It's not our choice, Ceris. We can't interfere directly. Neither can you."

"I can't leave him there," she insisted, her clear blue eyes shining with unshed tears. "He'll die. And this time, since he's still mortal, death will be forever!"

"You can't help him," another Fate said.

Ceris closed her eyes and buried her head in her hands. After a few silent moments, she let out a loud sob, and then stood upright. "Then I'll find someone who can."

As she left the cottage, the scene changed once more.

Under a thick tree with heavy leaves, hidden from prying eyes, I was seated on a park bench beside Ceris.

The Fates came out of a hiking trail and entered a small, veiled clearing, approaching Ceris.

"I've found who can help me," the goddess exclaimed, barely containing her enthusiasm. "She's beautiful and kind. He won't resist her, I'm sure."

"Why do you insist on jeopardizing his safety?" a Fate asked.

"Levi's not safe alone." Ceris raised her melodious voice. "He suffers. He needs my help. I cannot bear watching him wilt away."

"And what is your plan?" another Fate asked.

"As if you didn't know," Ceris said as a Fate shrugged. "I want to make a deal with you."

"Go on," a Fate said.

"I've found the girl Levi will have feelings for. Now I have to make her useful. I ask you to give her your most precious gift."

"And what do we get with this?"

She smiled. "Her soul will be mine. It's inevitable. Love for her family rules her life, which makes me her goddess. She will fall in love with Levi and will do anything to protect him. Once Levi remembers who he is and doesn't need her guidance anymore, I'll give her soul to you."

"Just like that?"

"Just like that," she said. Her eyes were eager and expectant.

The Fates joined their right hands and closed their eyes. For a few seconds, they remained still.

Seconds later, in unison, they said, "We agree."

Ceris jumped up and laughed in relief. After thanking the Fates, she left.

Then, the Fates turned to each other.

"Ceris has no idea."

"No, she doesn't. She thinks the girl is ordinary."

"Will we tell her?"

"No. Why spoil the fun?"

Before I could make sense of it, the scene changed.

My head spun, and I wasn't sure if what I saw were visions, things that happened in the past; I couldn't tell if it was my mind playing tricks on me, or if I was truly living these moments.

I closed my eyes, trying to gain equilibrium against the swirling thoughts that inhabited my brain. When I opened my eyes, I nearly screamed.

I was facing myself.

The other me hurried to an airport luggage claim area. I looked around, realizing I was in the JFK terminal. This had to be the day I first arrived in New York. The day my visions started.

I watched as the other Nadine twirled a strand of her long hair while impatiently waiting for her bags to appear on the track.

Inside myself, I felt a pull. Frowning, I followed it and looked back. Ceris was hiding in the crowd. What was she doing here? My curiosity made me stop watching the other Nadine. I followed the goddess, who retreated to a less populated area. When she was sure she was alone, her features changed. Her elegant white gown gave away to a neat suit, her pale skin acquired a slight tan, her long, white-blond hair shrunk to her chin and grew yellow. Her clear blue eyes became clearer, almost silver.

My knees gave away and the air flew out of me, as if a long-nailed claw had punctured my lungs.

Cheryl. Ceris had become Cheryl.

She was now walking to the luggage claim area, her eyes on the other Nadine.

The walls of the airport terminal melted away; a black cloud took me back to the Fates' cottage just as Ceris came in.

She took off her cloak from around her. "He is here."

"Who, child?" a Fate asked, rocking and knitting.

"You know who. Mitrus. He has been following the girl."

"Fascinating," the Fate by the fireplace said.

"He found out the girl can heal his pain," Ceris yelled, then added in a hushed whisper, "I still don't understand how she can do that."

"Interesting," the reading Fate muttered without taking her eyes from her book.

"Actually," Ceris said, then halted and stared at the fireplace, "what is interesting is that he knows something is going on. What's more, he can sense auras, I know it. Thank the Everlast mine is always concealed, otherwise he would have sensed me and known I'm not human."

"He's not entirely human either," the Fate stirring the kettle by the fireplace said.

"His body is," Ceris whispered. "Which means he could be killed."

"Ceris," the one knitting called out. "We already discussed that. Don't kill him. Levi may be the balance, but the circle needs every one of the gods to function by the Everlast law."

"I know." The goddess tapped her long finger over her chin. "But I have to do something. He can't stay here and mess with my plans. He can't be near the girl." Her eyes seemed focused on the fire. "I wonder how he can tap into his powers. He isn't strong enough, but he has some tricks. Seeing auras is one of them. Repelling the winged demons is another."

"What do you think happened?" the one by the fireplace asked.

Ceris tapped her chin. "I don't know. I can only think of one thing. He is the god of death and the dead. Perhaps he saw someone die." Then she gasped. "Or he killed someone! That's it! That would explain it. Accidentally, he performed the act that bound his properties and now he can feel and do things he can't explain. Oh, it makes sense now."

"Tell us what is in your mind," the reading Fate asked.

Ceris smile turned wicked. "I'll create a diversion. He can sense auras? So be it. He will sense the strongest aura around. That will also give a false lead to the others."

"Be careful, child," the one by the fireplace said. "There are things that happen because they should."

"No," Ceris yelled. "Mitrus is too close to Levi. He killed Levi once; he could do it again."

"Trust the Everlast energy, child," the knitting fate said.

"I do trust it, but that doesn't mean it couldn't use some help every now and then."

The scene changed. I found myself inside Morgan's office in Jacksonville. He was standing up and looking rather hypnotized. Beside me was Ceris—disguised as Cheryl.

Looking deeply into his eyes, she said, "One of the gateways to the Clarity Castle is Cathedral Rock in Arizona, a place of pure power. A couple will come to ask about it, and you will help them get there. You will do whatever you have to. You will sacrifice anything, even your life to aid them. Do you understand?"

Looking like a zombie, Morgan nodded.

Shadows rose from the ground and revolved around me, taking me to yet another place.

The goddess and I stood beside an incredibly blue lake inside a rocky cave. The ceiling was low and full of sharp points, though the overall extent of the cave seemed large. I couldn't see an exit and that made me nervous. The smell of wet plants was strong, but it died out as soon as Ceris ignited a log, creating a bonfire beside the lake's bed.

That was when a whimper made me turn. I saw a young girl seated against the cave's wall. Her mouth was gagged, and her wrists and ankles were tied by a shiny pink thread.

The girl was terrified. Every time Ceris moved, she recoiled and whimpered.

Ceris approached her and whispered, "I'm so sorry." She put her hand over the girl's chest. For a few seconds, the girl squirmed with wide eyes, trying to get out of Ceris's reach, but soon she stopped and seemed petrified.

Ceris's hand glowed. Slowly, the girl's chest opened.

Bile filled my throat and I gagged. My knees buckled and I sagged against the wall, wanting this vision to end.

But it wouldn't end. The girl's chest opened fully, and her heart appeared from inside the gap. The bloody mass floated forward, guided by Ceris's power. The heart kept coming until it rested over Ceris's palm. The girl's lifeless body slid sideways.

Ceris took the girl's heart to a steel plate that hovered over the pink fire. Then, she repeated the procedure over the girl's arm, grabbing one of the bones of the lower part. She placed the bone with the heart over the plate. Ceris focused on the heart and bone, and in her eyes was a heinous shine. What was happening to her?

Oh God, I wasn't witnessing this. No, no, it could not be true. Wasn't Ceris the goddess of love and family? Where was *her* heart now?

Ceris grabbed the bone and pushed it through the heart until it looked like a nasty and gruesome chicken leg—the bone inside the meat. She deposited it over the plate, and then using magic, she guided the plate over the lake. With a wave of her hands, the plate sank into the lake, taking the bone and the heart with it.

An intense dark light shone from where the plate had disappeared, blinding me for a second. Ceris chanted some incomprehensible words, holding her scepter tight.

It didn't take long for something to rise from the water: a Black Thorn.

Smoke ascended from the shadows of the cave and covered me. I screamed as a piercing headache shredded the inside of my skull. It felt as if my brain were being stabbed by thousands of needles. Through the black wall, some spots of light surfaced and grew, clearing my sight and bringing me back to Grandmother Rock.

I was kneeling inside my sign circle atop the rock. The wind whipped up and a cold fog brushed against my skin.

Ceris had her hands over my forehead. I kept screaming at the pain; it was as if she were extracting my soul with her long nails. I felt it in my toes, rising to my knees, my thighs, my abdomen. I put my hand over my chest when it passed over me there, as if I could hold it in. My eyes wide open, I observed the goddess drink from me. Then the pain passed through my throat and my forehead, finally leaving me as it was absorbed by Ceris's skin. I fell.

I gasped as the pain went away. I gaped at Ceris's elegant retreating form, wondering why I wasn't dead. I thought she had been sucking my soul and killing me.

"There." She halted in the center of the circle drawn on the ground. Her white gown ruffled in the wind. "I gave you the gift. I also took it away."

26

Wait a minute. Back up. I wasn't ready for this. In fact, I couldn't even stand up. My body shook so hard, beating and hurting against the cold rock of the mountain.

No, no. I had imagined it all, right? It had been bizarre dreams and not visions, right? Because, oh my God, Ceris couldn't be Cheryl. If she was, what did that mean?

"Besides," Ceris's voice broke through my woozy state, "you saw too much."

On my knees, still unable to stand, I blinked several times. My gaze flicked to Victor and Micah. Both still stood on the sign I'd assigned them. They stared at me, their lips tight, their eyes grave, their poses regal.

I squinted. There was something different about them. It was like they shone. Like their wisdom and strength now glimmered through them. Like they knew.

I stared at Victor and whispered, "Levi." He didn't confirm or deny the name. He didn't even blink. But he didn't need to. The fact that he was a god was written all over his features. I glanced at Micah. "Mitrus," I said. He gave me his trademark expression. A sly grin.

"Thank you, Nadine," Ceris started, getting my attention back. "I thank you for your help. Though, I don't understand how you were able to help with the pain. And I don't understand how Mitrus came to be here. But thank you for helping Levi come to this place. This was the only way to bring back his memories."

I fell to the cold ground again, nausea threatening to take over.

It was over. Everything was over. Victor was Levi. He was a *god*. He was Ceris's soulmate. The boy I fell in love with in a vision was actually a god. Everything had been a plan, a setup, and I had been a toy, a tool. Ceris had used me to get her lover back. Now, he would leave with her, and I would have to watch.

I wiped the tears that filled my eyes before they could spill. Victor moved toward me, his eyes gleaming with compassion. What? Now he was feeling pity and wanted to say he was sorry? Or perhaps he would say thanks, like his mate, for having helped him to get to her.

"Stop!" Ceris pointed a finger at Victor, and I thought she used her powers to keep him in place. "Stay where you are. The three of you. If you get out of your circles, Imha and Omi will know where we are."

"Imha is near?" Micah perked up. He struggled against Ceris's magic, wanting to get out of the circle.

"Micah," I whispered. "Mitrus. Whatever." I frowned. "Imha isn't on your side. Your death wasn't an accident. She planned it. In a manner, she killed you."

He growled. "What?"

I winced. "I just saw it in a vision. Cheryl ... Ceris knows this too."

"No, no." Micah shook his head. "It can't be."

"Oh, it can," Ceris said, smiling. A cruel smile on such a perfect face. "She betrayed you." Micah snarled and Ceris laughed. "Anyway, Imha is coming, but Omi and his demons are closer."

"What do you care?" I asked. "You're as bad as Imha. You're a murderer." I turned to Victor. "She was the one who orchestrated your parents' deaths. And Jason's and Lauren's."

Victor shook his head, his eyes wide. "No, she couldn't." He turned to Ceris. "You couldn't."

She inhaled sharply before looking into his eyes. "I did what I had to do."

"No," Victor whispered, trying to lunge at her.

"Don't waste your energy, love." A smile slipped over her lips. "You may have your memory back, but your body is still human."

"You're insane," I whispered. God, how I wanted to kill her. Kill her ... a god couldn't be killed without risking tipping the scale. My world was upside down because of it right now. And Ceris had forged a thorn capable of killing a god. "The Black Thorn," I said. Victor and Micah stared at me. "You made a Black Thorn. Who is it for?"

"She did what?" Victor returned his gaze to his mate. Or should I call him Levi? Oh God, what a mess! "You created a Black Thorn?"

"I did." Ceris raised her chin. "I found a pure, untouched, and untainted maiden and went to the Lake of Life. I used her heart and bones to create a thorn to kill Imha."

"But a god shouldn't be killed," I argued. "We have seen what happens if the gods aren't together." I extended my arms toward the dark skies above us. "The Fates told you this."

"I don't care what the Fates said," Ceris shouted. Her fury brushed against my skin. "Imha and you"—she pointed to Micah—"didn't respect the rules. I've been through the underworld, thinking Levi was genuinely dead. And if we don't find his scepter soon, he will die. Forever."

In her mind, Ceris acted out of love and for that I couldn't blame her. Nevertheless, I was furious. She had made *me* suffer. She had tricked me. She had orchestrated my life for more than eleven months.

"So now, to survive, we have to find our scepters?" Micah asked.

Ceris glared at him. "You're on your own now. Honestly, I hope you die." She looked skyward. "Time to go."

"Where?" I asked.

"You, I don't care about," Ceris snapped. "You served your purpose. Now forget about us and return to your pathetic life." She approached Victor, who tried to retreat but was prevented by magic. "Imha is getting close, love, and she won't be fooled by the circle."

"You think I'm going with you?" Victor asked.

She leaned toward him. "I'm certain you are going with me."

"I'm going with Nadine, and you stay away from me."

My breath caught.

Shocked by his statement, Ceris opened her mouth and gaped. "After all I did for you? You're my soulmate. You would choose to go with a mortal over your own goddess?"

"Yes," he shouted. "After all, in case you didn't notice, you killed, you lied, and you betrayed our rules, claiming it was for me."

"I did those things because I love you," the goddess whispered.

"Perhaps it's time for you to revise your definition of love." He crossed over the circle and headed in my direction. Instantly, screeches and ruffling of wings sounded overhead.

"By the Everlast, they're already here." Ceris turned to me. "Goodbye, Nadine. I hope the Fates don't treat you well." She waved her hand toward Victor, producing a vortex of pink wind that enfolded both him and her. Quicker than a blink of an eye, the vortex was gone.

And so was Victor.

I didn't have time to process it. Bats landed around the edge of Grandmother Rock, and I was alone with Micah.

For a second, I thought he would leave too. Instead, he came to my side and helped me stand. I was grateful for not being alone but I wondered how we would survive against the dozens of bats and other demons that climbed up the rock.

I kept myself frozen in place, hardly breathing, to avoid any rushed attack. I needed time to think, to come up with a plan, but I had no idea what to do.

The bats and demons formed a circle around the edge of the rock with us in the center. I tried not to flinch, but it was hard not to as they growled, shrieked, scratched their claws on the ground, and slobbered all over.

My muscles tensed when some of them started closing in on us. Micah held my arm and kept me close. I didn't relax even when the creatures moved aside so something or someone could come up the trail onto the rock top.

"Hello, Micah. Hello, Nadine." Brock approached us, an artful sneer on his face in between his reddened cheeks.

My mouth went dry. "You!"

"Yes, me. Am I late? I thought all of your friends would be here too. Where is the third one?" As if we would answer him. "All right, let's change the question. *What* are you three?"

Micah snorted. "Power Rangers, ever heard of them?"

"Amusing." Brock paced before us, his tone not amused. "You see, if you don't answer me, I'll have no other option than to take you both to Lord Omi." His eyes showed interest in that threat. Perhaps he was into torturing. He turned to me and I shivered. "Will you be a good girl and answer my questions?"

"Never," I snapped.

Brock shook his head and stepped closer to me.

Micah put himself in front of me and snarled, "Leave her alone."

"I'm afraid we're going for a ride." Brock snapped his fingers and the demons advanced.

Micah did his best to keep them off us, off me, but there were too many. In seconds, we were pulled apart.

Fear clawed inside me, making my body shake.

"No," Micah yelled, trying to get to me.

The bats closed in on me. I turned around, looking for a space to crawl through, and ended up face-to-face with Brock.

Then a fist met my face.

I woke with a loud gasp, only to have a blow to my stomach take the air out of me. I recoiled in time to escape a second kick.

"You're awake," Brock said. He knelt before me as I scrabbled backward until I hit a wall.

We were in some kind of classroom. A freezing, putrid, and deserted classroom. A long crack ran down the length of a blackboard and the windows were boarded. Broken desks cluttered the area, and spiderwebs coated the ceiling.

"Have you reconsidered?" he asked.

For a second, I was lost. What was he talking about? Then it all came rushing back to me.

I still couldn't believe it. Levi was Victor, Mitrus was Micah, Ceris was Cheryl. And I had been a toy in their hands. I felt sick and put my hand over my stomach in an attempt to soothe the turmoil. It still hurt from the kick, and it was quite painful to breathe deeply.

Brock touched my leg. I slapped it off. "Stay away."

"A feisty one." His gaze ran the length of my body. "Hmm, I bet you're delicious."

"Go to hell!"

He laughed. "My dear, Nadine, we already live in hell."

"Then why do you want to help Imha and Omi make hell even worse?"

"Because I won't be living in it," he answered. "I'll receive gold, women, a title, and a new home near the Clarity Castle if I deliver them any information that may justify the recent powerful episodes."

So, did the gods know about Victor and Micah and their true identity? I might be outside the situation now, but I wouldn't be the one to crack and tell who the guys really were—especially after Micah had stayed with me and tried to defend me from the demons. I wanted to ask where he was, but I didn't want to show Brock I cared. I was sure he wouldn't answer me anyway.

"You're wasting your time," I said.

"We'll see about that." Without taking his eyes from me, Brock walked to the door and opened it.

Two giant demons, larger than gorillas and smelling worse than skunks, entered the classroom and approached me.

I swallowed the bile that built up in my mouth and cringed. "No," I whispered. I pressed myself against the wall, wishing I could blend into the wood and plaster against my back.

They grabbed me and made me kneel, holding my arms outstretched. I squirmed against their cold, strong holds.

"Now, Nadine," Brock said, pacing, "be a good girl and answer me. What happened at Cathedral Rock?"

I didn't say a word. The grip around my arms tightened, and I clenched my teeth.

"Remember, you're asking for this," Brock said. He punched my stomach.

My vision blurred and I couldn't breathe. If the brutes hadn't been holding me, I would have crumpled to the ground and cried.

Brock readied himself to deliver another punch.

"No, please," I whispered.

"Where is your friend?" he asked. "Why wasn't the third one with you atop the rock?"

I shook my head. Brock hit me in the stomach again, then in my face, then in my chest. I clenched my teeth and swallowed back agonizing screams. I wouldn't humor him while he beat me or answer anything he was asking.

Then, he changed tactics. Instead of hitting me again, Brock produced a crystal vial from inside of his pocket.

I struggled against the brutes that held me pinned in place. "What is that?"

He glanced at the liquid inside the vial, a sneer taking over his features. "I'm the one asking the questions here. What happened at the rock?"

I bit my tongue and held his pretentious gaze.

"Suit yourself," he said, approaching me.

I jerked against the demons' hold, but one of them tugged my hair, causing my head to tilt back. The other used its ghoulish fingers to open my mouth. I fought them, but how did I hope to win? I was a domestic cat being squashed by two rhinos.

Brock let a few drops of the vial's liquid drip inside my mouth, which slid down my throat. Its taste was sugary and almost pleasant.

"Let her be," Brock ordered. They pushed me to the floor. "I'll give you some time to think."

He stormed out of the room, and the demons went with him. I was left alone in the dark classroom.

It was my chance to try and get away. Instead, I remained on the ground, weak and hurt and exhausted. I hugged my knees and let the tears fall.

Where was Micah when I needed him to come and save me?

That was when it began. The drops he'd given me burned and slowly made their way into my chest, then my stomach, and then it was everywhere. The drops scorched, prickled, and maimed every inch of my body.

I wished the pain would stop. Even if it meant I would have to die.

27

The pain did stop a couple of hours later.

By then, I was screaming for Brock to come in and kill me because I couldn't endure it anymore. He didn't come. Instead, he sent a demon inside to pummel me. It punched my stomach.

When the burning inside me was gone, I couldn't move. I could barely breathe.

Each time there were noises outside my door, I squirmed, afraid Brock would come in and give me more of that liquid.

I didn't want this. I didn't want any of this. My life didn't matter.

The last year of my life had been a lie. Why would I want to live it? Missing my family, I'd attached myself to someone not even real—my vision Victor—then had been nothing but an instrument in the plans of an evil goddess of love.

And Ceris thought she was better than Imha. Oh, boy, was she wrong. The ache in my soul outweighed the ache of my body. To know Victor, or Levi, or *whoever* he was, was with her now, making up for the time they had spent apart, ripped me to pieces in a way Brock's torture couldn't even come close to matching.

I felt incredibly jealous, even though I wasn't sure what else to feel. If it all had been a lie, weren't my feelings for Victor a lie too? I couldn't discern it right now, and I didn't want to discern it —ever. Why should I care about my life? It wasn't even mine anymore.

I'd given up.

The door opened, startling me. The demons pushed someone inside. The person stumbled and fell to his knees. I gasped when I recognized Morgan.

"Nadine," he groaned, crawling over to me. "By the Everlast, what have they done to you?" Being careful, he hoisted my head up and rested it on his legs. "Where is it hurting?"

"Everywhere," I croaked.

"This is bad." Morgan assessed my body, looking for visible wounds. Other than bruises from the punches and the scraped knee from the rock climbing, he found nothing. "Tell me how I can help."

"I just want to sleep," I said. But in my mind, I instead wished to die.

Morgan pulled me up to sit, propping me against a desk. "Did you get to Cathedral Rock?"

"Yes." I sighed and told him everything that had happened since last speaking to him—the circle I drew on the rock top, the visions, the revelations about Ceris and Victor and Micah, the end of my gift, the argument, and the way the goddess fled.

"By the Everlast!" Morgan's eyes shone. "I have been beside Levi and Mitrus these past few days!"

Yeah, I could see his point and understand his happiness. After all, the gods he worshipped so much were alive and had talked to him. More importantly, he had helped them.

But now we were here, trapped with Brock and the demons, missing Micah, and left to die.

"How did you get here?" I asked.

"They found me a few miles north of Sedona." He looked around the classroom. "We need to find a way to get out of here."

"The only way out is death, and I'm longing for it."

"What? You don't mean that."

I slid to the ground again. I had no strength to keep myself up. "I give up."

"No, you can't. Everyone wants to live. Everyone has a reason to live."

"My life has been a lie." I wanted to shout, but my weariness prevented my voice from being more than a whisper. "Victor, Micah, Cheryl. My feelings. The scholarship at NYU. The job at Langone. All a lie, and I was used."

"And if it was? You'll give up living because your heart was broken, because things weren't what you anticipated? Come on, I expected more of you. I believed you were a fighter."

How could he belittle the things that had happened to me?

Oh, and there was Micah. He had used me too. Had he known who he was and flirted with me just to be healed and led to Cathedral Rock?

Honestly, I wasn't sure I wanted to know.

A few silent minutes passed, during which I avoided looking at Morgan.

"Can I ask something?" he said all of a sudden. I shrugged. "I heard you have a great voice. Could you sing, please? The silence is kinda scary."

I stared at him. He was a man in his fifties who wasn't afraid of admitting he was scared, a man who had risked his life for me, a man who would do anything for his dear creed. For him, I agreed.

I sang a light, romantic ballad. Of course, the lyrics were about lost love.

On the first high note, I shivered. The music filled my hurting body, expanding my veins with hope, clarifying my thoughts. And I remembered. The joy of singing, the good it brought to me, the strength it gave me, the will to do more, to *be* more.

I remembered my family. And Raisa. And Olivia.

My family and friends needed me. I couldn't just die and leave them behind, alone to fend for themselves. I had promised myself I would work hard and support my family, provide them with a better future. I had to keep moving, keep living, forget about Victor, and dig into my original plan—to study and become a doctor and provide for my family. What's more, I didn't know if Omi or Imha knew who I was yet. But I knew if they figured out who I was, they could certainly harm my family to get to me, to learn the truth about the guys from me. I couldn't allow anyone to harm them. I wouldn't. I had to protect them.

I had to get out of here. I would get out of here. I would live.

At times, the visions had showed me what to do and saved me. This time I wouldn't have them, and I would have to make do.

By the end of the song, my face was wet with fresh, warm tears.

I sat up with my back against a desk and looked into Morgan's eyes. "How did you know?"

He smiled. "That singing would bring you back? I didn't. I just prayed it would."

I sighed. My body still hurt from the punches and the damned liquid, but my head was clearer. I wanted to feel better, to beat the weariness out of my body, and to find a way out.

I eyed the classroom, trying to find anything I had missed before—a back door, another unsealed window, a phone. "Any plans?"

"None yet. All I know is we're far away from Cathedral Rock in an abandoned school close to an interstate. Outside, there are demons everywhere, but I only saw two inside. The ones guarding our door."

"Did you happen to see Micah when you were being brought here?"

"I wish," he said, shaking his head. "My guess is Brock is keeping him somewhere else, some place special, with more protection. He's a god after all."

Yes, a god. It still was hard to believe. "We need to think," I said.

"You know, even if we come up with a plan, it won't be easy."

"We can't give up yet."

Morgan started to smile, but Brock burst into the room.

"Ah, the dear friends are reconnecting. How joyful! Nadine, I can see you're looking better. Ready to answer my questions, or do you want more of my elixir?"

"Does it come in strawberry flavor?"

His eyes registered the affront. "Insolent girl!" He raised his hand. I flinched, anticipating the blow, but it didn't come. He seemed to reconsider and asked again, "Last chance. What happened at Cathedral Rock, and where is your friend, the one who was with you at the bar?"

"He went to buy a smoothie, then he left on his flying carpet, and I stayed to play with your demons." I knew I was angering him, but since I wouldn't crack, I might as well enjoy it. I loved watching his cheeks redden in anger. "Give up already. I won't tell you anything."

Brock clasped his hands together. "Yes, I already figured that out. I'm preparing a rite to summon Omi. He will take you and extract the answers he needs from you. Very painfully."

Morgan's wide eyes met mine. Oh God!

"Brock," Morgan started. "Please, for our old friendship, let us go."

The other priest's evil laugh made the hairs on my arms

stand on end. "I haven't been your friend for years. I've been using your knowledge and your aura sensing power for my own advantage."

Morgan's lips tightened. Ouch, hearing all that from someone he had considered a friend hurt. I had felt that myself.

"How do you think I found Omi?" Brock continued. "With your ability. And you didn't even know it. Fool."

When Brock left the room, Morgan remained frozen, staring at the spot his former friend had been. I wanted to respect his feelings, but we didn't have time to waste.

"Morgan," I called in a soothing tone. "I'm sorry."

He shook his head and faced me. His eyes were hard as ice. "No, it's okay. I should have seen that coming. He has always been ambitious. Apparently, not in a good way."

"Are you okay?"

He let out a hollow chuckle. "Not really." He stood up and scanned the classroom. "We need to get out of here."

"I know." I propped myself up, holding a desk.

My legs could barely support my weight. I hadn't slept or eaten anything for only God knew how long, and the gashes on my shoulder stung and throbbed each time I moved. I could lie down and sleep for a whole week. "Omi is coming. Once he arrives, we have no chance of escaping."

The corner of Morgan's lips twitched up. "I have a plan. Not sure if it will work, though."

In the back of my mind music played. I hummed to the tune, letting hope flow through my veins. His half-thought-out plan had to be better than sitting around like a couple of victims.

I SANG AGAIN, LOUDER THIS TIME—A HAPPY POP SONG WITH HIGH notes that demanded more of my vocals.

Brock pushed the door open and marched in, his nostrils flared and fingers clenched. He slammed the door shut. "Will you shut up?"

"Why?" I asked, sitting on one of the few unbroken desks, trying to mask my motives with a scared expression. "The demons don't like it?"

"Your singing is ruining my concentration." He leaned closer. "Shut up before I knock you out again."

"I'm not afraid of you," I whispered, hoping to charge his ire.

He readied his hand to strike.

"Brock!" Morgan called in time. The evil priest turned, but Morgan slammed him in the head with a piece of broken desk. He fell on the floor beside me, unconscious.

Morgan hunched over his former friend, searching his pockets for useful tools and weapons.

I fought against my irregular breathing. Becoming nervous or scared wouldn't help our quest. "What now?"

"Now we wing it," he said.

"Excuse me? This is your plan? To improvise against dozens of demons? Oh God."

"Better than staying here and waiting for a miracle. Do you have a better idea?" He stood. In his hand, he held the vial with the strange brilliant liquid. He was staring at it, hypnotized.

"What is that stuff?"

"Well, if it is what I'm thinking, it's supposed to be the water from the gods' fountain. Omi probably gave it to him for this task. It has magical properties, responding to the thoughts of the person using it."

"We should hold on to that then, in case we need more help."

"We'll definitely need more help." Morgan gave the vial to me. "We still have to figure out how to pass through the demons outside without being eaten."

That made me think. "By the way, why aren't there more demons inside guarding us?"

"Demons can't stand being in confined spaces for long." Morgan continued to rifle through Brock's pockets. "I believe they trusted Brock would be able to contain us. Besides, demons aren't very bright, you know."

"Let's hope they're super dumb for the next few hours."

Morgan retrieved an odd looking dagger strapped to Brock's lower leg, under his pants. It was small and had a bright curved blade. The hilt was silver with encrusted red gems.

"The Crimson Blade," Morgan whispered, his eyes wide. "It is said that whoever possesses one of these"—he held the dagger up—"either is or will become a lesser god of war, a subordinate of Omi. I can't believe Brock went this far."

"Is it so bad to become a lesser god?"

"Well, if Brock forced his way into the position, he might have had to sell his soul to the god he wants to be subordinate to."

Now my eyes went wide. "Wow, that doesn't really seem like a fair trade."

"It isn't." Morgan shook his head and hung the dagger on his belt.

"What are you doing, taking the dagger? Do you want to become a lesser god?"

"It doesn't work that way. I probably can't use its magic, so it's not truly mine." He looked around one more time. "All right, I think it's time to go."

I took a deep breath. "We're going to attack the demons guarding the door, aren't we?"

Morgan nodded. "Yup."

It might have been our only option, but that didn't make me like it any better.

After he dragged Brock's body to the back of the classroom

and stashed it behind a few desks, I followed his directions and hid behind the door, then held my breath and stood still.

He bumped the leg from the broken chair against a desk, making a loud noise. It took a few minutes, but the demons eventually marched in, slobber hanging from their sharp teeth, and their long, dirty nails sprouting from their claws dragging on the floor.

With shaking hands, I closed the door as the brutes advanced toward Morgan. They didn't look for Brock. They seemed intent on attacking whoever annoyed them. And Morgan was doing a good job. He waved the wooden chair leg around and jumped on a wider desk to get out of their range. But the demons didn't stop. Morgan tried to keep their claws away by brandishing his improvised weapon.

That was my cue. I tiptoed to the brutes and opened the vial with the fountain water. I prepared to let a few drops fall on their back, but one of them lunged at Morgan, messing up our plans.

I froze, my mouth hanging open, as I saw Morgan get pushed to the wall and scratched on his face. Shocked, I almost dropped the precious vial.

The other demon detected my presence and turned to me. Adrenaline shot through my system, and I was able to move again. I backed away, putting a few desks between us. Not that broken wood and metal would detain the demon, but I needed time to think.

He kicked the desks out of the way and lunged at me. I slid aside—his claws grazed my shoulder—and let him break his head on the wall. A second later he was after me again, his head intact but the wall in pieces. Pain sliced across my shoulder. I swallowed hard and glanced at Morgan, who was wrestling the other demon, trying to stab him with the Crimson Blade.

My second-long distraction was enough for the demon to

slap me and send me flying. I hit my back on the edge of a desk, and he charged me again. He caught me by my neck and dragged me up, away from the safety of the ground. His huge hand choked me, and his nails buried into my skin. I worked on the vial, but couldn't get the stopper off. My hands shook, and his grip was too tight. I couldn't breathe. My vision went gray.

Just when I thought I was sliding into unconsciousness, the stopper popped off. With my left hand, I grabbed the demon's arm and pulled him close to me. With my right hand, I turned the vial upside down above his head. The liquid dripped out, touching his skin. Instantly, he dropped me and yelled, putting his claws over his face. A burnt smell reached my nose before I saw the fire spreading over his body.

He backed up, yelling and jerking, trying to find a way to put out the fire crackling his skin.

That caught the attention of the other demon, distracting him. With a roar, Morgan pierced the demon's chest with the Crimson Blade. Its body collapsed, and thick black blood spread over the floor, forming a large gooey pool. Crumpled in a corner, the demon I had set on fire stopped jerking. His melted skin was covered by blisters as the fire died out. I gagged.

"Two down." Morgan stood. "Two hundred more to go." He chuckled at his own dreary joke.

I turned to him and gasped at the sight of long, deep, bloody scratches on his cheek, his chest, and his thigh. "Morgan, you're hurt."

He pointed to me. "You too."

Blood dripped from my aching shoulder, but the wound didn't look as bad as his injuries.

"Can you walk?"

He limped to the door, gritting his teeth, and cursed. "It hurts, but I can walk."

We peeked out from behind the door. The corridor was dark,

but I could see the shape of a staircase ahead. A sign on the wall informed us we were on the second floor.

I pulled Morgan back inside the room. "Don't tell me you want to simply run out of here."

"I don't like it either. Do you see any other option?"

I shook my head. Without the visions, there was no other option. Besides, between staying here and fleeing, I would rather die during an attempted escape. I just hoped no more demons decided to come inside.

He put his finger over his mouth and beckoned me to follow him into the corridor. We tiptoed to the end of the hall where the staircase was. He peeped inside another classroom. "Come," he mouthed.

I followed as I didn't want to be alone and surrounded by demons again.

We stood in another dirty classroom, littered with broken desks, dim light pushing its way through cracks in covered windows. The desks had been pushed to a corner. In the center of the room, candles lit a circle drawn on the scarred and dirty hardwood floor.

"What's this circle?" I asked.

He searched a bag and a coat he found draped over a desk. "It's for summoning Omi."

My throat went dry. "What? So he did it? Brock called Omi?"

He showed me a car key in his hand. "Our way out."

I recognized the keychain. Morgan had found Victor's car key. "About the circle, Morgan."

He finally looked at the circle. "I can't tell. If we're lucky, we interrupted the summoning. Otherwise, we're wasting time talking. Omi could arrive at any minute."

After a quick peek out the door to make sure drooling demons were absent, Morgan and I sneaked to the staircase.

Halfway to the staircase, I heard a caw and froze. What?

Slowly, I turned toward a classroom with a half-opened door from where the sound came.

"What are you doing?" Morgan asked.

I opened the door the rest of the way and gasped.

Right in the center of the classroom, Micah was seated on a chair. He was bound by thick ropes around his bare torso, his ankles, and behind him, his wrists. His head hung low and he had several bleeding wounds spread across his body. And the raven, the one with the scar over an eye, sat on his shoulder.

Morgan shoved me aside and ran to him. "By the Everlast! We'll get you out of here, my Lord."

Micah grunted in response.

My heart squeezed. Among us, he had always been the strongest, the one who stood the tallest, the proudest. In truth, he was a god. Theoretically, an evil one. And now here he was, tied and hurt, small and weak.

Morgan tried to shoo the bird.

"D-don't," Micah said. "His name is Rok. He's mine."

Oh my. Swallowing my anger, I approached them and knelt beside Micah. This wasn't the time to be mad at him for sending the bird after me, or for being the immoral god of death.

"I'm ... sorry," he croaked, tilting his head to me. He looked terrible with pale skin and dark circles under his eyes. "For not being able to ... protect you."

"Don't worry about it." Gently, I cupped his face and held his head up. A cold jolt passed between us, and he inhaled deeply. Glad I was still able to heal him from his internal pains, I continued, "There were too many."

Startling me, the raven took off and hovered in circles above us.

From his waist, Morgan pulled the Crimson Blade out and cut the ropes. Micah started slipping to the ground, but Morgan and I held him. We put his arms around our shoulders and lifted him. Even weak, Micah stood and took most of his weight with him.

Morgan nodded toward the door. "We have to keep going."

Midway down the last flight of stairs, something jumped out at us. Morgan fell forward and rolled down the rest of the steps —Brock on his back.

With Micah hanging from my shoulder, I sprinted down to the wrestling men. Morgan stumbled up, kicked Brock's face and ran to the nearest door, pulling Micah and me behind him. He shoved the door open. All we saw were demons. Dozens of them. And they had seen us.

The taste of bile built up in the back of my throat. My heart pumped so hard my ribs hurt.

"Leave me here and go," Micah whispered.

"As if I would leave you behind, my Lord," Morgan said.

Brock caught up with us. "Lord, you say?"

Damn it. Now he would deduce Micah was one of the gods.

The raven dove toward Brock and, broken and hurt, Morgan punched the other priest in the face, then threw me the car keys. "Go," he yelled. I stared at the keys in my hands, frozen. "Run, Nadine. Go! Take him out of here."

I wanted to help him. I wanted to knock Brock down and carry Morgan to the car with me, even though Micah already weighed a ton alone. I wanted to be able to rewind. I wanted to go back in time with a note that said *don't trust Cheryl* and start the last year over. If I could do that, I wouldn't be watching a friend being punched to death while demons hunted and salivated for us.

But I couldn't rewind and I couldn't forget. I had to flee. I had to live. I had to take Micah out of here and deliver him to safety. My family needed me to live. *I* needed to live. But I couldn't leave Morgan.

"Nadine—they want you both, not me. I'll be fine. Go!"

Morgan was right—if I stayed, I'd die and Micah would be recaptured. If I ran, Micah and I just might live.

But Morgan was going with us.

In my pocket, I found the vial. I slipped Micah's arm from my shoulder and helped him lean against a wall. While both priests wrestled, I let some drops from the vials drip over Brock's back. In my mind, I saw Brock frozen as an ice sculpture for a long, long time.

"What the ...?" Morgan retreated a step from Brock's still hands and nodded a thanks at me.

Micah stumbled forward, took the dagger from Morgan, and without any ceremonies, stabbed Brock's heart. The priest's eyes widened and two seconds later, the ice melted and he fell on the floor.

My hand over my mouth, I gasped. "You killed him."

Micah stumbled again, clearly dizzy, and Morgan caught hold of him.

He fixed his black eyes on mine. "If we get out of here and don't kill him, he'll tell the other gods who we are, who you are, and they will come for you. For your family."

A shiver rolled down my spine.

He was right.

Still, I didn't like killing.

Blood oozed from the body, and I swallowed the bile building in my throat and the shock.

"We need to move," Morgan said.

Nodding, I walked to them and put Micah's arm over my shoulders again. We rushed back inside the building and down the hallway to the exit at the other end, the raven following us. Outside, we saw Victor's Audi parked about thirty feet from the exit. We darted to the car.

And that was when demons appeared from the corner of the building, running and flying toward us. I ducked, but a claw ripped at my already injured shoulder. I kept running. Escaping. Living.

Near the car, I pressed the button on the keychain. The lock popped up as I grabbed the handle. We slid Micah onto the backseat, and the raven flew in. Then I jumped inside as Morgan entered through the passenger door. With wobbly hands, I locked the doors and turned the car on. The demons bumped against the car. One broke a window. I yelled and stepped on the gas. Ahead, down the dry and dusty road, was a blinking traffic light—the interstate.

"Faster," Morgan coaxed, gripping my seat and leaning forward.

The wingless demons ran after the car until they couldn't keep up with the speed anymore, but the flying ones continued their pursuit. A bat scratched the car from front to back.

"Victor will kill me," I muttered, then shook my head.

What would *Victor* care? He was a powerful god. He'd never need a car again.

God, I was so stupid!

I pushed thoughts of Victor away. When I reached the interstate, I let out a short, puffed breath. I had no idea which interstate this was or which direction to go, but I hit the brakes and yanked the wheel to the right. The car fishtailed before the tires caught the pavement. I hit the gas, hoping the road would take me away from the demons. To safety.

I slammed my foot down and drove as fast as the car allowed. Now only a few bats flew with us. I kept an eye on them, turning the wheel and zigzagging away from their claws.

But they kept coming. A mass of bats zoomed down on us, flanking the car on both sides. I couldn't get us out of their reach.

"Morgan, I have an idea." I gave him the vial with the miracle liquid. "Splash that on us, on the car too, and let's imagine we're driving on another road, far from here."

A few bats landed on the car and started scratching the metal, probably looking for a way to peel it open.

He eyed the liquid. "Ok, let's try."

"Know any safe road?"

"How about I-95 near Jacksonville?"

"Sounds good."

Morgan opened the vial, tipped it sideways so his hand was full with the liquid, and sprayed it around. A few drops caressed my skin as my mind shifted to a safe, calm road in Florida.

Under my hands, the wheel of the car became soft, as if it were weightless. I closed my eyes for a brief moment, hoping we would arrive at our imagined destination rather than drive off the road and into the bats' claws.

When I opened my eyes, expecting to see an empty and safe road, I saw them. Three figures stood right in the middle of I-95 —accordingly to the bent sign along the interstate.

I stepped on the brakes with all I had. The tires squealed, and the car came to a stop inches away from the Fates.

28

___

THE THREE EERIE WOMEN LOOKED LIKE THEY HAD BEEN GARDENING in their yard, not standing in the path of a fast car. Their calm faces held hints of smiles, and their gray eyes never left mine.

The liquid had worked its magic. I was on I-95, inside Victor's car, with Micah and his bird, but without Morgan. Where the hell was Morgan?

I glanced back and found Micah struggling to sit up. "What's happening?"

One of the Fates gestured with her white hand. She wanted us to come to them.

I wasn't sure what to do. I had just escaped from Brock and his demons. I didn't want to be trapped again. Besides, as far as I knew, the Fates owned me now. I had no idea what they would want with me.

She gestured again.

Micah held on to my seat and looked ahead. "What do they want now?"

I gulped down my fear and exited the car. With the little strength I had, I helped Micah, putting his heavy arm around my shoulders. The raven flew out but hovered close.

"Where's Morgan?" I asked as we neared them.

"Safe somewhere else," the one on the right said.

"What now?"

"Now, you're both safe," the one on the left said.

I grimaced. Safe from demons, but not from them. Fates were the women who spun the wheel of destiny, which didn't let me know if they were evil or good. I decided to be on the defensive, just in case.

"What will you do with me?" I asked.

"We were thinking about leaving this place before we need to interfere more," the one in the center said. She extended her hand to me, and I squinted at it. "Nadine, your life is ours. If we wish to hurt you, we won't ask for permission."

She pushed her hand forward.

As I reached to take it, Micah held my arm. "What are your plans for her?"

"We're not obligated to answer your question, Mitrus," the one in the center said. "But rest assured we have no plans of hurting her. For now."

I looked up to Micah and nodded.

He shrugged, and I took the Fate's hand.

The world around us revolved. I felt as if I were having one of those revealing visions again.

That sudden thought saddened me. I realized I would never have another vision. Ceris had taken the gift from me. Yes, I had fought them at the beginning. After all, I'd thought I was hallucinating. That I was crazy. Insane. There were times I'd wished I didn't have visions, but now that they had been taken from me, I missed them.

The scenery settled. We stood on a tiny island with white sand and rocky shores that fought against angry black waves that crashed and bellowed. The wind whipped my hair, and I turned my face. A simple cottage that looked a lot like the one the Fates had in the woods stood before us.

I gawked at the view. It was so peaceful, so comforting. "Where are we?"

"On a Croatian island," one of the Fates answered.

I watched as the raven flew away. "Why did you bring us here?"

"To rest," the one closest to me said, smiling shyly. "You two will stay here for a week or two."

"What? Why?" I asked. "And my family? Raisa and Olivia will wonder where I am. I need to go back. And my job at Langone? It's supposed to start tomorrow." Wait. I forced my mind to slow down. I was sure the job at Langone had been arranged by Ceris. I didn't want anything to do with it.

"You deserve it, Nadine," the same one said. The others stood behind her and didn't seem to pay attention to our conversation. "You deserve the job at Langone. Ceris found out about the position and told you. You got it on your own. If you had failed to get it, she would have intervened, but it wasn't necessary."

Well, that was a relief. I needed that job. I needed it to get into med school and to move forward with my life. "Then I need to go back."

"The wheel of destiny has spun," she continued. "Your job at Langone will start in ten days. Raisa and Olivia have been told you are on vacation. And your other friends and family are safe."

Was this some kind of punishment? "What did I do to deserve this? I thought I had accomplished all Ceris wanted of me."

"Yes, you did." Her smile widened. "This is not a punishment. This is vacation."

She started walking away.

"Wait," I called out. Since arriving, I'd wanted to ask them more about Victor, where he was and what would happen now, but had held on to my curiosity.

The Fate faced me. "Yes?"

Instead I asked, "What about Morgan?"

"Morgan's destiny is set." She turned away. "Rest, child." Her words were carried out by the wind. "We'll be back soon."

The Fates walked toward the darkness at the back of the island until they disappeared.

Even hurt and bleeding, Micah looked down at me, a grin on his pale face. "Alone at last."

THE WIND BLEW STRONG AND COLD, AND I SHIVERED. I KEPT MY gaze glued to the spot where I had last seen the Fates until Micah shuddered against me.

"Let's get you inside." I helped him turn around, and we slowly inched to the cottage.

Like the Fates' house in the woods, this one was small and simple, with almost no furniture and no electronics. In the living room, the fireplace was lit. It would have been nice to stand there and warm up, but I had to drop Micah somewhere first.

Past a narrow doorway, we found a short corridor with four doors, two closed and two opened.

I pointed toward the door closest to us. "This one."

Slowly, we made it inside the bedroom, and I helped him lay on the bed. He was pale and some of his wounds had stopped bleeding, but now he was covered in dried blood and dirt. I took a few towels from the common bathroom off the corridor, wetted some, then went back to the bedroom and sat beside him.

"I feel loved," he joked with eyes closed, but smiling.

I dabbed the wet towel over his wounds, trying to focus on them and not on the muscles underneath them. "Shut up."

For some reason, it hadn't dawned on me that he was a god yet. After all we lived through, it was hard picturing him coming up with evil plans, helping Imha, and running around killing people. Wasn't that what the god of death did? I shuddered.

Trying to lighten the mood, I said, "So, the raven is yours. Did you have to send it to scare the hell out of me?"

He chuckled, coughed, and then grunted in pain.

Not the answer I expected. "Sorry, don't answer it."

"It's okay," he whispered. "I knew you were special ... because of your aura. So I sent it to watch over you ... in case something happened."

Understandable, but still a little creepy. If I had known it was his bird, maybe I would have been flattered, not scared all of those times.

"Did you know you were special?" I asked before I could think, and I felt heat on my cheeks when the corner of his lip tugged up. "I meant, did you know you were a ...?" I couldn't bring myself to say it aloud. I swallowed and tried again with a different word. "Did you know you were Mitrus?"

He pursed his lips. "No. I mean, I knew something wasn't right. I knew I was different, but I had no idea this shit went this far." He tsked. "It all makes sense now. After I killed those men in Israel, I accessed some part of my past, of my true soul, and some of my power seeped in. That's why I could repel bats, why I liked the dark, and how I could see auras."

"Yes, it makes sense," I repeated, trying to absorb all the info. There were a million more questions I wanted to ask him, but I had no idea how to phrase them.

When I passed the towel over the cut on his eyebrow, he held my hand and opened his eyes to look at me. "Thank you." He turned my palm over and kissed my wrist. A shiver started where his lips touched my skin, and ran up my arms. My heart lurched.

Quickly, I pulled my arm away. "You're too weak. You need to eat something."

"I don't ... think I can eat anything right now." He closed his eyes again and inhaled deeply. "I just want to sleep."

Trying to make no sound to disturb him, I tiptoed out of the bedroom and closed the door. In the bathroom I found a first aid kit. I picked it up and sat on the beat-up love seat in the living room with intentions to clean my wounds, take some Tylenol, and then find something to eat.

However, my eyelids felt too heavy. I gave in and closed my eyes for a second, relaxing my back on the love seat and willing the sleep away.

I WOKE UP ON A SQUEAKY TWIN BED. CONFUSED, I LOOKED around.

The simple bedroom was inundated by the dim lights coming from the almost closed door behind me, and I saw a bag beside the bed with what looked like some of my clothes inside. My shoulder was bandaged and most of my cuts were cleaned.

The memories of the previous day assaulted me, but I refused to be brought down by all that had happened. I just had to get through whatever test the Fates had prepared for me and then go back to my life. I would not think of Victor or Ceris. I would *not*.

I slid out of bed and peeked out the door. Across the corridor, the bed was made in the other bedroom, which meant Micah was up. I glanced down at myself and my torn clothes. Better to take a quick shower and change before showing up like a beggar before a god.

Holy shit. I said it as if it were normal, but it wasn't. My mind still couldn't wrap around the fact that Micah was a god. The god of death, actually. Wasn't he supposed to be evil? Didn't he plot with Imha to destroy the world?

Okay, one step at a time. First, a shower.

As I thought, I felt much better in a clean pair of jeans and a long-sleeved gray tee and my black boots.

I walked into the living room, holding my breath, expecting to see Micah somewhere. I frowned at the empty area and entered the kitchen next. There, seated around a wooden kitchen table, were the Fates.

I froze at the door as one of them gazed at me and smiled.

"Hello, child," she said. I swallowed, but couldn't find my voice or anything appropriate to say. "You're probably hungry." She pointed to the counter behind her, covered with bread, fruits, cheese, juices, and several other goodies. "Help yourself."

Slowly, I walked in, grabbed a plate, and picked some of the goodies. "Where's Micah?" I asked as I leaned against the counter.

"Mitrus is walking outside," the same one answered. The other two seemed to be meditating or simply not in this conversation. "He needs time alone to think."

Didn't we all need time alone to think?

I put my plate on the counter and took a deep breath, gathering courage. "What is going to happen next?"

The Fate smiled. "You'll stay here and rest. Soon, you'll go back to New York, to your classes, and to your new job."

"That's not what I meant."

"I know, but I can't answer your question." She lost the smile. "My sisters and I can't share our knowledge. The only thing I can tell you is that Levi and Mitrus will go on quests to find their scepters so they can become full gods again, but that you already knew."

I nodded. "Yeah."

"You don't need to worry," she said, standing. She walked to the coffee machine on the other side of the kitchen and took a steaming mug from it. With a new smile, she handed it to me. "It's not mochaccino, but it's coffee nevertheless."

Still a little wary, I took the mug from her. "What don't I need to worry about?"

She looked into my eyes deeply, intensely. "About you. About us. We won't harm you."

"I wish it was easy to believe," I whispered.

She patted my good shoulder. "You will." She turned and sat back between her sisters. "Now go. Mitrus is outside and he wants to talk to you."

That startled me and I almost dropped the mug on the floor. I sipped from it, left it on the counter, and rushed out.

I opened the front door, and the chilly wind whipped my hair around my face. I held on to it and looked around. It was easy to spot him. Standing tall on a rocky parcel about forty or fifty feet from the cottage, Micah kicked the rocks around with his hands tucked inside his dark jeans pockets and his shoulders stuffed under a black shirt.

I smiled, noticing he wasn't wearing black pants for the first time since I met him. But as I took the first step toward him, I erased the smile from my face and frowned. I had to remember he was not who I thought he was. I had to remember he had done bad things and probably would do more.

He turned to me as I approached him, his rough face serious and totally handsome with his hair messy because of the wind.

"Hey," I began, hoping my voice was steady, unlike what I felt. "Did you want to talk to me?"

"Yes," he said, but didn't go any further.

Honestly, I had no idea how I should behave in front of a god. I was worried I would say the wrong thing, and he would cast one of those magical bolts and strike against me. Being a mortal, they were certainly fatal to me.

"What is it, Micah ... uh, Mitrus?"

The corner of his lip tugged up. "Micah. Call me Micah, please."

I suppressed a snort. As if it would be easy to get used to this. "All right. Micah, what is it?"

He took his hands from his pockets and folded his arms across his chest. "I'm leaving."

"Excuse me?"

"I asked the Fates to take me away from here." The muscles on his jaw ticked, and his neck looked strained. "I wanted to go while you were sleeping, but they wanted me to ask you for something first." He pressed his lips together, and I tried to process the information. He extended his shaking hand to me. "Your touch. Please."

I gaped at his hand. Seeing he was shaking and probably in pain, I almost grabbed it with eagerness, but the I'm-being-used feeling returned and I held on to what little pride I still had.

"You're leaving. So, what are you going to do when the pains get worse? Come knocking on my door?"

He averted his eyes. "Not if I can help it."

Ouch. His admission that he wanted to stay away from me hurt more than I thought it would.

I retreated a step. "Well, you can start enduring them right now then."

Swallowing the enraged tears that were threatening to roll down my cheeks, I turned my back to him and walked away.

"Nadine," he called me.

I ignore him and kept on walking to the cottage.

He caught up with me, grabbed my arm, and pulled me so I was facing him. His black eyes shone with something I couldn't read.

"Please, heal me," he said through gritted teeth. Without warning he cupped my face with his hands, and the cold jolt spread through my skin.

With his mouth open, he tilted his head back and took it from me. I could feel it—something powerful, something energetic—transferring into him, as if I had an unlimited supply of whatever it was especially made for him.

I didn't think he noticed, but he pulled me closer to him and, when he leaned forward with his eyes still closed, I gasped—not because of the energy he drank, but because of his strong body brushing against mine, his sandalwood scent playing with my senses.

His forehead rested on mine, and I held on to his elbows for support. A few seconds later, he let out a relieved sigh and opened his eyes. They didn't have that strange shine anymore. Still, they were magnetic and I couldn't look away. I couldn't even move away. And Micah seemed relaxed where he was too.

His eyes still on mine, he slid his hands down my neck and my breath caught. A kiss on my forehead surprised me, but not more than when he let go of me and put several steps between us.

"Thank you," he said.

It was my turn to cross my arms. "You're not welcome."

He nodded, looking at the ground.

Without any more words or a look back, he walked away, to the beach on the farthest corner of the tiny island.

And I couldn't stop looking at him.

The Fates walked out of the cottage toward me. Two of them continued their path past me, toward the beach, but one of them halted by my side.

With her eyes on Micah, the Fate said, "Mitrus asked to leave for your own good."

I stared at her. "I don't understand."

"He knows he isn't a good man, a good god. He also knows your heart is a good one. Because of that, he wants to stay away from you."

Oh. He wanted to stay away from me because I was good, because he only associated with the likes of Imha and Omi. No wonder he wanted to leave. He would probably go running to the goddess of chaos, even after she betrayed him.

My gaze found him again. He stood on the beach with the Fates, his back to me. I still couldn't believe he was evil.

The Fate's hand squeezed my shoulder. "Take care of yourself, child. We'll be back soon."

She strolled down the beach and halted beside her sisters. Then the Fates joined hands, forming a circle with Micah in the middle. A second later, the four of them were gone.

And I was left alone.

Want to read more about Nadine, Victor, and Micah? Get *Soul Oath (book 2) now*!

THANK YOU

Thank you for reading *Destiny Gift*!

Reviews are very important for authors. If you liked my book, please consider leaving a review on your favorite retailer and/or on goodreads, please!

You can get the next books on the series now:

Soul Oath
Cup of Life
Everlasting Circle

Don't forget to sign up for my Newsletter to find out about new releases, cover reveals, giveaways, and more!

If you want to see exclusive teasers, help me decide on covers, read excerpts, talk about books, etc, join my reader group on Facebook: Juliana's Club!

ABOUT THE AUTHOR

While USA Today Bestselling Author Juliana Haygert dreams of being Wonder Woman, Buffy, or a blood elf shadow priest, she settles for the less exciting—but equally gratifying—life as a wife, a mother, and an author. She resides in North Carolina and spends her days writing about kick-ass heroines and the heroes who drive them crazy.

Subscribe to her mailing list to receive emails of announcement, events, and other fun stuff related to her writing and her books: www.bit.ly/JuHNL

For more information:
www.julianahaygert.com

facebook.com/julianahaygert

twitter.com/juliana_haygert

instagram.com/juliana.haygert

goodreads.com/juliana_haygert

pinterest.com/julianahaygert

bookbub.com/authors/juliana-haygert

ALSO BY JULIANA HAYGERT

To find links and more info, go to:

www.julianahaygert.com/books/

Shorts

Into the Darkest Fire

Tested

Standalones

Daughter of Darkness

Rite World: Blackthorn Hunters Academy

The Demon Kiss (Book 1)

The Hunter Secret (Book 2)

The Soul Bond (Book 3)

The Shadow Trials (Book 4)

The Infernal Curse (Book 5)

Rite World

The Vampire Heir (Book 1)

The Witch Queen (Book 2)

The Immortal Vow (Book 3)

The Warlock Lord (Book 4)

The Wolf Consort (Book 5)

The Crystal Rose (Book 6)

The Wolf Forsaken (Book 7)

The Fae Bound (Book 8)

The Blood Pact (Book 9)

The Wyth Courts

Winter King (Book 1)

Spring Warrior (Book 2)

Summer Prince (Book 3)

Autumn Rebel (Book 4)

The Fire Heart Chronicles

Heart Seeker (Book 1)

Flame Caster (Book 2)

Sorrow Bringer (Book 3)

Earth Shaker (Novella)

Soul Wanderer (Book 4)

Fate Summoner (Book 5)

War Maiden (Book 6)

The Everlast Series

Destiny Gift (Book 1)

Soul Oath (Book 2)

Cup of Life (Book 3)

Everlasting Circle (Book 4)

Willow Harbor Series

Hunter's Revenge (Book 3)

Siren's Song (Book 5)

Breaking Series

Breaking Free (Book 1)

Breaking Away (Book 2)

Breaking Through (Book 3)

Breaking Down (Book 4)

www.ingramcontent.com/pod-product-compliance
Lightning Source LLC
Chambersburg PA
CBHW021124190726

48288CB00008B/2494